Praise for D.
John Lloyd Branson

MURDER BY IMPULSE

"D.R. Meredith's High Plains mysteries started great and got better. *Murder by Impulse* is the best yet—delightful characters in a dandy story."

TONY HILLERMAN

"The crime is imaginative, the characters memorable, the West Texas locale evocative, and the story hair-raising.... Meredith has developed into a fresh, snappy voice of crime fiction."

Newsday

MURDER BY DECEPTION

"Meredith again demonstrates that sinister criminals and horrifying crime do not require London fog or New York streets to be exciting.... Branson and his lovely assistant keep the action and the humor flowing as the horror dances around the edges of the tale."

Fort Worth Star-Telegram

MURDER BY MASQUERADE

"A delight for the gourmet of mayhem: sparkling characters, a diabolically dovetailing plot, and some of the most brittle writing this side of McBain. Meredith is a bright new dawn on the tired horizon of the American mystery."

LOREN D. ESTLEMAN

Also by D.R. Meredith
Published by Ballantine Books:

MURDER BY IMPULSE
MURDER BY DECEPTION
MURDER BY MASQUERADE

MURDER BY REFERENCE

D.R. Meredith

BALLANTINE BOOKS • NEW YORK

 Published in the United States of America by Ballantine Books, a division of Random House, Inc., New York, and simultaneously in Canada by Random House of Canada Limited, Toronto.

Library of Congress Catalog Card Number: 91-91831

ISBN 0-345-36861-4

Printed in Canada

First Edition: July 1991

To the members of the Cosy Nostra,
too numerous to name.

AUTHOR'S NOTE

I am unaware of any murder ever having occurred in the Panhandle-Plains Historical Museum, and I am equally unaware of its staff being other than respectable, helpful, law-abiding, and pleasant—which explains why both the characters and the events in this story are fictitious. Although I have tried to be as accurate as possible in the physical description of the museum, I have deliberately, intentionally, and with absolute malice aforethought significantly altered the details of its security system. I leave it up to the reader whether or not Sarah Jane is a real live ghost.

ACKNOWLEDGMENTS

D. Ryan Smith—Director, Panhandle-Plains Historical Museum.

Suzanne Hewitt-Knorpp—Education Director, Panhandle-Plains Historical Museum.

Various members of the Museum Auxiliary.

Paul Youngblood—who provided invaluable advice on security systems.

Dr. Francis Clegg-Ferris and Dr. Mackie Allgood—who didn't object to discussing autopsies over dinner.

Certain "informed sources" at the Amarillo Police Department.

Mike Meredith—Assistant District Attorney and my husband, who checks my legal facts for free.

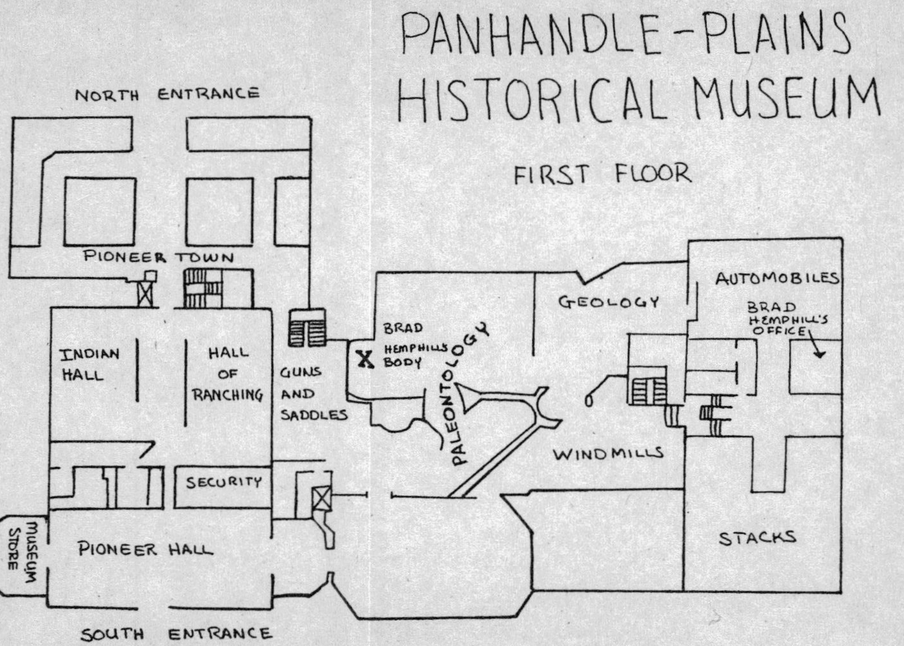
PANHANDLE-PLAINS
HISTORICAL MUSEUM
FIRST FLOOR
NORTH ENTRANCE
PIONEER TOWN
INDIAN HALL
HALL OF RANCHING
GUNS AND SADDLES
BRAD HEMPHILL'S BODY
X
PALEONTOLOGY
GEOLOGY
AUTOMOBILES
BRAD HEMPHILL'S OFFICE
WINDMILLS
STACKS
SECURITY
PIONEER HALL
MUSEUM STORE
SOUTH ENTRANCE

PROLOGUE

The Past

HIS MOTHER AND DAD BOUGHT IT FOR HIM THE DAY AFTER Halloween.

To comfort him, they said.

The grinning clown's nose glowed red in the dark. Not a friendly red, like a lollipop or an apple, or the shiny new wagon Santa Claus left under the tree last Christmas, but the ugly color of blood when the doctor pricked your finger.

The little boy hated his night-light.

He tried to tell his mother, but she couldn't see the difference in the shades of red. He couldn't *see* them, either, but he felt them inside when his mother turned off the overhead light. Once he'd thrown a shirt over the bulbous nose, but the red had seeped through the white cotton.

Like blood.

He'd rolled up that shirt and hid it in the back of his closet behind his box of Lincoln Logs and tried to forget it. But he couldn't forget. He knew the hateful garment was in his closet, knew it had a red splotchy stain from the night-light—even though he couldn't see it. You don't have to see things to know they're there. Finally he'd wrapped the shirt in an old towel and thrown both in the trash bin behind his house. He told his mother he'd lost the shirt.

At first he'd always covered up his head at night. Until his dad told him he might smother. He knew what smother meant. It meant you couldn't breathe anymore, and when you couldn't breathe anymore, you were dead.

Like Lindsey.

And when you were dead, the police came, and then the ambulance, with the red blinking lights that whirled round and round and shone through the window and reflected off the ceiling—and your mother started locking the door at night.

As if she could lock the scary things outside.

You couldn't lock outside what was already in.

CHAPTER ONE

Canyon, Texas—Halloween: The Present

WALTER GOODWIN BELCHED AND PLACED HIS APPLE CORE in the plastic Baggie that held the crusts of his Spam sandwich. Married thirty-five years, and his wife still didn't cut the crusts off his bread. He didn't like the crust. Never had. Didn't much like Spam, either; reminded him too much of the army and waiting in the chow line behind a bunch of other shavetails. He did like apples, though, and the crunch when he bit into one, the sound especially loud in the quiet museum.

That was something else he liked. The museum. Panhandle-Plains Historical Museum, to be specific, though nobody referred to it by its full name. There was no need. Everybody from Texhoma on the northern border of the Panhandle to just this side of Lubbock in the south knew what you meant when you said *museum*. It was a magnet; it drew crowds—rich and poor, black, white, and brown. There was no admission fee; folks paid what they could afford.

When Walter Goodwin worked the day shift, sitting at the desk by the big front doors, he'd watch some visitors drop a fifty-dollar bill in the donation jar. Other times he'd watch a man and his wife with a houseful of kids count out quarters and dimes until they had a couple of dollars' worth, and he'd figure their contribution was greater because it was harder to come by.

He especially enjoyed the museum at night, when it was hushed like a church during silent prayer. A man could let go of his imagination, pretend all kinds of things. Sometimes at night Walter would even stop to pass the time with one of the mannequins in certain of the displays. It didn't do any harm and it kept him from getting sleepy. He liked the camp cook standing by his camp fire with the chuck wagon in the background, and he always stopped to visit with Charles Goodnight's picture, the one taken when Goodnight was an old man and looked a lot like a bull buffalo.

He threw the scraps from his sack lunch into a wastebasket and screwed the top back on his thermos. Nearly midnight, and time to make his rounds again. There was no rest for an honest security guard. He'd start in Pioneer Hall at the south entrance and finish up with the stacks in the annex. He grinned to himself. Annex: funny how old names hung on. The annex had been part of the museum since 1974. Technically he guessed it was called the Transportation Wing, but nobody ever called it that; at least, nobody who'd worked at the museum for a while.

It was still the annex, though, and part of it, the part the public never saw, was still called the stacks. That was because the annex used to be the West Texas State University library, and the stacks consisted of a four-tier area where old metal shelving units remained. Some of them, the ones that still had shelves, held stored artifacts instead of books. Nothing was left of the other units except metal frames empty of their bookshelves and lined up row upon row, like old thigh bones.

He chuckled. The thigh bone's connected to the hip bone. Just like the old song, except in this case, the hip bone's the ceiling. Take away those old metal shelving units and the ceiling would collapse. Sometimes it didn't pay to disturb the order of things. He figured referring to that area as the stacks, instead of changing its name, fell into that category, too. Or maybe it was like crossing your fingers for good luck. Maybe it didn't help, but it damn sure couldn't hurt. Not that he was superstitious, but this area was strange, dark as the hinges of hell for one thing, even with all the lights on, and not quite empty-feeling for another. If a man let himself, he'd start thinking he could see things out of the corner of his eye. Himself, he always kept his eyes straight ahead. He liked to pick the dead folks he talked to; not the other way around.

He hoped he didn't find any doors open that should have been closed and locked. Not that an open door meant a break-in, just that the doors to the stacks had a way of opening themselves. He used to spend some of his off-hours in the security room watching the tapes made by the video cameras mounted in the annex—just to see if he could catch anyone unlocking those doors.

He never did.

Of course, none of the cameras were focused on those doors, but it was impossible to enter the annex without being filmed, and if you didn't enter the annex, you couldn't open the doors to the stacks.

Unless.

He wiped his forehead. Unless you were already in the stacks. You didn't need a key to open a door if you were already inside the stacks; only if you were outside.

It was Sarah Jane. That's what some of the other security guards called her, but never in front of Darrell Farmer or Dr. Rachel. Darrell didn't believe in ghosts, and neither did Dr. Rachel. Walter guessed that, as head of museum security, Darrell was in no position to admit it even if he did. As for Dr. Rachel, well, she was a nice lady, real professional, like a museum director ought to be, always talking about the "spirit of a museum," but she sure didn't mean a real spirit. She always shushed anybody who mentioned Sarah Jane, said that such careless talk "damaged the credibility of the museum and the validity of its artifacts."

Walter didn't much approve of calling the objects people lived with and worked with, and—hell!—fought with, artifacts. Folks put something of themselves into everything they touched, whether it was a buffalo hunter's gun, a little girl's china doll, or a chuck wagon. It was only natural that some of them, like Sarah Jane, lingered to see how the museum treated their possessions. The past didn't always stay in the past; sometimes, he thought, it folded itself up like a hanky and touched the present. Or maybe waited on the other side of a door or hid in the shadowy corners. If a man opened that door fast enough, or looked in those corners long enough, he might catch a glimpse of the past.

He chuckled at himself and stood up, hearing his knees pop as aging tendons stretched. He was getting fanciful in his old age. He'd be sixty next month and he was letting his mind wander a little more now. That was only fitting. A man had more to think about at sixty than he did at twenty-five, more worth remembering, maybe even sharing. Still, better not let anybody catch him talking to the displays or thinking aloud about ghosts. Some people might consider him senile, and that wasn't the truth. His mind was as sharp as it always had been; the body just sounded as if it needed to be oiled to take out the squeaks.

He patted his shirt pocket and felt his eyeglasses case. Another sign of age. He was a mite nearsighted, something else that proved life didn't always follow the predictable pattern. Man his age was supposed to be farsighted. Not him, though. But he wasn't bad yet; objects at a distance just looked a little out of focus. If he squinted, he could see just fine.

He lumbered out of the security wing and into Pioneer Hall, checked the closed gift shop, shone his flashlight at the mannequins all togged out in their uniforms representing eight periods of Texas military history, then turned toward the new addition to the museum. He didn't favor that part of the building as much as the older section. Not enough folks to talk to, he guessed, but a damn fine paleontology collection and the best exhibit on the petroleum industry he'd seen anywhere. But a man couldn't talk to an oil derrick or a dinosaur skeleton like that allosaurus. He couldn't anyway. He wouldn't mind if the camp cook came to life and answered him back, but he didn't much relish the idea of a dinosaur waving its bones and growling at him.

He stepped into the new wing, glancing at the two-story replica of an old wooden oil derrick that required an entire room to display; then he walked through an archway into a black-ceilinged exhibit hall. Circling around a curved wall, he entered the Hall of Pre-History—dinosaur room, he'd heard kids call it—stopping to stare at the diorama of a dimetrodon, a low-to-the-ground lizard with a spiny, sail-shaped fin, or whatever it was, running down the middle of its back. He wondered what color dimetrodons really were. Whoever made this model painted it dark green with a red chest and red sack around its neck. Ugly as a pit bull with a goiter, Walter thought, as he walked past it into the exhibit hall proper.

Here was a critter that made a pit bull look like a lap dog, he thought, glancing up at the allosaurus skeleton. The creature was reared up on its hind legs like nothing you ever met outside your nightmares, its huge head mostly mouth filled with needle-sharp teeth and open in a bony grin. Walter sketched a salute toward the monster and chuckled nervously. Maybe he was turning a little superstitious, saluting a skeleton, and not a real skeleton at that but a replica. Looked real enough, though, like it had just climbed out of the earth, its bones stained dark with age, shadowy life still lurking in its empty eye sockets. Besides, it never hurt to act respectful toward a species that had ruled the earth tens of millions of years, even if most of its members looked uglier and meaner than homemade sin.

And not all dinosaurs were flesh-eating devils. The triceratops, for instance. Just an eight-ton, twenty-five-foot plant eater, probably harmless as long as it didn't step on you, or hook you with one of its three horns, or slap you with its spiked tail. While most folks thought it resembled a rhinoceros, he had always leaned more toward thinking of it as a spiny-backed, reptilian cow—ugly maybe, but not necessarily mean. Might have been a friendly enough critter, maybe even docile.

Walter glanced toward one end of the raised platform that

curved around two sides of the hall. On this platform the triceratops skull was mounted on top of a small pillar, the bony frill around the skeleton's neck looking like one of those Elizabethan ruffled collars. He squinted at the blurry object perched atop the skull.

First the hair on the back of his neck stiffened, then shivers rippled along his spine as he fumbled in his pocket for his spectacles. "Halloween stunt. Must be. Damn kids must have hid out in the bathroom," he muttered to himself as he pulled his glasses from their case. "That's what it is. Sure it is."

His hands shook so hard, he dropped the glasses on the tile floor. He bent down, not even hearing the popping of his joints as his fingers grasped a piece of unshattered lens. He held it close to his right eye and closed his left one. The dinosaur sharpened into focus.

"Holy shit!" Walter Goodwin screamed.

CHAPTER TWO

JENNER'S HEAD SNAPPED FORWARD AS SERGEANT ED Schroder's old Ford skidded around the corner and slammed to a halt in front of the museum, its front bumper just inches short of ramming a Canyon police car. Jenner leaned back in the seat and drew his first deep breath since the two police officers had left Amarillo twelve miles—and a few minutes—earlier. He didn't want to know just how few. He didn't get a kick out of knowing how close he had been to a motor fatality. Schroder only recognized two speeds: stop and Damn the Torpedoes.

Schroder unbuckled his seat belt. "Shake your butt, son. The body's waiting."

Jenner released his own buckle. "What's the hurry? He's sure as hell not going anywhere, is he? Besides, the van's not here. You probably blew it off the road when you passed it doing Mach one, and we can't do much crime-scene investigation without all the paraphernalia it carries—like the disposable clothing, for instance. I'm not touching a bloody corpse without that white suit on."

Schroder lit an unfiltered Camel and peered at Jenner through the cigarette smoke. "I wouldn't let you touch a body without supervision anyway. You ain't had enough training.''

''Good, then I'll just sit in the car and wait for the Special Crimes van. That way I can help the evidence tech carry in her tape measure.''

''Out of the car, son, and quit whining. You're just pissed off that the chief temporarily assigned you to the Special Crimes Unit as a condition for your reinstatement on the force.''

''Yeah, and whose fault was that? Chief Mostrovich was ready to forget about my suspension, since I'd done such *outstanding police work*—his words, not mine—going undercover to hunt down the Boulevard Butcher. Then you suggested that you'd keep an eye on me for a while just to be sure I learned to work through the proper channels. Proper channels, my ass! You didn't go through any channels when you suspended me. I should've asked for a review board.''

Schroder exhaled a cloud of smoke. ''You'd have been thrown off the force once the chief found out you went undercover without authorization. The chief doesn't like rogue cops going off on their own. Bad for discipline.''

''I'm not a rogue cop! I'm a traffic cop, and I'd like to get back to doing my job before I forget how to drive a patrol car!''

''Most cops in Potter and Randall counties would give their left nut for an assignment to Special Crimes,'' Schroder reminded him brutally. ''You just don't know when you're well off. Now, quit your bitching and get out before I kick your ass.'' He mashed out the minuscule butt of his cigarette in the overflowing ashtray.

Jenner looked at the older man. Built like a square block—with, as an afterthought, arms, legs, and a head—Sergeant Ed Schroder had sandy-red hair thinning on top and pale blue eyes surrounded by stubby lashes. He customarily wore prefrayed shirts that wouldn't stay tucked in his pants, even if they had been pinned to his underwear. On this occasion he was dressed in cuffed slacks with a shiny seat and a brown tweed sports coat, complete with sagging pockets, that dated back to the Carter administration.

He was a cigarette-smoke-scented slob.

He was also the premier homicide investigator for the Potter-Randall Special Crimes Unit, and the man who had pushed the hardest for its creation. Since Amarillo straddled the county line between Potter and Randall, and killers didn't always check to see in which county their victims would land, Schroder argued that a single investigative unit staffed by personnel from law enforcement agencies in both counties was needed. He was right.

That was another irritating trait Schroder had; he was usually right.

Jenner climbed out of the car. Schroder was right about something else, too. He, Sergeant Larry Jenner, the cop who prided himself on his generous good nature, had turned into a whiner. What he couldn't understand was why Schroder endured it. It wasn't as if he and Schroder were friends. Schroder didn't have any friends, or none that Jenner knew of. Schroder wasn't interested in people until they were dead.

Except for himself, of course, and that worried Jenner. The only thing worse than an uninterested Schroder was an interested one.

Jenner reluctantly followed Schroder up the sidewalk to the museum's massive front doors, mentally bracing himself for what lay behind them. God, but he hated corpses.

A young Canyon police officer let them in. Judging by his white, stiff face, this rookie, Jenner decided, was another cop who didn't like corpses.

"Where is it?" asked Schroder, shaking a cigarette out of a crumpled pack. The burly detective never smoked at a crime scene, but he was never without an unlit cigarette. Jenner figured he couldn't talk without a Camel in the corner of his mouth, waving up and down like a conductor's baton.

"In the new wing, the prehistoric exhibit."

"Anybody touch anything?"

"No, sir. It's just like the security guard found it. He's kind of shook."

Jenner could understand why. He and Schroder stood looking up at the young man grotesquely straddling the triceratops's skull, his body wedged in the narrow space between the horns and the bony frill, like a bull rider in some surrealistic rodeo. A faint red smear stained the tip of one huge horn, as if the creature had just gored the victim and had been interrupted before it could buck him off and impale the body to the tile floor.

Gray eyes like black-flecked bits of gravel peered out from under the half-closed lids of the corpse, and Jenner stepped out of the direct line of sight. He decided the thing he hated most about murderers—other than the basic fact that they *were* murderers—was that not one of the bastards ever closed his victims' eyes.

"No visible wound," grunted Schroder, peering closely at the corpse. "Not on the front part of him anyway. His back may be as full of holes as Swiss cheese, but we won't know that until we get him down."

"Jesus Christ, Schroder!" said Jenner, leaning over so the blood could run to his head and maybe he wouldn't faint.

Schroder glanced at him. "While you're close to the floor, check for scuff marks, footprints, scratches, or skid marks."

Jenner took several deep breaths and swallowed the bile that threatened to choke him. "What for?" he asked, and wondered what had happened to his voice. He croaked like a ruptured frog.

"All that extra blood ain't helping your brain a bit. That body didn't climb on that skull by itself. Somebody put it there, and unless that somebody had wings, he had to walk across the floor, step up on this curved platform—that's eighteen inches, maybe two feet—then tuck the body on top that skull, like the poor bastard was out for a Sunday ride. Now, if you've ever carried any dead bodies—"

"God, no!"

"—you'd know it's awkward work. Not the same at all as carrying somebody live. Disconcerting, too, if you ain't used to it. Or even if you are. The average person isn't comfortable around the dead. Reminds us too much of what we're facing."

"Damn it, Schroder, get to the point!"

Schroder frowned at him. "Even if he's cold-blooded as one of these dinosaurs and dead bodies don't bother him, he's still carrying dead weight. Maybe his foot slipped; maybe he left some scuffs on the floor. Check it out."

"Yeah, sure, be glad to, anything to help. I'll just squat here and look at the floor and remember how happy I was handing out traffic tickets. You won't find any dead bodies riding on prehistoric skeletons out on I-40."

"If you find anything, mark it for the evidence tech."

"I can handle that, Schroder," he said, doing a quick mental check on the state of his physical well-being. Stomach still cold and tight-feeling, as if he'd swallowed a block of ice, but better than it was. Voice stronger, dizziness gone. Nothing calmed the nerves faster than knowing you didn't have to stand around looking at a stiff.

"As soon we finish photographing, measuring, and otherwise processing the victim in situ, so to speak, I want you to lift him down."

CHAPTER THREE

THE HOUSE DID ITS BEST TO IMPERSONATE A NORMAN CAStle. Constructed of gray stone, with an artificial moat lapping against its foundations on three sides and carefully trained ivy crawling up its walls, it more or less succeeded, depending on whether or not one ignored the fact that outside its gates stretched the flat plains of the Texas Panhandle, broken only by the gullies and canyons, mesas and cliffs, that lined the Canadian River to the northwest. In spring, mesquite trees, sagebrush, cholla, prickly pear, and yucca lurked outside its walled boundaries like invading armies, ready to storm the ramparts to infest the manicured lawns and carefully tended flower beds while gardeners armed with herbicide and trowels readied their defenses.

Not that their defenses ultimately won the war.

The cacti were on no environmentalist's endangered list, although anyone who ever spent hours plucking the fine needles of cholla or prickly pear out of his body, or treating a stab wound administered by a yucca leaf, might wish they were. And in spite of millions spent in research, no herbicide known to man was more than nominally effective against the mesquite tree. As for sagebrush, one admired its pungent odor and learned to live with it.

Man adapted to his environment. Not the other way around.

Unless one was John Lloyd Branson, thought Lydia, surveying his six-feet-four-inch frame clad in its customary black Western-cut suit and boots. His only concession to the occasion was a pearl-gray silk waistcoat instead of his usual vest, and a black Stetson instead of his gray one. He looked like a riverboat gambler or a wealthy Victorian Age rancher. He *always* looked like a gambler or a rancher, depending on whether he wore a string tie or a bolo. Tonight it was a string tie.

He didn't adapt to his environment; he created his own.

Juries loved him.

Which was probably a good thing, Lydia decided. He was, after all, the Texas Panhandle's most famous, most successful, most eccentric attorney. Also the wealthiest. Exactly where or how he became wealthy remained a mystery—at least to Lydia. If his neighbors in the small town of Canadian, Texas, knew, they weren't telling.

Nor would anyone tell how and why, and most particularly *who*, shot John Lloyd in the knee, leaving him with a limp. In fact, no one told Lydia much of anything about him—except legends. He was the only person she knew in danger of becoming a myth while still in his mid-thirties. Even Howard Hughes couldn't claim that distinction.

"Miss Fairchild, do I have something caught between my teeth?"

"I was just . . . just contemplating something."

John Lloyd's deep Texas drawl irked her. The bland expression in his obsidian-black eyes irked her. Both meant he was thoroughly pleased about something, thoroughly at ease, thoroughly in control of himself—while she stood in the enormous foyer of this phony castle feeling like a fool. A five-feet-ten-inch blonde, dressed in a clown costume, complete with curly orange wig, white greasepaint, a false nose, and floppy shoes, clashed with the decor. If she had any doubts about her status as social misfit of the season, she dismissed them after glancing at the butler's expression. He looked as though she'd tracked in something nasty on her oversize shoes.

John Lloyd tucked his silver-headed cane under one arm and plucked an invitation done in flawless calligraphy from his coat pocket, his eyes not quite so bland. "In the five months you have been in my employ, Miss Fairchild, I have learned to be wary of your contemplative moods. They generally lead to disruptive actions, frequently result in physical injury, and always disturb my peace of mind. Might I inquire as to exactly what action you are contemplating this time, so that I may metaphorically gird my loins?"

That was another of John Lloyd's habits that irked her. He never used contractions and always structured his sentences like a nineteenth-century novelist. Arguing with him involved simultaneous translation into modern English.

"I was trying to decide whether to brazen it out or to retreat, and I think I'll opt for cowardice. I'm going back to the car. You'll find me huddled in the backseat under a blanket when you're ready to leave."

John Lloyd handed his invitation to the butler with one hand and grasped Lydia's arm with his other. "For a woman of your intellect and beauty, Miss Fairchild, your social insecurity amazes me."

"My beauty is buried under an inch of greasepaint, and I misplaced my intellect, or I'd never have let you railroad me into this, John Lloyd."

"As I recall, it only required a phone call inviting you to accompany me to a Halloween masquerade ball."

"You said Halloween party!"

John Lloyd Branson arched one blond eyebrow, a feat of fine motor control that irritated Lydia. "I fail to grasp the difference."

"A Halloween party is chips and dip, drinking punch from plastic cups, bobbing for apples, dancing to taped music, or maybe somebody brings along his guitar or plays the piano. It's relaxed, for God's sake! But this!'' She waved her arm toward a living room (hall? stronghold? keep?) slightly smaller than Cowboy Stadium. ''Caviar and champagne, pewter goblets, enough live musicians to rival the Amarillo Symphony Orchestra. As for apple bobbing—forget it! The women in those designer Halloween costumes wouldn't chance mussing their hair unless their stylist was standing by with hot comb and blow dryer. This isn't a party, John Lloyd. It's a Social Event—capital *S* and capital *E*—and I come blundering in looking like a refugee from Barnum and Bailey.'' She saw the butler nodding his head in agreement.

''I believe I did try to dissuade you from applying the greasepaint, Miss Fairchild, but to use a colloquial expression, you had the bit between your teeth. However, with the proper self-esteem, one can feel comfortable in any gathering.''

''Maybe you can! You're John Lloyd Branson. You'd be welcomed if you clipped your toenails at the dinner table. Without you I wouldn't be invited past the false portcullis of this ostentatious pile of rocks.'' The butler nodded again.

''Miss Fairchild, you are a snob.''

''What!''

He released her arm and clasped her around the waist, drawing her tight against his side while he gestured with his cane toward the other guests, many of whom were beginning to stare curiously toward the foyer. ''You are judging these people by outward appearances.''

''Their outward appearances must equal the budget of a Third World country. Look at those women's outfits. I'd bet my last dollar they all have designer labels. For God's sake, John Lloyd, all those women need is a Gucci label on their behinds, and you could sell them as matched bookends on Rodeo Drive. Like the witch in the pointed hat swishing this way in black silk and sequins.''

''That, Miss Fairchild, is our hostess, and her husband is a close friend of mine.''

His voice had lost its drawl, Lydia noticed. It was always

an ominous sign when he started snapping off his words. It meant he was on his way to being royally pissed off—usually because someone disagreed with him, and as usual, that someone was she.

"John Lloyd, we're so glad you came," cooed the witch in the pointed hat in a low, intimate tone Lydia suspected she only used with men between the ages of puberty and senility. "Bill and I've looked forward to seeing you"—she looked at Lydia and hesitated—"and your guest, of course." Lydia doubted that.

"Mrs. William Bancroft Whitney, may I introduce my legal clerk, Lydia Fairchild. Miss Fairchild is presently finishing her degree at Southern Methodist University School of Law, and will join my firm as a partner upon her graduation."

All very stiff and proper, thought Lydia. Typical John Lloyd—except for the proprietary tone. She wondered if he expected her to curtsy. "Mrs. Whitney," she began.

"Please call me Monique."

"Monique," repeated Lydia, certain that whatever name her hostess had been christened, it wasn't Monique. More than likely she adopted the name on the advice of her interior decorator.

"Amarillo is such an informal society," continued Monique Whitney, her smile as firmly glued on as her false eyelashes. Lydia suspected that Monique Whitney last appeared in her natural state at birth. From that point on she braced, capped, sculptured, exercised, dyed, implanted, tucked, plucked, and hot-waxed herself into a flesh-colored figurine of such perfection that she looked real only in a very dim light.

"Such a change from Dallas," said Lydia uneasily, since what she knew of Dallas society could be written on the head of a pin and still leave room to copy the complete works of Shakespeare. Society leaders seldom shower third-year law students from undistinguished middle-class families with invitations to the annual debutante ball.

"I hope you don't think we're provincial."

Lydia wondered how long the woman had practiced in

front of a mirror before she perfected a smile that showed her teeth without crinkling the skin around her eyes. "I think Amarillo is a wonderful city." She did, too. Amarillo had a symphony, ballet, theatre, opera, art galleries, writers—and its quota of phonies, of which Mrs. William Bancroft Whitney was one.

"What a unique costume, Miss Fairchild. I couldn't help noticing it from across the room." Monique's voice subtly changed from a coo to the purr of a cat unsheathing its claws, and Lydia felt her stomach clench with tension.

"John Lloyd did say it was a Halloween costume party, Monique, and I've always loved clowns. I just had to beg Maurice to finish it in time." No need to mention that Maurice owned a costume rental shop, and the clown outfit was the only thing still in stock in her size.

"Maurice is the designer?"

"Yes," she said, and smiled.

Monique smiled back. "You must give me his address."

Lydia coughed and wished she were back in her shabby apartment across the street from the law school. She even wished she were in class listening to Dr. Simmons lecture on the Uniform Commercial Code, which she supposed was a truer measure of how trapped and helpless she felt. The Uniform Commercial Code had to be the single dullest body of law in the American jurisprudence system, especially as propounded by Dr. Simmons. His monotone could reduce a class to semiconsciousness faster than an overdose of Valium. She wished she were semiconscious now; in fact, she wished she could pass out on the floor. Anything was better than being caught in a lie by Mrs. William Bancroft Whitney.

"Absolutely not." John Lloyd sliced off his words with the precision of a cleaver.

Lydia jerked her head up to stare at him. "W-what?" she stuttered, then caught her breath when his arm tightened around her waist like a vise.

"Have you forgotten your promise, my dear?"

Lydia felt as if she were trapped in a boat at the top of a

waterfall and John Lloyd had just tossed her a lifeline. The problem with his lifelines was that they so often dragged her into the rapids. "Uh, my promise?"

"Not to disclose his identity to anyone without his consent," he coached. "Remember? He is not accepting any new clients."

"Uh, that's right. Maurice is busy, overwhelmed, swamped, inundated, stressed out. He's personally involved in every design."

"I see," Monique said, her grass-green eyes—colored contacts, Lydia decided, since they matched the glitter sprinkled over her eye shadow—shifting from John Lloyd to Lydia and back again as though debating whether to try another frontal assault or retreat gracefully.

She retreated. "Let me get Bill."

Lydia watched Monique weave her way through the crowd, a glittering thread in a shimmering tapestry of silk, satin, and sequins. She felt reprieved. Also ashamed. "Thank you, John Lloyd, and I-I'm sorry."

"You are not a good liar, Miss Fairchild."

"I wasn't lying—exactly."

His mouth twitched as if he were about to grin. (John Lloyd seldom indulged in such an expression.) "Oh? And what exactly were you doing?"

"Exaggerating. Embroidering. Interpreting the facts. There really is a Maurice—except his name is Maury—and he does make his own costumes. Actually, his mother does, but Maury picks out which McCall's pattern she uses."

John Lloyd's mouth twitched again. "I see."

Lydia rubbed her thumb over the web of red scars on her left palm, reminders of the September night she'd fought off the Boulevard Butcher, a serial killer who'd strewn bodies in the alleys of Amarillo's red-light district. She swallowed back a hysterical laugh. She'd survived a murderous attack by a psychopath, only to lose a trivial game of one-upmanship to an artificially enhanced snob. It was a game she wished she'd never played—because it had forced her to admit what she'd been denying for weeks: the Butcher had left her more than a legacy of scars; he had left her fear.

She was afraid of everything—including Mrs. William Bancroft Whitney's ridicule. But most of all, she was afraid John Lloyd Branson would guess she was a coward and pity her. She might be frightened of her own shadow—not to mention the dark, strangers, sudden noises—but she had some pride left. Not much, but enough to resent being an object of pity, particularly John Lloyd's. Better that he consider her a socially maladroit fool; he suspected that already.

She swallowed again and forced herself to meet his eyes. "Aren't you going to tell me that I made a fool of myself?"

"I hardly think it necessary to point out the obvious," he replied, the soothing drawl back in force.

Lydia distrusted that viscous tone. It was the same one he used to reassure a frightened client. "That's never stopped you before. Whenever I make a stupid move and fall, you always lecture me on how I could've avoided tripping in the first place. What's different about this time?" she demanded, proud of her belligerent tone.

Just like old times.

Before the Butcher.

John Lloyd released her and stepped backward, his limp barely perceptible, and then only if one watched closely. "Mitigating circumstances, Miss Fairchild."

"What mitigating circumstances?" she asked, and heard her voice shake. She cleared her throat and repeated the question.

"Self-defense. You retaliated against a venomous barb, somewhat ineptly, I might add, certainly not up to your usual standards of repartee. Then you inexplicably froze, like a rabbit staring hypnotically into the eyes of a reptile, and I intervened to prevent your being swallowed whole. Why did you freeze, Miss Fairchild?" he asked suddenly.

Lydia blinked—like the animal he'd compared her to, she thought—then wondered if rabbits blinked. Not if John Lloyd

Branson's black eyes were staring at them, she decided. "Would you believe I had liar's block?"

It was the first time she'd ever seen John Lloyd Branson stunned into silence.

CHAPTER FOUR

"WHERE ARE WE GOING?" ASKED JENNER, FOLLOWING Schroder out of the paleontology wing, past the two-story replica of a wooden drilling rig, and into Pioneer Hall. He didn't really care as long as the trip took him out of the immediate vicinity of the corpse.

"To talk to the guard while the evidence tech is working the crime scene. She's got enough help without us, but don't worry; you ain't going to miss anything. I told her to come tell us when it's time to lift the body down." Schroder pushed open the door to the security wing, which also housed the staff room and the Auxiliary Room—or volunteers' lounge as it was designated by certain staff members who believed *auxiliary* more properly described hospital pink ladies.

The volunteers' lounge was a large, comfortable-looking room furnished with couches, easy chairs, end tables, some with lamps, a coffee machine with cups, and a long conference table down its middle. It beat the hell out of most employee lounges Jenner had seen, but then, you can't expect volunteers to sit on Goodwill furniture that's been recycled for the second or third time. Employees, on the other hand, are paid to put up with crap like that.

Huddled under a saddle blanket that Schroder had pulled out of an exhibit, and hovered over by a young Canyon cop, Walter Goodwin sat in the middle of the longest couch in the room. Someone had loosened his belt and undone the first three buttons on his shirt, exposing graying red chest hair that matched what remained on his head. Jenner sensed that the old man would be embarrassed as hell at his own appearance—just as soon as he was capable of noticing it. Right now he had all he could do just to hold himself together. Finding dead bodies in unexpected places tended to loosen every bolted-down place you thought you had in your head.

Goodwin had both hands wrapped around his coffee cup, as if he had frostbite and needed to thaw out his fingers. Either that, or he had the shakes too badly to hold the cup in the ordinary way. Or both.

Jenner suspected both.

Shock always froze a man's fingers and toes—something to do with constricted circulation, Jenner supposed—and leached the warmth right out of his guts. That was why you always wrapped a shock victim in blankets or heating pads. To keep him warm—and alive. Otherwise he could freeze and shake himself to death. A sort of hypothermia without the low temperatures.

The guard's flaccid skin was the color of gray lichen and sparkled with droplets of sweat that Jenner, drawing on ten years' experience dealing with accident victims, knew were cold and oily-feeling. A cold sweat always left a man's face looking as if it was layered with Vaseline. What with Walter Goodwin's slack facial muscles, wattled neck, and greasy skin, his features were melting together and sliding off his skull. While Jenner didn't think Goodwin would die, the old man certainly didn't look any too chipper, either.

"Jesus, Schroder, maybe we ought to call a doctor. I've seen autopsied bodies that had a healthier color than this guy."

Schroder lit a cigarette, exhaled, and stared at him through the smoke. "How the hell would you know, Jenner? You spent most of your last autopsy out in the hall puking up in a bedpan."

"It was a wash basin!"

"Never have understood how you can pull mangled bodies, whole or in pieces, out of car wrecks without a quiver, but you can't sit five minutes in the morgue without recycling a week's worth of your wife's cooking."

"It's different, that's all," protested Jenner, wishing Schroder would ease off the subject of autopsies. Just thinking about it made his stomach queasy.

Schroder rolled his unfiltered Camel to the other corner of his mouth, a procedure that Jenner had heard other smokers insist was impossible. Evidently no one had ever told Schroder. "Sometimes I think you just do it to piss me off, son—"

"I'm not your son!"

"—but then I remind myself that you're just not seasoned yet."

He walked over to the couch and tapped a thick forefinger on the ID badge clipped on his coat pocket before the young Canyon officer had a chance to open his mouth. He then leaned over the security guard and touched his shoulder. "Can you answer a few questions, Mr. Goodwin?"

The old man licked his lips and peered up at Schroder, or at least peered in that direction. Jenner wasn't certain the guard was seeing anything, since his eyes had the fixed stare of a blind man.

"He's still kind of dazed, Sergeant," interjected the young Canyon officer whose nametag identified him as D. Evans. Jenner wondered if the *D* stood for Dale. "I guess he was real surprised to find the body."

"No shit," muttered Jenner under his breath.

"Mr. Goodwin," repeated Schroder insistently. Schroder expected people to be dazed on their own time.

Walter Goodwin blinked, licked his lips, and looked

around the room like a man returning from a long journey. His eyes said he hadn't enjoyed the trip.

"Mr. Goodwin, I'm Sergeant Schroder, Potter-Randall Special Crimes Unit. This is Sergeant Jenner—"

"Son of a bitch!" Goodwin spat out the words along with a shower of saliva. "Leaving something like that on one of my displays. He done it on purpose and for pure cussedness, and I'm gonna wring his neck like he was a chicken. Don't do no good to talk to a man like that, just got to wring his neck."

Jenner sucked in a breath, held it, and crossed his fingers for a little extra luck. Some cases were sweethearts; the answer just came and cuddled up in your lap without much effort on your part. If the old man knew the killer, then Special Crimes could wrap up this one in a hurry, and maybe there wouldn't be another for a while. Maybe not until next year—when he, Sergeant Larry Jenner, traffic cop extraordinaire, would be back on the expressway handing out tickets.

He noticed that the young Canyon cop—D. Evans—had bolted off the couch and was looking wildly around the room and unsnapping the flap on his holster as if he expected the murderer to walk through the door. Idiot kid! Nothing was *that* easy. He circled around to the end of the couch for a better view of both Goodwin and Schroder.

Schroder sat down on the coffee table in front of the couch and exhaled another cloud of smoke. Jenner hoped he didn't asphyxiate Goodwin before the old man could name the killer. "Who was it?" asked the burly detective, his voice sounding a little hoarser than usual.

Goodwin set his coffee cup down and clasped his hands together. Jenner noticed he was still shaking. "Young Brad Hemphill. Curator here at the museum. Takes care of Pioneer Town—what we used to call Pioneer Village. Nice a young man as you'd want to meet. Last man you'd think would end up in trouble. Always real polite. Said thank you whenever a man did something for him, even if it was something a man was supposed to do and didn't need no thanks for, like handing him the clipboard so he could sign out at night. Real nervous sort of a fellow, though. If a man walked up behind him and he wasn't expecting you, he'd jump six feet in the air. But he'd apologize for it, like it was his fault he was nervous. Talked real quiet and walked real quiet, too, like he was in a library. Or scared he was going to wake up something in this old building.'' Goodwin wiped at his eyes with one shaking hand. ''He damn sure did, didn't he? Woke something up, and it killed him!''

Jenner decided later that Schroder's mouth didn't exactly fall open; more like his upper lip curled away from his bottom lip, so that both canine teeth emerged as yellowed fangs. His cigarette tilted downward at a ninety-degree angle, clinging precariously to the detective's lower lip, and releasing an inch of ash to cascade down his shirt.

''Hemphill's the victim?'' asked young Officer Evans, his round blue eyes even rounder and his voice sliding up the scale and cracking.

Goodwin stared at Evans, his face gradually turning from gray to plum-purple. ''Christ Almighty! Who did you think I was talking about? No wonder this country's got a crime wave. If I wasn't an honest man, I'd take up a criminal profession. Might be damn lucrative if you're any example of the cops who might be trying to catch me. You couldn't catch your own spit in a five-gallon bucket.''

''But I thought you knew the perpetrator,'' protested the cop.

''Officer!'' The tone of Schroder's voice would have stopped a major riot, much less one young cop. ''Officer, sit down and don't *think*. It appears you don't have any aptitude for it.''

Jenner considered pointing out that the kid hadn't said anything that the three of them, including Schroder, hadn't thought, but decided against it. The old man already suspected they were fools. No need to confirm his suspicions.

Schroder turned back to the guard. ''So the body is this young curator, Brad Hemphill.''

''That's what I said!'' Jenner decided that Goodwin's voice

could only be described as testy. Nothing like a little righteous indignation to counteract shock.

"Did you touch the body or move it?"

"Lord Almighty, no! You think I'm an old geezer who lost my smarts when I lost my hair? I'm a security guard, Sergeant, not a cop, even if I did take some law enforcement courses up at Amarillo College. I know better than to mess around with dead bodies, maybe destroy evidence. I called the university police, my boss, Darrell Farmer—he's head of museum security—and the Canyon police. I could've just hit the alarm button—the system's hooked up to both the university police office and the Canyon Police Department, but I didn't want to scare off the killer. The burglar alarms on the doors ain't been updated to the silent kind. They make a hell of a racket. Maybe the killer was still in the museum, and everybody could kinda sneak up real quiet like, cover all the doors, and maybe catch him trying to leave. I even turned off the alarm system so the cops could get in without having to diddle around with turning it off from the outside. You see, both the university and the Canyon cops have keys to the doors and to the alarm."

He paused to catch his breath before continuing. "I was trying to save a little time, see, and keep things quiet so he wouldn't know I'd found Hemphill. Didn't work, though. First man through the door set off the alarm. He must have turned on the alarm thinking he was turning it off. Anyway, I was standing in the doorway to the paleontology exhibit—just in front of that allosaurus skeleton—with my back to Brad when that alarm went off."

The old man wiped his face on his sleeve. "I don't remember much after that. That alarm going off shorted out my brain." He looked up at Schroder, his eyes apologetic. "I'm ashamed of myself, Sergeant, going crazy like I did. I was in the Korean War. I've seen dead bodies before, a lot worse-looking than Brad's, but something just came over me."

Schroder dropped his cigarette butt in Goodwin's coffee cup, his eyes never leaving the humiliated figure on the couch. "How did you know Brad Hemphill was dead?"

The old man jerked his head back as if he'd been hit on the chin. "Of course he was dead! Do you suppose he'd been sitting up there on that skull if he wasn't dead? Brad had a lot of respect for this museum. He never would've climbed on one of the displays, not for no reason."

"Not even to play a joke?" asked Schroder, his faded blue eyes expressionless, but then, they always were. Schroder didn't believe in giving away his thoughts.

The old man shook his head. "Brad Hemphill never had no sense of humor. You know the kind. Tries hard, but you have to explain a joke to them. Besides, his eyes were half-open and his mouth was gaping. He was dead all right."

Schroder lit another cigarette and snapped his Zippo lighter shut. "If you never touched the body, Mr. Goodwin, how did you know he was murdered?"

The security guard stared at him as if he hadn't heard the question. "I don't understand what you're getting at," he finally said.

Jenner didn't either. In fact, he didn't understand any part of Schroder's interrogation.

Schroder leaned forward, his square, thick hands braced on his knees. "There was no wound on the front of the body, Mr. Goodwin. No bullet hole, no stab wound, the front of his skull wasn't crushed—nothing that said Brad Hemphill didn't crawl up on that skull and die of natural causes. So why are you so certain he was murdered?"

Jenner felt sorry for Goodwin. If the guard was guilty, he was about to stumble into a sizable hole in his story. If he was innocent, he was learning that being a good citizen and reporting a murder didn't always rate a good-citizenship award. Usually, it earns you first place on the list of suspects. There is always the possibility that the reporter of a corpse is also its dispatcher. It happens—a lot.

Goodwin rubbed his jaw and shifted back on the couch. His face still glistened in the fluorescent light, but Jenner noticed he wasn't sweating anymore. "I don't know if you're gonna believe this or not, but it's the truth. It was because he was *here*, in the museum, at midnight. Brad Hemphill never stayed past closing time. All the other staff did sometimes—I know 'cause I had to check them out and turn off the alarm—but Brad never did. Oh, he'd work Saturdays and on Sunday afternoons when the museum was open, so he wasn't lazy, but since he started work here four years ago, he'd walk out the south entrance at exactly five P.M. You could set your watch by him."

"Did you see him leave at five this afternoon?" asked Schroder.

"I wasn't on the front desk this afternoon. I usually work four to midnight, but we've got two men out on vacation, so I've been relieving Darrell Farmer around eight and working till eight in the morning." He stopped and grinned. "Twelve-hour shifts ain't bad so long as you don't have to work too many in a row. But tonight was different."

"Yeah," said Jenner. "You found a dead body." He ignored Schroder's look that meant there was apt to be another body on the premises if he didn't shut up.

The old man looked solemn again. "Besides that. I reported in about six because Darrell had to go to a big party up in Amarillo tonight, one of them benefit things for the Panhandle-Plains Historical Society. All the staff was supposed to go. The society raised most of the money to build this museum, and it still has a pretty big say in how it's run, so going to the benefit is kind of in everybody's job description. Of course I didn't go. Neither did the cleaning crew."

"So who was still here at six o'clock?" asked Schroder, pulling his notebook out of his coat pocket.

"Every living soul had checked out of this museum. There was nobody left but me and the cleaning crew. Maude Young and her folks come in just about six every night. Most folks is either gone for the night, or at least out for supper before coming back, so Maude can get the offices cleaned without bothering anybody. She and her ladies generally finish up at ten-thirty or eleven, and I let them out. Tonight it was about eleven. Then I had my supper break and started my walk-through to check everything. I'll tell you something, Sergeant. There was no body on that skull when I got here at six, because I always do a walk-through when I come on duty. There was no body on that skull at ten when Maude was mopping the floor. But at midnight Brad Hemphill was sitting there deader than any of the museum's old bones. I want to know where he was between six and midnight.''

CHAPTER FIVE

THE WHITNEY LIVING ROOM WAS NOT AS LARGE AS LYDIA had first supposed. If one counted the paved terrace visible through the four sets of French doors set into archways along one wall, it was merely the size of a basketball court. A balcony jutted out over one end of the room, while a fireplace large enough to cook wild boar carcasses dominated the opposite end. That evening several logs smoldered fitfully in its stone-lined depths. The gray stone walls were dotted with woven tapestries depicting, alternately, battle scenes replete with rearing horses and clashing swords and Biblical scenes of martyred Christians whose tortured expressions made Lydia doubt the benefits of religion in medieval Europe. Evidently the secular life was no more peaceful—as displays of dusty medieval weaponry were succeeded by tapestries that conjured up images of maimed bodies and castles under siege.

Groupings of carved wooden benches with high backs, uncomfortable wooden chairs with tapestried seats, and three-legged footstools that doubled as end tables were scattered about on the polished stone floor in what were intended to be conversation areas. Wall fixtures designed to resemble flickering torches and two gigantic chandeliers, each holding dozens of candle-shaped bulbs, cast the only light in the cavernous room and failed utterly to dispel the shadows lurking in its corners. Lydia decided domestic life in the Middle Ages was a barrel of laughs for masochists who enjoyed darkness, discomfort, disease, and death, not to mention the numb behinds that must have resulted from sitting on that god-awful hard furniture.

The room was ludicrous, grandiose, oppressive—and empty. There was no sense of timelessness, no sense that the original owners of the weapons, the tapestries, the furniture, had temporarily stepped out and might return at any moment. In spite of the musicians, in spite of the crowd of guests who strutted about like restlessly pacing actors waiting for their cues, the room was a vacuum, a carefully dressed set for some pageant that had been canceled.

If this was the home of Monique Whitney's dreams, Lydia decided she must be a restless sleeper.

"How do you like my house, Miss Fairchild?"

Lydia turned to face her host. William Bancroft Whitney was dressed like a not very convincing Dracula. Judging by the leathery creases around his eyes and a fleshy slackness about his jaw, Lydia estimated him to be at least ten years older than John Lloyd, perhaps more. Still, he was an attractive man with a pleasant voice who smiled as if it was something he did often. Too bad the effect was ruined by his sorrowful eyes. Like a man who looked on life and saw too many things he couldn't change.

"Miss Fairchild is speechless," said John Lloyd, squeezing her arm in warning.

Bill Whitney laughed. "No, she's not, John Lloyd. I've seen that same expression on too many other faces. She's deciding whether to lie and tell me this room and this house are just wonderful, or to tell the truth, that both look like an amusement park spook house. Except there aren't any spooks. No self-respecting ghost would haunt this pile of stone. That's left to the living. Go on, you can say anything you want, Miss Fairchild. I've probably said worse myself."

Lydia laughed, heard the incipient hysteria in her own

laughter, and felt John Lloyd staring at her. She rubbed her sweaty palms on the bloused legs of her costume and felt trapped again. Whatever she said, it couldn't be the truth, that William Bancroft Whitney had hit the nail on the head: the living often became specters without the inconvenience of dying first. That had nothing to do with his question. "Why the particular style?" she finally asked.

Whitney shrugged and gestured toward his wife. "Monique wanted it, didn't you, my love?"

Monique Whitney curled her fingers around her husband's arm. She reminded Lydia of a vulture wrapping its talons around a tree limb. "I'm a student of genealogy, Miss Fairchild, and this is a replica of my family's castle in France. My ancestor who built it accompanied William the Conqueror to England in 1066."

Probably in search of better accommodations, thought Lydia. "I guess everybody has a looter or two in their family. One of my ancestors was supposed to have been a pirate."

Monique Whitney frowned, and her eyes took on a hard glitter, like the sun reflecting off a sheet of ice. "There's a difference between a soldier of William the First and a common pirate."

Lydia agreed. William won, which legitimized his looting the natives, and her ancestor was hanged as a thief for doing the same deed. However, voicing that distinction didn't seem either diplomatic *or* safe—not with Monique Whitney standing so close to a wall full of weapons. "So this is the medieval equivalent of the old homestead," she said instead.

"Not exactly. I did have to compromise. The French doors, for example, are from a much later period, but some light was necessary. I couldn't very well have skylights put in. Of course, the rest of the house isn't so authentic, but my architect managed to keep the ambience of the period. Bill really does love the house. He's just teasing you. Aren't you, darling?"

People who called people darling in public always made Lydia feel as if she were trapped in a 1930s drawing room comedy. But it wasn't the 1930s, this wasn't a drawing room, and there was nothing comic about the distaste in Bill Whitney's eyes.

He took a sip of his drink. "It makes a good place to give a party, I guess, and I've got my own study with furniture you can actually sit on without stiffening up like that rent-a-servant who's been answering the door all evening. The man must double-starch his jockey shorts. Come on back, John Lloyd, Miss Fairchild. Rachel's there."

"No, she isn't," interrupted Monique, tapping one deep red fingernail against her goblet. She smiled at her husband. If a barracuda could smile, thought Lydia.

Whitney studied his wife's face. "Where is she?"

"She went back to Canyon."

"Why?"

Monique shrugged her narrow shoulders. "How should I know? Dr. Rachel Applebaum doesn't confide in me. Perhaps she thought she should take the money back to the museum and lock it up."

Whitney's fingers tightened around his glass. "Rachel wouldn't do that. Even though most of it will go to the museum, the money belongs to the historical society. It's deposited in the bank by the treasurer. This isn't a cookie-jar kind of organization. The museum director can't dip into the funds anytime she pleases, and Rachel knows that. We're audited every year, for Christ's sake. How am I going to explain that I allowed somebody to walk off with a satchelful of uncounted money?" He glanced at his watch. "At ten-thirty at night? By herself? With all the damn crazies who would kill you for a nickel, she drove back to Canyon with all that money? At two hundred bucks a ticket to this benefit, I figure we've probably made close to forty thousand dollars for the museum."

"Really, darling, your museum director will be perfectly safe. The money's mostly in checks anyway."

Lydia choked. "Two hundred dollars a *ticket*?"

"Certainly," snapped Monique Whitney. "Didn't John Lloyd tell you? This is a benefit for the Panhandle-Plains Historical Society. Those who contributed received an invitation to this evening's event. But don't worry, Miss Fairchild. John Lloyd paid for you."

Her insinuation made Lydia feel like one of her ancestor's serfs that John Lloyd had bought cheap at some medieval estate sale. "You paid two hundred dollars a ticket?"

Whitney ran his fingers through his hair, a distracted expression on his face. "I'd better phone and make sure she got there all right. Excuse me, John Lloyd, Miss Fairchild." He turned and elbowed his way steadily through the crowd toward an archway leading to the rest of the house.

"Bill worries too much. A big museum security guard and some curator dressed like a conquistador went with Rachel. If you'll excuse me, I'll go calm him down. Besides, I may be mistaken. Perhaps Rachel didn't take the money with her. I'm sure you two can entertain yourselves." The sound of Monique Whitney's laughter lingered behind her like a bad smell.

Lydia didn't bother acknowledging her departure. "You paid two hundred dollars a ticket?"

"Are you repeating yourself, Miss Fairchild, or am I hearing an echo?"

"Don't answer my question with another question! I want to know if you paid two hundred dollars for my ticket to this benefit."

"I made a charitable donation in our names to the historical society."

"From the office account?"

"From my personal account," he answered, his black eyes probing hers.

"Then the tickets aren't a business deduction?"

"You are sounding unpleasantly like an Internal Revenue agent, Miss Fairchild, but I shall answer your question anyway. No, the tickets are not a business deduction."

"Then this is personal? You paid two hundred dollars to bring me to a *social event* I wouldn't have been invited to otherwise and wouldn't be caught dead at if I'd had any choice." She took a deep breath. "I'll write you a check. I pay my own way and make my own choices. I'm not some helpless female languishing away waiting for some male to take charge of her social calendar."

John Lloyd's eyes never shifted, but Lydia sensed his focus had sharpened. "You should update your language, Miss Fairchild. For a woman living in the last decade of the twentieth century, your word choice is archaic—"

"I must have caught the disease from you. You use words not heard by the human ear in the last hundred years, not to mention never using contractions—"

"—not to mention inaccurate. Languishing, as it pertains to a lady's behavior, has been unfashionable almost as long as the whalebone corset, Miss Fairchild. Cowering is the better word."

Lydia's stomach clinched. "I've never cowered in my life. Women my size don't need to. We punch somebody's lights out instead!"

"According to the dean, you've been cowering in your apartment every hour you're not in class, Miss Fairchild."

"The dean?" she asked, feeling like a cornered rabbit again. "What dean?"

"Dean Johnson of the Southern Methodist School of Law, Miss Fairchild. He has been very concerned about your behavior. It seems there has not been a single demonstration, petition, or riot instigated by you in support of your version of truth, justice, and the American way since you returned to school. The dean reports that he has gained fifteen pounds as a result of your extraordinary deportment. It seems that, heretofore, he relied on you to spoil his appetite."

"The dean reports? Who is he? A CIA agent? Or *your* agent? Does he turn in weekly reports? Daily ones? Just because I've been spending time studying *in* my apartment is no reason for your spy to make a big thing out of it. Besides, it's an invasion of privacy, John Lloyd, and I don't like it. Just who the hell do you think you are?"

John Lloyd flinched, whether from her profanity or the fact that her loud voice was drawing the other guests' attention, Lydia didn't know. Furthermore, she didn't care. She hadn't said anything really obscene, and as for the other guests, let them stare. They would anyway.

"Well?" she demanded.

"Lydia, in spite of my best intentions, and against your best interests, I find myself growing fond of you."

Lydia felt the backs of her thighs tingle, a physical reaction that occurred every time he called her by her given name or confessed to caring for her. "An uncontrollable sudden passion is no excuse to manipulate my life, John Lloyd."

He flushed. "I believe my passion, as you term it, has never been uncontrolled."

"I have raised your blood pressure a few times, though, John Lloyd. Admit it," she interrupted.

"However, my behavior is not the issue. Yours is. Human behavior is perfectly explicable, Miss Fairchild, if one considers it as a series of references that have significance only within a certain specified context. Your odd behavior this evening, for example. Your obsession with your costume, your unaccountable failure to put Mrs. Whitney in her place, when you have never before suffered snobbish fools gladly, your reaction to my buying you a benefit ticket to a perfectly acceptable charitable function—all are understandable when considered in a certain context. When confronted by a seemingly illogical or incongruent act, reread the references. I have done so, Miss Fairchild, and have concluded that you are afraid."

"I am not afraid, damn it, and you're reducing me to a mathematical formula, John Lloyd, and I don't like it!"

He arched an eyebrow. "Mathematics is a rational science, Miss Fairchild. I never said your behavior was rational, merely understandable."

"So now I'm crazy! Is that what you're saying?"

He squeezed her hand. "No, but you are suffering from delayed stress syndrome, flashbacks to a time when you felt helpless, trapped, afraid, flashbacks to the Butcher, Miss Fairchild."

Lydia felt sweat pop through her thick white makeup. "I had a right to be afraid then. That sadist was planning to carve me up like a Sunday roast, for God's sake! But that's in the past; it has nothing to do with now."

"It has everything to do with now. The past is not some

fixed point; on the linear progression of time, it impinges on the present and sometimes the future. Otherwise the superstitious would not believe in ghosts.'' John Lloyd released her hand and gestured at the room. ''The past can be a prison, Miss Fairchild—as this house is to Monique Whitney, as your memories are to you.''

''But the Butcher is dead,'' she whispered.

''And you killed him, Lydia,'' he replied softly, ''but you have not exorcised his ghost.''

CHAPTER SIX

THE EYES, EARS, AND—JENNER SUPPOSED—THE MOUTH OF the museum were contained in a room not much larger than a walk-in closet right next to the volunteers' lounge. Most of it was occupied by a table covered with a double bank of video monitors and a control board containing enough switches, dials, buttons, cables, and wires to send a security expert into ecstasy and a thief to jail. At least, that was the gospel according to Darrell Farmer, the head of museum security, who sat in a wooden folding chair in front of the table, expounding chapter and verse.

"You see, Sergeant Schroder, the days of a tired museum guard with his trusty flashlight shuffling through darkened halls and checking barred doors are over. Museum security is high tech now. We have video cameras, sound and motion detectors, burglar alarms connected to both campus security and to the police and fire departments, checkout sheets for the staff, strict control of the keys to the back, front, and side doors—"

"Who's got keys?" interrupted Schroder.

Farmer looked disconcerted for a moment. He wasn't accustomed to being interrupted. "I have one; the director;

Goodwin here, or whoever's on night duty; the president of the historical society because he's a member of the museum committee that governs the museum; the campus security office; the police department; the fire department''—he ticked off names on his fingers—''and that's all.''

''What about the museum staff? Don't they have keys?''

''Absolutely not. If they work late, the night guard lets them out. If they go home for dinner and come back later, then they make arrangements before they leave the museum to be back at a certain time, and the guard watches for them. Control of access is my first rule of security, Sergeant.''

''No spare keys laying around?''

''Of course there are—three I believe—but those are locked in a cabinet in my office, along with extra keys to all the offices and display areas. *And* I check those keys every day, Sergeant, including today. No one has substituted keys. No one has stolen keys. Control of access again. Even if there were keys missing, and someone tried to break in, there are always the video cameras, the motion and sound detectors. This is an efficient operation. Nothing enters or leaves this museum without being heard and filmed.''

Schroder cocked his head, a lighted cigarette hanging from his mouth, his face expressionless. ''Then how come you still have a night guard?''

Darrell Farmer glanced at Walter Goodwin, who stood leaning against the back wall and glaring at his supervisor. ''Backup, Sergeant, much as NASA installs redundant systems in our space vehicles, just in case a sudden power loss should occur.''

''Redundant, my ass,'' muttered Goodwin just loud enough for Jenner to hear.

''Did you say something, Goodwin?'' asked Farmer, squaring his shoulders and looking at the guard. Jenner would have bet a month's pay that Farmer was ex-military. He had that stiffness about him, as if he had a steel rod for a spine, and he looked spit-and-polished from his burred gray hair to his mirror-shiny shoes. He operated strictly by the book and was not, Jenner suspected, very patient with a subordinate.

All in all, Darrell Farmer was definitely not a warm and cuddly person. Those in charge seldom are. Like Schroder.

"I said, it's a good thing we've got a backup system, even if it is a tired old guard," replied Goodwin, his shirt buttoned, hair combed, but still looking haggard.

"What's that supposed to mean, Goodwin?" asked Schroder, his nose twitching slightly, as if the detective had caught a whiff of, not a lie, but a truth carefully glossed.

Farmer interrupted. "Goodwin's been with the museum a long time, Sergeant. He doesn't trust some of our new technology. Prefers the personal touch."

"So does Dr. Applebaum," insisted Goodwin.

"Dr. Applebaum doesn't have the benefit of our training, Goodwin. Any glitch in the system, and she lets her imagination run away with her."

"Such as?" asked Schroder. Jenner noticed that the sergeant's nose wasn't twitching anymore, but his eyes had narrowed. Not a good sign for somebody.

Farmer's eyes narrowed, too. "Such as *what*, Sergeant?"

"Such as what kind of glitch, Farmer? What goes wrong with your security system that makes your director nervous? I been around awhile, too, long enough to hear what everybody says about Dr. Rachel Applebaum. A fine-looking woman and bright as hell, too damn bright to be jumping at shadows. So how about you cut the bullshit and tell me why you got a night watchman."

Farmer's face turned scarlet. "We have lost power a few times," he said reluctantly.

"How many times, and why?"

"The last six months, maybe four times during the day, twice that many at night. Why? Well, the security company isn't certain, but we suspect a strong wind's responsible for most blackouts. We rewired, put the electric cables underground, corrected the problem."

"No more power losses?"

Farmer shook his head. "None."

Schroder twisted around to look at Goodwin. "What about it, Goodwin? No more glitches?"

Goodwin hesitated, glanced at Farmer, then straightened

his shoulders. "Not exactly, Sergeant Schroder. The motion detectors in the annex short out every once in a while, and the video cameras there flicker sometimes. Nothing serious, and it sure don't mean a break-in, not in the annex anyhow. Funny things are always happening there."

"Name some," said Schroder, stubbing out his cigarette butt on the bottom of his shoe and dropping the butt in his coat pocket. Some cops in the department measured the length of an investigation by the number of discarded cigarette butts in Schroder's pockets.

Goodwin swallowed and looked at his boss. Farmer laughed and answered the question. "The annex is an addition to the museum, Sergeant. It was the West Texas State University library until 1974. It's an old building with a lot of artifacts stored in the stacks. Staff members are always in and out of that area, changing artifacts in the displays, and forgetting to lock the doors. Or they'll try to carry too much, drop something, or set an artifact down and forget it. Another staff member, or one of the cleaning crew, sees doors open that should be locked, or objects where they have no business being, and all of sudden we have a bunch of people upset. You have the same situation in any organization, but it's more sensitive in a museum. With a collection worth millions of dollars, nobody wants to admit he was careless, so stories get started."

"What kind of stories?"

Farmer patted his forehead with a handkerchief—sparkling white and pressed, Jenner noticed—and took his time replacing it in his pocket. "Just rumors. I can't remember any specific ones, but the open doors in the stacks disturbed Dr. Applebaum enough that she insisted I continue the old practice of a night watchman in the museum. But it's foolish to be wasting time like this. You want your murderer, Sergeant, just play back the videotapes. His picture will be on one of them. These top three monitors on the left are the only ones that concern us. From left to right screens, we have front door, back door, and side door."

"What about the other monitors, Farmer?" asked

Schroder, plucking another cigarette from a crumpled pack. "Why are they blank?"

"I'd rather you didn't smoke in here, Sergeant. This is very delicate equipment. Cigarette smoke can build up a nicotine film and interfere with efficient operation."

"So I won't light it. Now, what about the blank screens?"

Farmer looked at the unlit cigarette in Schroder's mouth and shrugged. "That's a bad habit, Sergeant. You ought to consider breaking it."

The detective grinned, or at least grimaced, which for Schroder passed for a grin. "You know one of the nice things about investigating a murder, Farmer?"

"The satisfaction of seeing justice served?"

"Yeah, that's the first nice thing. The other one is that my bad habits ain't important. It's other people's habits that matter—like your habit of not answering questions."

Farmer's mouth tightened momentarily, then relaxed. "We generally turn the other cameras off at five, when we close. No point in watching films of an empty museum. We depend on the sound and motion detectors instead, detectors which are not generally on during museum hours except those focused on certain open, very valuable displays. If somebody reached over a railing and grabbed an artifact, like upstairs in the petroleum exhibit, for example, we'd know it. Of course, we'd see it, too, on the monitors."

"That's good," Schroder grunted. "Because unless your motion detectors are a grid of light beams too high to be crawled over, and too low to the floor to be crawled under, they aren't worth jack shit. You got a grid, Farmer?"

The head of museum security was beginning to look as if he wished he'd never heard of the museum, security systems, or Sergeant Ed Schroder. "Not exactly, but we have more than one beam. You have to understand our difficulties here, Sergeant. Too many beams, and any kid who stumbled against a display would set off an alarm. Too few, and the detectors are worthless. Then there are staff members working on displays in the evenings, so detectors have to be deactivated. If people would just follow the rules, there wouldn't be any problems."

Schroder scratched his chin. "Thieves and murderers don't follow the rules, Farmer. Now, let's get back to business. I don't know what your security consultants told you, but unless your sound detectors are sensitive enough to pick up a fly crossing its legs, they aren't worth jack shit, either. Of course, if they *are* that sensitive, you've got the opposite problem. A mouse scratching between the walls, a cricket tuning up, a mosquito buzzing, you got alarms going off everywhere."

"Like the fire alarms," said Goodwin abruptly.

Schroder's nose twitched again. "What about the fire alarms?"

"Goodwin, I wish you'd let me handle the details of our security. You keep interrupting with nonessential information."

"I like Goodwin's interruptions," said Schroder. "What about the fire alarms?"

Goodwin was sweating again, Jenner noticed. Not shock this time, but conflict. The guard was a good man and a loyal employee, but Jenner suspected his loyalty was more to the museum and its director than to Farmer. "You better ask Mr. Farmer, Sergeant," he finally said. "He can tell it better than me."

Farmer ran his hand over his close-cropped hair. "We've had problems with the fire alarms shorting out, but there's no reason to read anything into it. I'm afraid you're getting the wrong idea, Sergeant. This museum has had fewer problems than most others its size, but when something unforeseen occurs, like this murder, people lose their sense of proportion. Small defects, glitches, are exaggerated. This is a good security system, and I have a trustworthy staff operating it. I'll stake my job and reputation on it. Damn it, I'll stake my life on it!"

"Brad Hemphill did," remarked Schroder. "Didn't work for him. Let me kind of summarize what you and Goodwin have told me so far. You know where all the keys are—or think you do. None of the spares have been stolen or substituted—or you think they haven't. You've had power losses—but not lately. Fire alarms going off, sound and motion detectors shorting out, video cameras flickering in the annex—but there's no problem. Everybody signed out of the museum by six o'clock, including Brad Hemphill—''

''No!'' interrupted Farmer. ''Brad Hemphill didn't sign out while I was on duty, and Goodwin didn't relieve me until six.''

''But he had, Darrell,'' said Goodwin, looking confused but insistent. ''I looked at the checkout sheet first thing, and everybody was gone.''

''He didn't leave while I was here!'' stated Farmer. ''You must have missed seeing him, Walter.'' Jenner wondered why Farmer had switched from calling the guard *Goodwin* to addressing him as *Walter*. Was he cajoling the guard into admitting a mistake—or into taking the blame?

Whichever it might be, Walter Goodwin wasn't cooperating. ''I didn't miss him, and I locked the doors at six, right after Maude and her ladies came in. He couldn't get out after that without a key—and he didn't have a key!''

Schroder looked at each man in turn. ''Ain't this nice. We got Hemphill as the little man who wasn't there—not inside the museum trying to get out, or outside trying to get back in. That either of you know of, that is. Let's add that to our summary: checkout sheet—worthless. Looks like your back's to the wall, Farmer. Down to the last defensive position. Now, what say we rewind these videotapes and see who broke into your museum tonight.''

''I have to go across the hall to my office. We have the recorder in there. It's a recommended procedure to keep your recorder locked up in a different location from the monitors. We use eight-hour tapes, inserting new ones once every shift. I put in a fresh tape at five, just before the other guards left.''

Jenner and Schroder followed the security chief into a tiny office and watched as he unlocked a large cabinet behind his desk. Farmer hit switches and pushed buttons, and a whirring sound filled the air as hours of tape rewound. ''How do you want to do this, Sergeant? We can watch seven hours of tape at regular speed, or we can fast-forward it, watching for a movement or a figure. If we see anything, we stop the tape, rewind, and watch that segment.''

He looked at Schroder, his face seeming younger than it had a few minutes before. Jenner suddenly felt sorry for him. Darrell Farmer trusted machinery too much and men too little. It ought to be the other way around.

"Do it," said Schroder. "Fast-forward—back door."

Farmer hit the switch and Goodwin called out from the monitoring room. "There's no date on this tape."

Farmer checked some buttons on the recorder. "Damn it, the date wasn't set."

"Another glitch?" asked Schroder, a sarcastic note in his voice.

Farmer wiped his forehead on his sleeve. "No, just carelessness. Can't blame anyone but myself. But damn it, I remember punching in the date. Must be a short or malfunction. It doesn't matter. We still have the tape."

Jenner squeezed between Schroder and Goodwin as the three men crowded around Farmer. The room was silent except for the sound of four men breathing and the occasional shuffle of feet. The room reeked of Schroder's tobacco smoke and the musty odor of antiquity. Age had its own peculiar smell.

"Nothing there except Walter checking the door," said Farmer as he finished playing the first tape.

"Front door next," said Schroder without expression.

"Nobody would choose that door. It's right by a busy street, lots of light. I think we'd be wasting our time viewing that one."

"Do it," said Schroder.

Farmer looked as if he might argue, but, instead, he shrugged his shoulders and stepped back into his office and punched a button.

Schroder leaned closer to the monitor. Jenner watched the screen with equal attention. He yawned as Farmer walked back and forth between his office and the monitoring room, slowing the tape, rewinding it, and playing it back at regular speed at Schroder's direction. He straightened when he saw Brad Hemphill appear on the tape.

"That's him, Sergeant," said Farmer, pressing the pause

button. "That proves it. Hemphill did check out just like the sheet said."

Schroder rubbed his chin. "Kinda funny, ain't it, Farmer. You just got through swearing he didn't check out while you were on the desk."

Farmer looked puzzled. "I don't remember him, but that's why we have video. It's better than fallible human memories."

"That's so, I guess," said Schroder. "Who's the guy behind Hemphill?" He pointed at a tall, thin young man whose curly brown hair was neatly bunched in a ponytail that hung past his shoulders.

"Abe Yates, assistant curator, works—worked with Hemphill. He needs a haircut, but that's his only flaw. He's been here eight months or so. Came to work right out of college. He follows the rules exactly, I'll give him that. Always confers with me personally when he's going to work late or needs the detectors turned off so he can change an exhibit. The rest of the staff ought to be that conscientious. Jesus, that Roberto Ortiz thinks the rules are for everybody but him. He's always bragging about some ancestor of his who came to Texas almost before God created it." Farmer tapped the monitor. "That's him, just behind Hemphill. Light brown hair and blue eyes. Never did look very Hispanic to me, but what the hell! If his family's been here as long as he insists, he's as much a mongrel as the rest of us. I'll bet the only Germanic heritage you have left is your name, Sergeant Schroder."

Schroder took his limp, unlit cigarette out of his mouth. "Probably so, but I'm not a mongrel. I'm a junkyard dog. They're twice as mean. But that's enough of genetics. Point out the rest of the staff on the tape. I like to have the advantage when I meet somebody for the first time. That's the junkyard dog in me."

Farmer obediently turned back to the screen, and Jenner decided the guard was definitely ex-military. He recognized authority when he heard it. "That's Dr. Applebaum, the woman with the black curly hair. To be precise, she has a lot of gray in her hair, but it's all in the front. Always wears a suit with blouses that have frills and ruffles. Now this one, the woman at the end of the line, with her hair in a knot or bun or whatever you call it, is Margaret Clark, our archivist. Glasses, doesn't smile much, acts like a dotty old woman, but good at security, almost a fanatic, in fact. I never find her door unlocked. The librarian from hell, you might say." He chuckled at his own joke.

Walter Goodwin frowned. "Mrs. Clark's had a hard life, Darrell. She lost her only daughter twenty years ago this month. She's always a little grim-looking in October. But she's friendly enough, always helpful, and speaks politely to everybody. She just doesn't get close to people. Except Brad Hemphill. He was her favorite. Sort of mothered him, she did, which was fine. He always looked like he needed it."

Farmer pointed out the rest of the staff—secretaries, assistant curators, guards, volunteers—none of them summoning one of the guard's pithy personality profiles. Jenner realized that Farmer hadn't said anything about Hemphill, either. While it might have been out of respect for the dead, Jenner doubted it. More likely, Brad Hemphill simply didn't register on Darrell Farmer's scale, dead or alive.

"Side door," said Schroder after Farmer fast-forwarded the rest of tape.

Farmer hit another button, and the four men watched the last tape. Again nothing—not even staff members or visitors leaving. The side door was always locked, day or night.

"That's it, Sergeant," said Farmer. "Nobody came in any of the doors."

Jenner slapped the burly detective on the back. "Guess what, Schroder, you've got a locked-room mystery. Beats the hell out of blood and guts, like the Butcher case."

Schroder looked at him and shook his head. "Son, are you being deliberately stupid just to irritate me, or is your brain shrinking?"

"Which means I've got a security break somewhere. A window maybe, in the stacks area," continued Farmer.

Schroder grinned, like a shark about to take a bite out of a swimmer. "You sure as hell do have a security break, Farmer. Somebody switched your damned videotapes."

"That's impossible!" exclaimed Farmer, a hysterical note in his voice.

Schroder lit his cigarette and inhaled. He let the smoke trickle out slowly before he spoke. "Any of you happen to notice that the tapes didn't record the entire Canyon police department busting in through those doors after Goodwin reported the body? Now, how do you suppose they got in without getting their mugs on videotape?"

CHAPTER SEVEN

LYDIA SQUIRMED AROUND ON ONE OF THE BENCHES IN search of a comfortable position. She'd tried one of the cushioned chairs first, but decided the rock-hard and lumpy stuffing hadn't been changed since the First Crusade. The bench was rock-hard, too, but it wasn't lumpy. In this mausoleum you took your advantages where you found them.

She also decided that one reason women in the Middle Ages wore so many petticoats and other under- and overgarments had nothing to do with modesty. They wore the damn things for padding, and she wished she had some. It was just as she thought: five minutes on the bench, and your behind went numb. However, the alternative to sitting on the bench was standing, and whenever she stood, some fool either made a crack about her costume or stumbled over her shoes. She could slip off the shoes and go barefoot, of course, but it was October, and the stone floors were like ice. Frostbite must have been a problem in castles.

She took another sip of her bourbon-and-water and tried to remember if it was her second or third. Her third, she concluded, though only her second to consume—since she'd spilled one on a silicon-injected redhead who had gazed in pseudo-shock at her costume, then asked if she bought all her clothes at Wal-Mart. Actually she did, but she wasn't in the mood to defend her shopping habits, particularly to someone too stupid to realize the only attractive redheads were the ones to the color born, so to speak. Red hair from a bottle always looked false, like a cheap print of a Rembrandt.

Lydia leaned her head against the tall back of the bench and closed her eyes. At least she wasn't cheap. Not at two hundred dollars a pop. She wasn't false, either; not anymore. She'd washed off her clown makeup in a bathroom that had a marble tub large enough to swim laps in and a toilet with gardenias floating in its bowl. She'd ripped off her wig, combed her hair, had a good cry, and now felt considerably better.

Throwing up on the gardenias helped, too.

She opened one eye and looked over toward John Lloyd holding court. It seemed that every female of every conceivable shape, size, age, and Clairol color had ogled, cooed, simpered, and pawed over him for the past hour—or however long it had been since she'd told him to go to hell and locked herself in the bathroom. She seemed to remember telling him to go away and drop dead, not necessarily in that order, but she'd been vomiting into the gardenias at that particular time, so it was possible her memory was faulty.

But not likely.

It sounded exactly like something she'd do—send away the only person on the premises who might care whether she lived or drowned among the gardenias. Just because he'd told her the truth.

"And you killed him, Lydia, but you have not exorcised his ghost."

She sat up and swallowed the rest of her drink in one gulp. He was right, damn it, but he could have been more subtle, something on the order of "My dear Miss Fairchild, it has come to my attention that your behavior has been uncharacteristically subdued. May I offer myself as a kindly audience of one?"

She'd have snickered in his face and denied acting any differently.

No, she thought, shifting on the hard bench and rubbing first one numb hip, then the other, subtlety wasn't the proper strategy, and John Lloyd knew it. So he'd tried shock treatment. She'd turned hysterical, locked herself in the bathroom, and sent him away. Her solitary accomplishment was making sure that John Lloyd never invited Lydia Fairchild to any party more socially selective than a cow chip–throwing contest.

"And you killed him, Lydia, but you have not exorcised his ghost."

She couldn't. How can you exorcise the ghost of a man you can't remember killing? To her subconscious the Boulevard Butcher was alive, and she was still helpless, still trapped, still afraid.

She set her empty glass on the little wooden footstool and clenched her fists. It was as if at the moment she killed him, she'd released a malevolent spirit, a ghost, determined to survive by blanking out her memory of its death.

"Do you mind if I sit down?"

Lydia jerked her head up to stare at Mary Todd Lincoln. "Uh, uh."

"Thank you. I'm so tired. I didn't want to come, but I had to. It was my responsibility. And I don't blame Bill Whitney for the party. Bless his heart, he knows this is my anniversary. It's that wife of his. She knew, but she didn't care. She was always like that. I knew them both as children. They were my daughter's friends."

"Uh, uh," said Lydia.

The plump little woman settled herself on the bench beside Lydia and peered at her through small wire-rimmed glasses. "Are you all right, young lady? You look as if you'd seen a ghost."

Lydia cleared her throat and wished she had another drink. "Uh, no, I'm fine. I haven't seen a ghost. Ghosts don't exist."

"Oh, you do talk. I was afraid you suffered from a speech impediment. You were gargling your words a moment ago."

"I had something caught in my throat," said Lydia, studying the elderly woman more closely. The plump round face, the slight double chin, and the black bonnet complete with mourning veil gave the casual observer the impression of looking at Mrs. Lincoln's twin. The resemblance disappeared on closer examination. Whereas Mary Todd Lincoln's features, at least in her photographs, had looked too close together and too small for the plump roundness of her face, this woman's were more generously spaced and bolder: more distance between the eyes, a more prominent nose, a wider, fuller mouth. While not beautiful, it was a perfectly proportioned face, strong, solid, determined.

The woman's dress was black silk, with long, tight sleeves and a high neck. A brooch at the neck of the gown looked as if it were woven of hair. Lydia swallowed noisily. It *was* woven of hair, and Lydia didn't think it was rabbit or mink or from the woman's favorite Persian. It was human hair, and that was a mourning brooch. God, how morbid!

"That's an unusual costume," remarked Lydia, looking desperately for a waiter. She wanted a drink, any kind of drink.

"It's a mourning dress from the 1860s," replied the woman, scooting carefully back on the bench so her hoop skirt wouldn't tip up and expose her undergarments. Lydia surmised they must be black, too.

"I thought I recognized it," said Lydia. "From museums, biographies of uh, Queen Victoria, old paintings. I've never worn one, of course." She snapped her mouth closed before she sounded more flighty than she already did. Flighty? Did she actually think that word? John Lloyd Branson's vocabulary was contagious.

"They knew how to mourn then," continued the woman, looking into the fireplace, or rather, beyond it at something Lydia couldn't see and didn't want to imagine. "Black clothing, mourning veils, keepsakes of the loved ones." She clutched her brooch. "I wove this myself from my daughter's hair. It wasn't like today, you know. Today we bury the dead quickly so we can forget them and go on with our lives. We deny death. That's what we do with our elaborate funerals and perpetual-care cemeteries. We must face death in order to appreciate the fragility of life."

Lydia briefly wondered: If I wear a mourning brooch, would the Butcher finally die? Then she shuddered with revulsion.

The woman touched her arm. "Are you cold, young lady? You're shivering."

"No—yes, just a little. Sudden draft from those French doors. I don't know why Mrs. Whitney leaves them open. It's Halloween, for God's sake! It couldn't be more than forty degrees outside. It's cold as a tomb in here." Damn it, why had she used that simile?

The old woman was staring into the fireplace again. "I've always thought a tomb must be as cold as that woman's heart." She turned suddenly and grabbed Lydia's arm. "What possessed her to have this party tonight? She knew I'd feel obliged to come."

Lydia gently pulled herself out of the woman's grasp and moved a few inches down the bench. "Why didn't you just send in your contribution and not attend? Believe me, that's what I would have done if I'd been given a choice."

The woman shook her head. "I couldn't. I'm on the staff. I'm sorry. I've been so impolite. I always am this time of year. My spells, you see. My name is Margaret Clark. I'm the museum archivist." She waited expectantly, a plump little lady who was either very eccentric or slightly mad.

"I'm Lydia Fairchild, John Lloyd Branson's, uh, associate." She'd almost said date, but caught herself.

"I know John Lloyd. He's on the museum committee. That's the governing board of the museum under the Board of Regents. He's also on the executive committee of the historical society."

"He does a lot of charity work," agreed Lydia.

"He's a kindly, understanding, generous man," Margaret Clark said. "Almost a saint."

Lydia's mouth gaped open. John Lloyd Branson a saint? Absolutely, positively not! She glanced across the room at him. He looked up at that moment, and she felt the backs of her thighs tingle again. Even if John Lloyd weren't arrogant, stubborn, devious, and frequently overbearing, no man who could induce tingles with a single high-wattage glance from across the room would ever qualify for sainthood. She glanced away and heard the end of the Margaret Clark's sentence.

". . . my son-in-law."

"John Lloyd was your son-in-law?" she gasped. The lawyer had never mentioned having been married. But that didn't mean anything; John Lloyd Branson dispensed personal information about as freely as a miser parted with a dime.

Margaret gave her a sharp look. "Of course not. Bill Whitney was nearly my son-in-law, but it didn't happen. Still, I was surprised when he married his present wife. I think he pitied her. She was such a desperate little thing, but pity is no basis for a relationship. Don't you agree?"

Lydia nodded, so relieved that she didn't trust herself to speak. But she wished the archivist hadn't mentioned pity. In fact, she wished the garrulous old woman would just go away. She glanced down at the footstool, on which lay a book bound in leather. *History of the Bancroft Whitney Family* was engraved in gold on the front cover. Idly, Lydia picked up the book and glanced at the title page. Privately published, she noted. What else? The Bancroft Whitneys might be hot stuff in the Panhandle, but not to the commercial publishing houses. No Bancroft Whitney had ever been president, a ball player earning the equivalent of the national debt, a corporate executive, a film star writing of past lives, an astrologer, or a serial killer—so the American public presumedly wasn't interested.

Margaret Clark droned on, something about her daughter, who, like John Lloyd, evidently possessed all the virtues of a saint. Lydia glanced through the Bancroft Whitney history, stopping to look at the photographs. Studying pictures of total strangers was better than listening to the museum archivist.

She leaned over her book, looking closely at the photograph of a much younger Bill Whitney, twenty years younger judging by the car he was sitting in, snuggling up to an attractive girl with curly black hair. Thinking it must be Margaret Clark's daughter, Lydia glanced at the caption and frowned. The girl's name had been neatly blacked out with what looked like India ink.

Several other young men and women crowded into the car, but the faces meant nothing to her. Except one. A young girl sitting alone on the hood of the car, her face pinched and forlorn, was the present Mrs. Whitney. Lydia glanced back at the caption and mentally apologized. Mrs. Whitney's name really was Monique.

She slammed the book closed and laid it back on the footstool. So she was wrong about the name; that didn't mean she was wrong about the woman. Monique Whitney was the kind who only had fun at someone else's expense, like at a beheading.

"She died tonight," said Margaret abruptly. A tear slid down her plump cheek.

Feeling disoriented, Lydia jerked around to stare at the woman, trying to grasp the threads of their conversation. "Monique? No, she didn't, not unless Bill Whitney just killed her in the study with the rope, knife, or candlestick." Lydia giggled.

"My daughter," said Margaret Clark, looking directly at Lydia while another tear slipped down her cheek.

Lydia's giggle turned to a gasp of horror and she stared at the mourning brooch. If Margaret Clark's daughter just died, how could she weave the brooch so quickly? The images that question evoked gave Lydia another chill, but whatever the truth was about the daughter, Lydia didn't intend to cross-examine an obviously demented woman. Best to humor her. And get John Lloyd! Let him deal with Margaret Clark. Lydia couldn't cope with her own ghost, much less anybody else's.

Cautiously she reached over to pat the older woman's shoulder. "I'm so sorry. I didn't mean to sound so callous, but I didn't know you were talking about your daughter when I made that silly joke. John Lloyd keeps telling me my behavior is inappropriate sometimes. So is my mouth. God, I feel awful." She rose to her feet, congratulating herself on how she'd handled the woman. "Let me find John Lloyd, and we'll take you home. Don't worry about a thing."

Margaret Clark grabbed her wrist with the strength of a much younger woman. "Don't bother John Lloyd."

Lydia froze. "Why not? John Lloyd's accustomed to dealing with crises. I have them all the time." She saw John Lloyd watching them and tried to look as desperate as possible. It wasn't hard.

The woman sighed and released Lydia's arm. "John Lloyd knows all about my spells, Lydia. He's helped me through them often enough. Sit down, please. I'm getting a muscle spasm in my neck from looking up at you."

Lydia hesitated, saw John Lloyd advancing toward them, and collapsed on the bench. The calvary was coming. All she had to do was hold the battle line. "I don't understand."

Margaret removed her bonnet and put it on her lap, gently smoothing the mourning veil so it wouldn't be crushed. "I know you don't, Lydia. I was too incoherent, I'm afraid. I often am, except at my job. I'm very organized at that, very professional."

"Good evening, Margaret." John Lloyd's voice was deep and very slow, his drawl pronounced. "Are you well?"

"If you mean am I coping, then no, not very well. I managed to confuse and frighten your young lady, and now I have to apologize before she thinks I'm mad." She patted Lydia's knee. "I am mad, my dear, but I'm not dangerous, although I could be if I ever discovered who murdered my daughter, Lindsey."

"Oh, my God!" breathed Lydia, her hands groping in the air. For what she didn't know.

Margaret Clark knew. "For goodness' sake, John Lloyd! Sit down and hold the girl before she flails around and knocks over a precious antique. Then we'd have Monique Whitney threatening her with a lawsuit and wanting you to file it."

"Let her interior decorator file it," said John Lloyd, kicking the footstool aside and sitting down to grasp Lydia's hands. "Miss Fairchild, are you all right?"

"Uh, uh," replied Lydia.

"She's lost her voice again," said Margaret. "Does she do that often, John Lloyd?"

"No!" shouted Lydia, jerking her hands out of his grasp,

then cringing when several other guests turned to look at her. "No," she said more quietly. "I didn't lose my voice, John Lloyd, and you can stop examining me for symptoms of insanity. I'm perfectly fine. I've already had my quota of hysterics for the evening. I was disconcerted for a minute, that's all. Happens every time I have a conversation with somebody who looks like Mary Todd Lincoln and talks about murdered daughters."

"I do, don't I?" asked Margaret in a pensive voice. "I've always felt so sorry for Mrs. Lincoln, losing all those sons, then her husband in such a horrible manner. It unbalanced her, poor woman. I can sympathize with her, since my only child was murdered, then my husband, of course."

"Your husband was murdered, too?" asked Lydia, feeling sorry again for this poor tortured woman. No wonder she was addled.

"Oh, no, my dear. He divorced me and married some youngster. I thought at the time he should be arrested for child molestation, but I'm more philosophical now. I was quite distraught over Lindsey, and he just couldn't take it, kept fluttering around telling me to pull myself together. I'd always taken care of him, you see, and when I couldn't, he left. He never was a strong person, and I couldn't prop him up anymore. I was broken myself. That's why I came over to sit by you, Lydia. You looked broken, too. All that business with that horrible man you killed."

"What!" gasped Lydia.

Margaret tilted her head to one side and peered at Lydia. "It was in all the papers, my dear, and I'm a very literate person, although I must admit that sometimes I sneak home with those awful tabloids from the supermarket. There's something so satisfying in all that scandal. I suspect it's because people at heart are such gossips. Oh, I'm being incoherent again. Or is it disconnected? At any rate, I read about you, and how young and sensitive and sheltered you were, and I felt so sorry for you. A young girl from a nice family isn't raised to kill people, but it's infinitely better than letting them kill you. It does take some getting used to, though. I was going to tell you so, but before I could stop myself, I began talking, and my own story came out in bits and pieces, not like a story at all, and I'm sure you believe I'm the one who should be committed. But I've been through that—commitment, I mean—completely voluntary, of course. And it didn't help. All those counselors sounded just like my husband, except their vocabularies were more refined." She finished her sentence in a rush and pressed her hand over her breast. "My, I'm nearly breathless, and I still haven't explained. You'd better tell her, John Lloyd."

"Margaret's daughter was murdered twenty years ago on Halloween, Miss Fairchild, and the crime was never solved."

"Twenty years! And you're still talking as if it just happened?" asked Lydia, staring at Margaret. "I appreciate your concern, but I don't want to spend every day for the next twenty years reliving my experience."

Margaret removed her mourning brooch, gently touched the braided hair, then dropped the piece of jewelry in a tiny beaded black reticule. She pulled the drawstrings tight. "Oh, I don't do that, my dear. I really would be mad, wouldn't I? I only mourn on Halloween night. The rest of the year I'm completely sane. Well, maybe not completely, but functionally sane. Is there such a condition, John Lloyd? Of course there is. Why am I asking? Many people are functionally sane for the same reason I am. Compromise, Lydia. I compromised with my grief. I wallow in it one day a year, tell my story to whoever will listen. Like the Ancient Mariner. The rest of the year I perform my duties at the museum. My spare time I devote to my avocation. I solve murders."

"My God, John Lloyd, now she thinks she's Miss Marple!" said Lydia.

Margaret frowned. "Of course I don't, my dear. I don't knit, and I hate gardening. I told you, I'm an archivist. That means I know how to organize a body of records and information. It also means that I know how to find things. Archivists make first-rate detectives. Remember the credit card receipt for the fish aquarium, John Lloyd?"

John Lloyd chuckled, gazing at the woman with affection. "Margaret's detective work saved my client from a life sentence for murder, Miss Fairchild. She is what the police call an informed source. Her information enables the police to obtain grand jury subpoenas for evidence that might otherwise remain beyond their knowledge and beyond their reach."

"I track a criminal by following his paper trail, my dear," said Margaret. "A property sale, a credit card purchase, tax records, phone calls, banking transactions."

"References again, Miss Fairchild," said John Lloyd. "Seemingly unrelated bits of information that have meaning only when considered within a specific context."

"I prefer to call them secrets, my dear," said Margaret. "People will murder to keep the silliest secrets. Like the woman who murdered her husband so he wouldn't find out she'd exceeded the limit on her Visa card."

"How do you find some of these references?" asked Lydia.

Margaret looked uneasy, then shrugged her shoulders. "I'm computer literate."

"What?" cried Lydia. "You're not saying what I think you're saying."

The archivist looked indignant. "If a schoolboy can plant a virus in our national defense mainframe, surely I can peek at a suspect's phone bill."

"But it's illegal!"

"I prefer to think of it as justifiable technological vigilante activity," replied Margaret firmly.

"John Lloyd, for God's sake, tell her she could go to jail if she gets caught," demanded Lydia, twisting around on the hard bench to face the lawyer.

But John Lloyd had risen and was walking to meet a solemn-faced Bill Whitney.

CHAPTER EIGHT

SINCE A PLASTIC BODY BAG CREATES STATIC ELECTRICITY that disturbs contact evidence such as hairs and fibers, Special Crimes never places the victim inside the bag. Nor do they actually cover the body with sheets for the same reason. Unless, of course, the corpse is in an advanced state of decomposition—in which case they can't get it wrapped and bagged fast enough.

Brad Hemphill's body, however, was fresh. It rested atop two clean white sheets for all to see. A murder victim was its own best witness if nothing disturbed its silent testimony before Special Crimes could examine it inch by inch under magnifying glasses and argon laser, taking fingerprints and samples of hair, blood, saliva, fibers, and fingernail scrapings. There were swabs of body cavities in the case of suspected sexual assault. There were the measuring and photographing of wounds, cuts, abrasions, burns, and bite marks. If one planned to commit murder, he or she had best not do it in Potter, Randall, or Armstrong counties of the Texas Panhandle. The men and women of the Special Crimes Unit were meticulous and formidable.

Very formidable.

Which was one reason Larry Jenner knew he had no business in Special Crimes.

He wasn't formidable.

Dressed in disposable clothing from head to foot, including cap, goggles, and face mask, Jenner leaned against one of the waist-high pillars in front of the allosaurus skeleton and scrubbed his hands with his handkerchief. The justice of the peace had come, pronounced Brad Hemphill dead, ordered an autopsy, and left, all within five minutes and all without getting any closer to the body than the doorway. Jenner didn't blame the guy. A JP wasn't a medical examiner or a pathologist. He wasn't formidable. He was just a poor schmuck whom the taxpayers of his precinct elected to perform a variety of necessary duties, one of which was to examine bodies whose occupants had departed without benefit of medical supervision and to order autopsies to determine if the departure was voluntary or involuntary. No point in the man poking around on the body just to appear official, a point of view with which Jenner agreed. He certainly had no intention of touching it again. He had already lifted the body off the triceratops skull with the help of another cop from Special Crimes. As far as Jenner was concerned, that constituted poking, and once was enough.

He scrubbed his hands again to remove the feel of dead flesh. Not that he'd actually touched the body with his hands—he'd worn two pairs of disposable gloves, which he'd immediately peeled off. He wasn't sure why touching a murder victim bothered him so much—God knows, he touched enough dead bodies as a traffic cop—but it did. He figured it had something to do with his own sense of outrage at the deliberateness of murder.

"Jenner, quit washing your hands like Lady Macbeth and get your ass over here." Schroder squatted by the body, pulling on a second pair of surgical gloves. "I want to take a quick look-see at the body."

Jenner considered not moving but decided against it. Right now Schroder was as unpleasant as a snapping turtle with a sour stomach. He shuffled toward the body, his paper booties making a whispering sound on the tile floor. "What do you want me to do? Hold your coat for you?"

Schroder flexed his fingers and looked up at the sergeant. "Jenner, you look like somebody wrapped you up in toilet paper."

Jenner folded his arms. "I don't mess around bodies without protective clothing."

The investigator shrugged his shoulders. "Suit yourself, but as long as you're all decked out, squat down and get some hands-on experience, son."

Jenner's mouth dried up. "What?"

"I want some idea of what killed this boy."

"Good God, Schroder! That's the pathologist's job."

"I can't wait three or four hours for the autopsy."

"Why not? It's better than stumbling around blind."

"I got a three-story museum full of lethal weapons to search, Jenner. I want some idea of what I'm looking for. There's every kind of gun from old muzzle-loaders to modern automatics—"

"I didn't see any sign of a bullet hole, Schroder, and Goodwin didn't hear any gunshot."

"—and then there's bowie knives, buffalo-hiding knives, scalping knives, butcher knives, bayonets, arrows, and damn Indian lances."

"But that stuff's all locked up, Schroder."

"So was the goddamn museum, but that didn't stop somebody from running in and out, like it had a revolving door." Schroder tugged the victim's collar down and examined his neck. "He wasn't strangled—no marks at all."

"And he wasn't stabbed, either, Schroder. No blood, no holes in his shirt."

"Roll him over."

Jenner's mouth dried up all over again. "What!"

Schroder frowned, and his eyebrows met in one long bristly line across his forehead. "I want to see the victim's back. I saw you lift him off that skull. You had your eyes closed. He could have a hole the size of your fist in his back, and you wouldn't know it. Now, roll him over, but put on some gloves. Duded out like a roll of Northern toilet tissue, and you don't have on gloves. What's your idea of safe sex, Jenner? Putting a rubber over your head?''

Jenner gritted his teeth when he heard the snickering from the other cops—campus security, Canyon police, Special Crimes—all watching and listening. He knelt down and pulled on another pair of surgical gloves. ''Did you have to make a crack like that, Schroder? Listen to those jackasses laugh.''

''They're just releasing tension. Working a murder scene's stressful business.''

''Jesus, Schroder, what about my stress?''

''You work it all out by bitching. Now quit screwing around and turn Hemphill over, but carefully. We don't want any postmortem bruising.''

Jenner glanced at the body and felt a chill slither down his spine, like a snake in a hurry. He swallowed, put one hand under Hemphill's shoulder, the other under his hips, and gently shifted the body onto its stomach. ''Sorry,'' he muttered under his breath to the corpse.

''What'd you say?'' asked Schroder.

''Nothing, just clearing my throat.'' No way was he going to admit to anybody, particularly Schroder, that he felt he was invading Brad Hemphill's privacy. Which was ridiculous. Hemphill was dead, and just because a tired, overimaginative cop, who shouldn't be investigating homicides in the first place, sensed some kind of presence that needed reassurance damn sure didn't mean that presence really existed. A good cop doesn't believe in ghosts, and he, Sergeant Larry Jenner, was a by-God good cop.

Schroder gave him the same look that Jenner's high school principal used to favor him with, the one that said: *I know you're lying, but I don't have time to stop what I'm doing to wring the truth out of you.*

Which was all right with Jenner.

Schroder rocked back on his heels and examined the body. ''No visible stab wounds.''

''I told you so!''

''No, son,'' continued Schroder. ''I don't believe a knife

killed you, but we'll find out what did. You can rest easy." He stroked the victim's hair.

"Jesus Christ, Schroder!" whispered Jenner. "You're talking to him like he's still alive."

"Sometimes I wonder if murder victims let go of life all at once, or if something stays behind for a while to protest their manner of leaving."

Jenner glanced around the dimly lit exhibit hall filled with its fossil record of extinct life forms and wondered if each skull, each skeleton, had really turned its empty sockets and bony frame toward him as if waiting for his answer. Or if he imagined it. The other cops were certainly waiting, but oddly enough, none of them looked as if they were about to laugh.

Jenner shivered. "You mean, like ghosts?"

"I don't believe in ghosts. But it never hurts to have a little compassion." Schroder's fingers gently pressed Hemphill's skull just above and to the back of his right ear. "Son of a bitch," he exclaimed softly. "Jenner, I'm losing my touch, getting the cart before the horse. I'm worrying about modern murder weapons like guns and knives."

"There's nothing very modern about a knife, Schroder. Cavemen had them."

Schroder shook his head. "Before men had knives, they had clubs, Jenner. The old blunt instrument. Feel Hemphill's head. He's got a soft spot just above the left temporal ridge. Bone's crushed."

"I'll take your word for it," said Jenner, his stomach feeling queasy again.

"Blunt force trauma, Jenner. Subdural hematoma—blood clot to you—victim goes into a coma and dies. Surefire way to murder someone. A good solid blow to the temporal ridge—right or left—or to the back of the skull above the brain stem is damn near always fatal. Even when it isn't fatal—which ain't often—the victim's brain is so scrambled, he can't remember his own name, much less who hit him. We've got so many assholes running around shooting people that we tend to forget that the oldest method of murder is still one of the best. It's quiet, efficient, you don't need any special skills, and you don't have to be Superman. Any ten-year-old kid with a baseball bat and a decent swing can kill."

"God, Schroder," breathed Jenner.

"*He* didn't have anything to do with it, son," said Schroder, lifting Hemphill's head, then gently manipulating one of his shoulders. "But I would appreciate His help keeping my head above the shit I'm fixing to walk into."

"What are you talking about, Schroder?"

Schroder stood up, his joints creaking like a windmill in a gale, and stripped off his gloves. "This is what they call a high-visibility case. Curator murdered in a museum, and not just any museum but the Panhandle-Plains Historical Museum, which is about as sacred a place to this part of Texas as a church. The whole damn population is going to be screaming for blood. What's worse, Hemphill's neck is stiff, and his shoulder's getting that way. Rigor mortis, son, and rigor sets in anywhere from four to six hours after death. That ain't a hard-and-fast rule, but it fits the circumstances."

"What circumstances, Schroder?"

"Hemphill dying sometime between six and eight tonight after the museum's locked up—or, at least, after the public is locked out. It ain't logical to suppose that some visitor whacked Hemphill on the head, hid himself and the body so well that Goodwin didn't find them when he made his rounds at six, sabotaged the security system, and had keys to the doors. My gut tells me somebody on the staff did it, and the staff is damn near as respected as the museum itself. That means, in case you haven't figured it out, that the shit is going to hit the fan when we start interrogating them. These are law-abiding citizens, or at least they were—until one of them took a blunt instrument to Brad Hemphill's skull. People like that aren't used to police procedure. At first they'll be cooperative as hell. Then, when we ask specific questions, like where were you when Hemphill was killed, they start getting scared and feeling guilty and surly, and finally, they make phone calls, and we're going to be ass-deep in alligators. Or lawyers. Same difference."

"You missed your calling, Sergeant Schroder. You should have been one of those . . . alligators, I believe you called us. Your knack for brilliant and succinct summation would be welcome in the legal profession.''

Jenner scrambled to his feet and stared at the tall, lean man who stood a scant three feet away. Then he turned to Schroder. The detective's right eyelid blinked furiously in a nervous tic. ''What the hell are you doing here, Branson?''

CHAPTER NINE

NOTEBOOK IN HAND, LYDIA WAITED OUTSIDE THE EXHIBIT hall for John Lloyd. She had planned to enter with him—right up to the minute he'd walked past the diorama of the dimetrodon that guarded the paleontology exhibit. But when the time came to take that last step around the corner, she couldn't.

John Lloyd had stopped, his head tilted to one side as if he'd been listening to her footsteps. "Miss Fairchild?" he asked without turning his head.

"I can't." Her voice was so soft, she could hardly hear it herself.

He turned to face her, that same intense look in his eyes that always seemed to pierce her skull and read the thoughts inside. "Ghosts again, Miss Fairchild?"

She turned and stumbled back the way she'd come, glad she'd changed into tennis shoes in the car on the way to the museum. Now she could run faster and quieter—it was important all of a sudden that she be quiet. She had made it as far as the foyer between Pioneer Hall and the glass-fronted room with its oil derrick when John Lloyd caught her.

He clasped her arm. "Miss Fairchild, whom are you running away from?"

She twisted away to shrink back against a wall, pressing both hands against her chest. Her heart pounded until her whole body felt buffeted by the rhythm of its beat. She wondered that John Lloyd couldn't see her shaking. Chills tingled over her skin. She felt unintegrated, a being of disparate parts. She tried to swallow, but her tongue felt swollen. Call it anxiety reaction or call it flashback, she knew that if she walked around that corner into the paleontology exhibit, the Butcher would be waiting.

She saw John Lloyd, his face taut with frustration and concern. "I'm sorry, John Lloyd." Her voice wavered and cracked.

John Lloyd muttered a four-letter profanity Lydia didn't know he knew and whipped a handkerchief out of his pocket. "Sit down, Miss Fairchild, here on the floor, since my grandmother's fainting couch is unavailable. Close your eyes and take four deep breaths. No more than four, please. Remember that."

Lydia let herself slide down the wall to the floor. She might as well sit down. Her legs weren't functioning anyway. Carefully she inhaled, watching John Lloyd as he nodded encouragement. With a touch as delicate as a rose petal he stroked her eyelids and she obediently closed her eyes. She felt him cradle her chin in one hand as he blotted her face with his handkerchief, drying her skin and warming it at the same time.

"Steady, Miss Fairchild. One more breath, please, then you may rise."

Again she inhaled deeply, filling her lungs to capacity. Then she relaxed and opened her eyes. Her hands still trembled, she noticed, and she felt weak and shaky, but otherwise all right. The crisis was over, and the patient was stable—until the next time. "I'm sorry."

John Lloyd rose with only a slight awkwardness and reached down to help her up. "As always, you are welcome, Miss Fairchild."

She wiped her damp palms on the trousers of her clown

suit and cleared her throat. "Was that one of your grandmother's home remedies for a gentlewoman suffering a spell, John Lloyd, or is inhalation therapy the latest treatment for hysteria?"

"My grandmother would most likely have thrown a pitcher of cold water in your face, Miss Fairchild, immediately followed by a glass of lemonade heavily laced with gin, administered orally, of course. Having neither cold water nor gin, I improvised. Counting breaths distracted your mind from fear and prevented a more embarrassing situation from developing. I do not believe my reputation would survive my future law partner's locking herself in the bathroom twice in a single evening."

She felt herself blush from her hairline to her breastbone. "I'm sorry about that, too, John Lloyd."

He tucked his handkerchief back in his pocket. "Please, Miss Fairchild. While two abject apologies from you in the space of five minutes may feed my fragile masculine ego, such groveling is not necessary. I forgive you."

"Fragile! *Fragile!* Your ego is cast iron, John Lloyd. And my apologies were not abject. And I do not grovel!"

He chuckled. "Anger is another potent restorative, is it not, Miss Fairchild?"

"You were baiting me!"

"And you rose to it as surely as a rainbow trout after the fisherman's fly." He stroked her cheek. "Your color is high, your back is straight, and your fists are clenched. Much better than the passionless little creature you have been most of the evening."

She slapped his hand away. "What would you know about passion, you Victorian stuffed shirt. You never even shook my hand when I got off the plane this afternoon."

"You were expecting an embrace?" he asked.

She evaded his eyes, which always saw too much and too deeply, and considered his question. What had she expected? A quiet party with congenial neighbors, followed by a long, intimate conversation interspersed with light lovemaking in front of his fireplace, sipping white wine between kisses? God, but she must be slipping farther from reality than she realized. In the first place, John Lloyd didn't have congenial neighbors. Two aging spinsters who always baked him apple pies and acted as if they suspected her of some unspecified but unseemly behavior lived on one side, and a retiring bachelor who stuttered whenever he saw her lived on the other. In the second place, how could they have an intimate conversation when John Lloyd guarded his private thoughts with polysyllabic sentences—and she couldn't talk about the Butcher? In the third place, they both hated white wine.

They were soon-to-be law partners, nothing else. She might as well save face before he accused her of attempted seduction. Or in his grandmother's parlance, of acting like a shameless hussy.

She straightened her shoulders and peered at him. "Of course not. Aren't you always telling me that anything but a business relationship between us would be inappropriate? It's just as well. Breaking through your icy reserve always gives me a chill anyway."

He nodded, his face a mask concealing any effect her words might have had. "Then if you have sufficiently recovered your composure, Miss Fairchild, shall we beard Sergeant Schroder in his den?"

Her throat clamped down and she had difficulty forcing her words past her frozen vocal cords. "I can't go in there."

"Because it is a crime scene?"

That wasn't the reason, but it would suffice. "I can't handle it yet, John Lloyd, I'm sorry. I'll follow you as far as the entrance and lean against the wall out of sight, listen, and take notes. See"—she fumbled in her shoulder bag—"I brought my notebook."

"If I needed a secretary, I would have called my own. However, I try to keep Mrs. Dinwittie away from scenes of violence whenever possible. She is easily upset."

"Mrs. Dinwittie chopped up her husband with an

axe. What kind of violence could bother her after that?''

His lips quivered, as if he considered smiling and decided against it. ''Perhaps I should say she is easily stimulated. I do not wish her to suffer a relapse.''

Lydia grimaced. ''Mrs. Dinwittie suffering a flashback with an axe in her hand would be bad for business.''

''Exactly,'' he said. ''And so is an associate who fears what lies behind every corner, Miss Fairchild. I am a defense attorney who specializes in murder. I always view crime scenes. They are often an important reference in the context of the crime.''

She licked her lips. ''We can divide our responsibilities. I can stay behind in the office and prepare briefs. I can try cases when they come to court.''

''You cannot,'' he said, tapping his cane for emphasis. ''I do not need a briefing clerk, and if you cannot face a crime scene, then neither can you face the evidence of that crime when it is presented in a courtroom.''

''It's not the same,'' began Lydia.

''It is! You cannot avert your face from autopsy photographs, from bits of bloody clothing, from weapons, and most especially from our clients, many, if not most, of whom are guilty—just because you are afraid of being reminded of your own ghosts.''

''I can be objective!'' she protested.

He leaned his cane against the wall and grasped her shoulders. ''I do not want you objective! I can hire a thousand objective attorneys who'll wave a bloody shirt about and never sense that it is more than a remnant of fabric. It is a remnant of a life! Our law schools are graduating hundreds every year, Miss Fairchild, hundreds of hollow men who view the law as an abstract. It is not! Every statute is written with someone's blood.''

He pulled her closer. ''I want you involved, Miss Fairchild. That means I want you to feel the fear, the regret, the remorse, the rage of violence.''

''I do! That's why I can't go in there!''

He shook his head, his eyes bright as though a fire smoldered in their depths. "You only feel the fear."

She leaned her forehead against his shoulder. "There's no point in lying to you anymore, is there?"

"None at all, Miss Fairchild," he replied, stroking her hair.

She slipped her arms around his waist, expecting him to pull away. He didn't. One arm circled her shoulders and held her against him. "I can't get past the fear, John Lloyd."

His chest rose as he took a deep breath and his body tensed, like a long distance runner waiting for the starter's gun. Then she felt his cheek press against her own. "Tell me about it, Lydia."

She froze. "About what?"

"Killing the Butcher," he said, his breath stirring the hair above her ear. "Your account at the time we found you with his body was curiously incomplete, a fact I noticed, even if Sergeant Schroder did not. You never discussed the actual killing then, and you have never talked about it since—not even in your deposition to the police. What really happened in that room?"

She pushed against his chest, but she might as well have tried to push the Rock of Gibraltar into the sea. Finally she gave up and stood still in his arms and stared over his shoulder at the wall. "Leave me alone, damn you! You're sick! The truth is, you're fascinated with violence. It turns you on. That's why you handle so many murder cases. You feed on violence like a vampire feeds on blood. But not this time. You're not biting me on the neck, Dracula. No gory details to gorge yourself on."

He sighed. "If I wanted the gory details, I would read the autopsy protocol. What are you hiding, Lydia?"

She recoiled from the question and jerked her head up to find his face poised just above hers. Too close. His eyes, those black intense eyes, held her captive as surely as if they touched her. "Nothing," she whispered.

And knew suddenly that she lied.

She *was* hiding something; she could sense it like a guilty secret. Something *had* happened in that miserable little room where she fought the Butcher, something so horrible that she was afraid to remember it. But what? What could be worse than killing another human being?

"God help me, John Lloyd. I can't remember!"

"You must. Your fear of remembering is like a cancer; it is consuming your strength, impoverishing your spirit. It is killing you! Feel my strength, Lydia," he said, pulling her closer. "I will not let you walk that dark passage of memory alone. Lean on me! Trust me! Tell me! Remember!"

She felt the sexual tension in his lean body, felt the strength of his compassion, the power of his indomitable will, and knew that whatever else they might be to each other, they would never be equals. Not as long as she depended on him for her strength instead of finding it within herself. Dark passages were meant to be walked alone. He could wait at the other end, and when she remembered—if she remembered—she would walk into his arms a whole woman.

She kissed him lightly, but pulled back before he could respond. "I appreciate your offer, but I'll help myself."

He released her instantly, as if he had just realized that not only was he aroused, but the object of his arousal had just spurned his offer of help. "I must talk to Sergeant Schroder. Your behavior has distracted me long enough, Miss Fairchild."

"My behavior, John Lloyd? I didn't grab you in a sexually suggestive way. You grabbed me."

He tugged down his waistcoat and smoothed his hair. "You misconstrued my actions."

"There was one action I didn't misconstrue."

A flush stained his high cheekbones as he picked up his cane. "I find you a threat to my self-control, Miss Fairchild."

"Then try taking four deep breaths the next time you feel horny."

She could still feel the arctic stare he gave her as he walked away. Anyone who denied that looks could kill, or at least seriously maim, had never been on the receiving end of one of John Lloyd Branson's glares. She hadn't thawed out yet.

CHAPTER TEN

"WHAT THE HELL ARE YOU DOING HERE, BRANSON?" REpeated Schroder, as if the attorney hadn't heard him the first time.

John Lloyd Branson inclined his head as politely as if Schroder's question had not been couched in what Jenner called his grizzly-bear-with-hemorrhoids tone of voice. "I am here because I am legal counsel for the Panhandle-Plains Historical Society, and, by extension, for the museum."

Schroder's eyelid quivered once more. "When I decide to arrest the dinosaur, you can stick your long nose in. Until then, keep out of my way."

"Might I ask, as the dinosaur's attorney, of course, what admissible evidence you have uncovered?" asked Branson, his black eyes mesmerizing. A blond like John Lloyd Branson ought to have blue or maybe gray eyes, thought Jenner; not obsidian-black ones that burned or glittered, depending on the lawyer's mood or the object of his gaze.

The object of his present gaze was sticking out his chin belligerently. "This ain't funny, Branson," said Schroder.

"I never suggested it was, Sergeant Schroder. I am merely

pointing out that I represent the inanimate objects that comprise the museum as well as its more corporeal employees.''

''Meaning what, Branson?''

''Meaning that from the facts covered in your aforementioned summation, the dinosaur seems to be your strongest suspect. He at least has what appears to be blood on his horn. The rest of your case seems to rest on the alleged rigor mortis, which I do not need to remind you is a dubious means of determining the exact time of death.''

''Alleged, my ass!'' interrupted Schroder. ''You try bending the victim's neck.''

''However, you did mention keys and a sabotaged security system, which do support your contention, at least superficially, that a staff member was involved.''

''Superficially! I suppose you can explain away video cameras that record nothing and doors that unlock themselves and burglar alarms that don't work, and a body suddenly appearing at midnight in a place it hadn't been two hours earlier, a body that was, by God, dead long before that!'' Schroder nodded decisively.

The expression in Branson's eyes changed from intent to watchful. ''Security systems have malfunctioned before, Sergeant.''

Schroder shook his head. ''Not like this, Branson. Somebody substituted prerecorded tapes, with no date on them, which means he'd already screwed with the recorder once before to make the tapes, and the security guards didn't know it. They never review the previous night's tapes if nothing suspicious has happened, just label them and lock them up. Our murderer knew where the tapes were stored, pulled out the ones already recorded without the date from days or weeks before, hit the play button on the recorder, and Walter Goodwin spends his evening watching a rerun. The control board was rewired, so the motion and sound detectors didn't work. Tell me somebody outside the staff had the opportunity to do a high tech fuckup job like that.''

Branson glanced down at the body for a moment, his eyes hidden by his half-closed lids. ''Interesting,'' he murmured.

"It damn sure is. Can you explain it?" demanded Schroder.

Branson looked up. "Of course not, Sergeant. I never believed that I could. I presumed from the outset after overhearing your conversation with Sergeant Jenner that your evidence was conclusive. I only wished to know what it was."

Schroder sucked in a deep breath that whistled through his clenched teeth, and the other cops moved back to give the two men room. It seemed a good idea to Jenner. He stepped backward and closed his eyes, waiting for the explosion. What he heard was a chuckle, then Schroder's voice. "Branson, have I ever told you that you're a son of a bitch?"

Jenner opened his eyes in time to see Branson smile. "Frequently—when you are not calling me a crooked shyster."

"I'd planned on telling you what I've uncovered."

Branson arched one eyebrow. "But only after a long, tedious, and quite possibly acrimonious argument, and we do not have time to waste."

Schroder absently dropped the surgical gloves in his pocket and pulled out a crumpled pack of Camels while he studied the lawyer. "What's this *we* business, Branson? I'm the cop. You're the lawyer. I'm in charge of the investigation. I arrest people for breaking the law, and you defend them. That's what we do, and I like my job better than I like yours."

Branson hesitated, and Jenner sensed that he was choosing his words carefully. "I have considered our adversative positions, Sergeant, but I believe we can cooperate without compromising our individual responsibilities. It may be an unholy alliance, but not an unethical one."

"You propositioning me, Branson?"

"Yes, and I am finding it difficult."

Schroder grinned. "Tell you what, Branson. Why don't you just say what you've got in mind without all the four-syllable words? I'm like an old whore; I don't need pretty palaver."

"I am offering to assist you in this investigation."

"Before I throw your ass out, how about you tell me why you think I need you. As soon as I finish collecting the evidence and interviewing the staff, I'll know who to point the finger at."

Branson shook his head. "Not if you are depending on DNA fingerprinting on the alleged blood on my client's horn to determine at which suspect you point your finger."

Schroder's grin turned into a scowl. "I was planning on it, and I suppose you're going to file some injunction to stop me."

"I will not have to, Sergeant, since I doubt the substance is blood. More likely it is paint."

Jenner squinted at the horn. Branson was right. The smear was too red and too shiny for blood. It was almost as red and shiny as Schroder's face.

"As you remarked to Sergeant Jenner, the staff—your suspects—are law-abiding people," continued Branson, an intent expression in his eyes. "What you did not mention is that they are quite, quite brilliant. They also collect and label, examine and classify bits and pieces of physical evidence much in the way you do and for much the same reason. They re-create the past as you re-create a crime scene. *And someone has done so now!*"

"What the hell are you talking about, Branson?" demanded Schroder.

"Someone created a diorama of a murder scene. A dead curator found sitting on a prehistoric skull, blood smeared on the creature's horn, as though the artifact had gored its keeper and tossed him skyward only to have him land astride its neck. How appropriate for a museum, Sergeant."

Schroder walked toward the triceratops skull and thrust his chin out as though about to question it, then jerked back around to confront the lawyer. "Why, Branson? Why the hell go to all that trouble?"

"Even the court does not require you to prove motive, the why of a crime, Sergeant. Only the means and opportunity—the how, when, and where of a crime—the facts, so-called, which so frequently prove the who."

"Goddamn it, Branson, I consider motive every time I investigate a murder."

"But as the last factor in your equation, Sergeant. First

you find the fingerprint, then you match it to a suspect, then you ask why. I ask why first. A fingerprint is only a reference to a crime, not the crime itself. Sometimes a fingerprint on a murder weapon is perfectly innocent when considered within a certain specified context. I look for those contexts. It is what I do."

Branson glanced down at the body again and nodded, a movement so slight as to be almost imperceptible, and Jenner shivered. It was almost as if the lawyer were acknowledging a comment by Brad Hemphill that he alone heard.

Branson looked at Schroder again. "You see Brad Hemphill and ask when he died and how. I see Brad Hemphill and ask why he died. I submit to you, Sergeant, that how, when, and where, provided you ever discover where, will not reveal the answer to the most important question: who murdered Brad Hemphill?"

"I suppose your damn *whys* will?" asked Schroder, his head hunched forward like a football tackle ready to sack the quarterback behind the line of scrimmage.

"Yes, when supplemented by your facts."

"You got two facts: how and when. What kind of why can you answer with them?"

"The most obvious question, of course. Why did someone move Hemphill's body?" The lawyer's voice was soft, but no one had trouble hearing it in the hushed room, where everyone stood motionless staring at the dead curator and the two men who flanked his body.

Schroder cleared his throat. "Well, are you going to tell us?"

Branson shrugged. "Someone wanted his body found, but not before midnight. It is obvious when considered in the proper context, Sergeant."

"It sure as shit is not, Branson. I can think of better answers than that. For instance, someone has an alibi for midnight, or thinks he does. More probably it was because the cleaning crew was here until after eleven. He had no chance to move the body at all until after that." Schroder noticed he was still holding his cigarettes and dropped the pack into his pocket. Either he had decided to observe the NO SMOKING signs posted in the museum, or Branson had the detective too riled up to know what he was doing. Jenner bet on the latter.

Branson sighed. "Sergeant, you are confusing facts with motives when you discuss alibis and opportunities. Consider the act of moving the body in the context of its murder. Murder is a terrible secret best left hidden. And it was hidden, hidden so well the cleaning crew didn't discover it. Why expose the secret? Because someone wanted us to know. But why murder Brad Hemphill at all? Why do so in the museum?"

"Damn it, Branson, I don't know," exclaimed Schroder.

Branson nodded. "Neither do I, but I will—eventually. At present we have more whys than facts, Sergeant, and facts are your responsibility in this marriage of convenience."

Schroder stared at the triceratops for a moment before turning back to the lawyer. "I don't remember accepting your proposition, Branson."

Branson held out his hand. "But you will, Sergeant Schroder, if for no other reason than to keep the other alligators away."

Schroder reluctantly clasped the hand. "Yeah, but you're still a son of a bitch."

"But I am your son of a bitch, Sergeant Schroder, at least for the duration of this case."

He touched the brim of his black Stetson hat in farewell and walked briskly toward the entrance, his limp barely noticeable. Jenner decided the lawyer carried his fancy cane as much for image as for practicality. John Lloyd Branson looked like an elegant gambler, and the cane added to the effect.

Branson stopped by the entrance and glanced back at Schroder. "Sergeant, I do not mean to interfere in your sphere of fact collecting, but I have one *why* about which your examination of the body at the Special Crimes lab might provide information. Why did the murderer change Brad Hemphill's shirt?"

Schroder's eyelid started jerking again. "What?"

"The victim's shirt is white and clean and appears to have

been freshly pressed, while his brown-and-gray-checked trousers are somewhat dusty. Another interesting anomaly in a bizarre case.''

Schroder watched him leave, then stared down at the body. ''If Branson weren't already a lawyer, and if he weren't such a pompous bastard, I'd recruit him for Special Crimes.''

''How come?'' asked Jenner.

Schroder took his cigarettes out of his pocket. ''Because I think he's right about the shirt.''

CHAPTER ELEVEN

JOHN LLOYD WALKED OUT OF THE PALEONTOLOGY EXHIBIT, his expression that of a hangman testing his rope for an eagerly anticipated execution. Lydia hoped it wasn't hers. "Come along, Miss Fairchild, do not dawdle. I want to talk to the staff before Sergeant Schroder confronts them."

She whispered a quick thank-you to her Maker for her reprieve and hurried after John Lloyd. "Wait a minute. I was listening at the door. I heard every word you and Schroder said. I thought you had an agreement with the sergeant."

"I do."

"How can you advise the staff and still assist Schroder? Isn't that a conflict of interest?"

"My client is this museum, Miss Fairchild, first and foremost, and it has been profaned by murder. I will cleanse it by discovering which of its caretakers is guilty by using whatever means I deem necessary. Sergeant Schroder is one of those means. I must have access to the facts, and I do not have the luxury of time. This institution is funded by the state as well as by the historical society, and the politicians who guard the public trough do not like scandal. The potential for scandal in this instance is virtually unlimited.''

''Why? It's not the museum's fault that somebody killed that curator. You're acting like somebody's running a white slavery ring on the side.''

He didn't answer, but she saw his mouth tighten, and she suddenly knew why an attorney like John Lloyd Branson, who never cooperated with the police, who prided himself on being an obstacle in their course, and who scoffed at nonprofessionals playing detective, decided to do both. ''That's it, isn't it? You know something about the staff members, don't you? Something really dirty that might not look proper in the newspapers? You're playing both ends against the middle. You're protecting the staff while at the same time trying to finger one of them for the murder.''

''*Finger* one of them? Really, Miss Fairchild, your use of slang is inexcusable.''

''Don't try to change the subject! You aren't cooperating with Sergeant Schroder. You're manipulating him. Who's got a skeleton in his closet, John Lloyd, besides Margaret (Miss Marple) Clark? I don't think it would do the museum's reputation, or funding, much good if the legislature in Austin found out that the archivist is a computer pirate in her spare time.''

''The staff, with the exception of the murderer, are not guilty of any felonious act, Miss Fairchild. However, they are not altogether innocent, either. Everyone has secrets which he or she would rather not have served up as a breakfast entree for the newspaper-reading public, secrets that have nothing to do with their abilities to fulfill their duties.''

''And I suppose you are the sole judge of whose secret is innocent and whose is harmful?''

He glanced down at her, one eyebrow cocked at that regal smartass angle she hated so much. ''Yes, I am, with the proviso that no secret is innocent to the person who holds it. I can be objective.''

''I thought you said you didn't believe attorneys should be objective.''

''Miss Fairchild, I do wish you would not take my words

out of context. I am simply in a better position than Sergeant Schroder to make a value judgment as to whose secret is too innocent to be the motive for murder. There is no need to wash all the dirty laundry in public when only one napkin is soiled.''

''Aren't you worried about being accused of unethical behavior?''

He stopped so suddenly she bumped into his shoulder. He whirled around, his face so stiff, it looked frozen. ''I am never unethical, Miss Fairchild.''

She swallowed, then plunged ahead. One could only drown once. ''No, but sometimes you're so devious, it's hard to tell the difference,'' she retorted.

''*I* know the difference.''

''But will the bar association, John Lloyd?''

His answer was another maiming look.

Lydia stepped into the volunteers' lounge and saw Margaret Clark, wearing her Mary Todd Lincoln garb and slumped on a couch, wiping her eyes. ''Oh, Lydia, my dear. It's terrible, just terrible. Such a wonderful boy. Such an awful thing for you.''

Lydia started toward her. ''But I didn't know him—''

''Hey, lady. You in the clown suit, are you a staff member?''

Lydia turned to face a young Canyon police officer. ''No, but—''

''I'll have to see some identification, ma'am.''

''Miss Fairchild is with me, Officer—''John Lloyd peered at the man's name tag''—Evans.''

''Excuse me, sir, but I'll have to see your identification, too.''

''I am John Lloyd Branson,'' he pronounced in such an imperial tone that Lydia expected to hear a drum roll and see young Evans genuflecting.

However, Officer Evans's expression never changed, and it amused Lydia that he obviously didn't recognize John Lloyd's name from Adam's. ''So much for notoriety,'' she whispered.

''For God's sake, Officer, he's my lawyer,'' exclaimed Bill

Whitney. "John Lloyd, we're cooped up in here like calves in a branding pen, and Evans here is about as talkative as that doorman Monique hired for the party. Probably use the same brand of starch in their drawers. I'd like to know what the hell is going on. And I want to know it now!"

"Murder's what's going on," muttered a redheaded older man in a guard's uniform.

"Mr. Goodwin, sir," said Evans. "Please don't discuss the case. Sergeant Schroder's orders."

"Officer Evans," said John Lloyd, pointing toward the door, "out, please, and close the door behind you."

"Sergeant Schroder said—" began Evans.

"I damn sure did, Branson." Schroder walked through the door and looked around. "Hello, Miss Fairchild. When I didn't see you earlier with Lawyer Branson, I figured you'd abandoned ambulance-chasing and found honest work defrauding savings and loans." He switched his attention back to John Lloyd. "Our handshake ain't even cold, and you're already going behind my back."

Lydia would never have believed that John Lloyd Branson could look guilty, but for just an infinitesimal flash he resembled a gambler caught with an ace up his sleeve.

Schroder must have thought so, too, because his eyes narrowed. "What were you fixing to tell these fine folks, Branson?"

John Lloyd smiled. He always looked so innocent when he smiled, thought Lydia, just like a con man selling beachfront property in West Texas. "I intended to inform the staff that Brad Hemphill apparently died from a blow to the back of the head and that I had given you permission to search the museum for your blunt instrument."

"I don't need your permission to search a crime scene, Branson, or had that slipped your mind?"

Lydia thought it more likely the Pope would forget he was Catholic before John Lloyd forgot the laws governing search and seizure.

"Christ on a crutch, John Lloyd!" exclaimed Bill Whitney. "Do you know how many millions of dollars this collection is worth? The insurance company could refuse to pay any damages if some ham-handed cop broke an artifact. Rachel, tell him.''

A slender woman in her mid-forties, with pale green eyes, rose gracefully from the couch. Two wide silver streaks that Lydia would swear were unbleached by human hands waved from a center part down to her shoulders on each side of a strong-featured face. She was stunning without being beautiful. She was also familiar. She was the girl in the Whitney family history, the one a young Bill Whitney was always photographed embracing.

''John Lloyd, there must be thousands of so-called blunt instruments in this museum. We have everything from Indian clubs to guns to iron farming implements. I imagine even the Chinese vase collection on the second floor contains several items that could qualify as blunt. Searching this museum would take days. Surely there's another way.''

''Dr. Applebaum,'' said Schroder in a respectful tone of voice that surprised Lydia. She'd never known the burly detective to display much respect for anyone he believed might be guilty of murder. ''Dr. Applebaum, there's no other way to find a weapon except by looking for it.'' He smiled.

''Yes, there is, Sergeant,'' interrupted John Lloyd. ''The one who wielded it can step forward.''

Schroder jerked his head around to look at the lawyer. ''You thinking somebody's going to confess, Branson?''

Lydia saw John Lloyd tighten his fingers on his cane, and knew that was exactly what he'd hoped. In fact, she was certain that was why he'd wanted to talk to the staff before Schroder; he believed the guilty one would be suffering remorse for his actions.

That was the kind of naive invitation Lydia would extend—not John Lloyd—and she wondered when their roles had been reversed.

When no one stepped forward, John Lloyd walked to the conference table and sat down. ''So be it,'' he said. ''If the sergeant will permit me, I, as the museum's attorney, will inform you of several unpleasant facts of life that those involved in a homicide investigation must face. In the first place, Brad Hemphill almost certainly died after this museum closed—which logically excludes a casual visitor as the murderer. In the second place, the security system was sabotaged—which also logically excludes a casual visitor. The consequence of these two facts is that each person in this room, with the exception of Mr. Whitney, is a material witness, and the museum is a crime scene. Each of you will be asked to account for your time between the hours of five and midnight."

"This is outrageous!"

"Who the hell are you?" demanded Schroder, turning his head toward the voice.

A tall, slender man of that indeterminate age between forty and sixty before character lines become merely wrinkles and a thickening waist descends into a paunch rose from the couch and marched to the conference table. His chin thrust forward and upward at what Lydia was sure he meant to be a regal, commanding angle. Instead he looked like a man performing a facial exercise to minimize a double chin.

"I am Roberto Ortiz, curator of art, and I am insulted by your insinuation, Mr. Branson. I am from an old and honorable family—my ancestor rode with Coronado when he explored Texas—and I resent being treated like a common villain."

"There is nothing common about your treatment, Mr. Ortiz," answered John Lloyd. "Sergeant Schroder is smiling—or was—a most uncommon occurrence. I suggest you reinforce his pleasant behavior by cooperating."

A lanky, ponytailed youth sitting on the floor, wearing a Bart Simpson T-shirt, chuckled. "Ease up, Bob, or the gendarmerie will think you're hiding something."

"My name is Roberto," insisted the older man, his head tilting backward to an even more regal angle.

"Yeah, and mine's Abraham, but Abe's easier to say and sounds a hell of a lot more friendly." The young man stood up. "Abe Yates, Sergeant Schroder. Brad Hemphill was my immediate boss, and I'm pissed off about what happened to him. He was one of those harmless, earnest little guys, a nerd I guess you'd call him, until you remember how, well, good they really are. They never like to hurt anybody, and that's a little uncommon, too.''

His carefree, mocking grin disappeared, and Abe Yates looked pensive for a moment. Then he blinked and shook his head, a self-conscious grin appearing, as if he surprised himself with his observations. Lydia doubted that assistant curator Abraham Yates wasted much time reflecting on good and evil; his eyes were too cynical.

''So what can I do, Sergeant? I'm cooperative.''

''Give the sergeant your keys, Mr. Yates, and tell Miss Fairchild your timetable and what color shirts Brad Hemphill customarily wore,'' said John Lloyd, gesturing Lydia toward the chair next to his.

Yates lost his grin again, and his face suddenly looked older and sharper. ''Why should I do that, Branson? Am I a suspect?''

''Should you be, Mr. Yates?'' asked John Lloyd, his drawl disappearing, which Lydia knew meant he was at his most dangerous.

''I didn't kill Brad Hemphill, Mr. Branson.''

''Then you have nothing to fear. To ease your mind, though, everyone is required to step forward and surrender keys. The police cannot search a building in which a majority of the doors are locked, is that not true, Sergeant Schroder?''

Schroder opened his mouth to answer, but John Lloyd interrupted whatever the detective was preparing to say. ''Of course it is. I am certain that all of you are most anxious to cooperate in this matter, since noncooperation might be misconstrued as an attempt to obstruct justice. Also remember to include Brad Hemphill's preference of shirt color in your statement to Miss Fairchild.''

''Keys I can understand,'' said Yates. ''But his shirts? Why?''

John Lloyd's face looked as bland and innocent as a newborn baby's. ''Let us say that I have an interest in the gentleman's customary attire.''

In the ensuing silence, Yates dug a key ring out of his pocket and tossed it to Schroder, who deftly caught it and deposited it in a plastic bag he pulled out of his pocket.

"Good catch, Sarge," he said as he winked at Lydia and sprawled in a chair next to hers. "Ask me anything, sweet lady: name, address, phone number, marital status, Stanford Benet score, references from former lovers."

"Do you know a good undertaker?" asked Lydia.

"Why?"

"Because you're going to need one if you make another sexist remark to me."

He held up his hands. "Sorry, lady. Pax, all right? I'm just a little nervous. I never anticipated murder or the Gestapo when I signed up for this cruise."

"Farmer said you came to work after you graduated from college. You're a little older than the average college graduate, aren't you, Yates?" asked Schroder, sitting at the head of the table and removing a handful of plastic bags from his coat pocket.

"How come you're hitting on me, Sergeant? Is it the hair?" He stroked his ponytail and grinned, but Lydia noticed an angry glint in his eyes.

"I got more to worry about than whether you're boycotting barber shops, Yates. Everybody else has been here for years. They're a known quantity. You're not."

"I'm the new kid in school, so you're naturally suspicious?"

Schroder rubbed his chin. "Let's just say I'm naturally curious."

Yates sighed. "You can find all this out by reading my personnel file, but for Brad Hemphill's sake, I'll save you the time. I bummed around a few years, worked in antique stores and for a few private art collectors. That's what made me decide I wanted to work for a museum. I've been here about eight months. It's a worthwhile job. Not a lot of money, not what some of the big museums pay, but this place has a reputation, and the collection is outstanding. I'm lucky to be here, and I'm going to prove it by being cooperative. Get my point, Roberto?" His face suddenly looked not only older, but harder, almost threatening.

"You don't need to explain my duty," answered Roberto, pulling his key ring from his pocket and handing it to

Schroder, then bowing politely to Lydia as he sat down opposite her. Lydia straightened her shoulders and smiled at the vain little man. Nobody who bowed to a lady could be all that bad.

"I'll do my part," said Margaret Clark, standing up and rustling over to the table in her black silk mourning dress. "Gracious, this is such a nightmare. Poor, poor little Brad. It's like losing my Lindsey all over again. Good evening, Sergeant Schroder, how's your neuritis? My daughter was his baby-sitter. Such a dear child."

"Your daughter baby-sat Sergeant Schroder?" asked Lydia.

"Of course not, my dear. John Lloyd, this child simply doesn't track well. Does she have attention deficit disorder? It's the latest buzz word for youngsters with short attention spans."

"Your daughter baby-sat Brad Hemphill?" asked Lydia, rubbing her forehead. Margaret Clark in her Mary Todd Lincoln disguise was hard to take at three in the morning. Margaret Clark without her disguise and after a night's sleep probably wouldn't be much easier.

"That's what I said, dear. Little Brad lived right next door to Lindsey. And he died on the anniversary of her death. And he was murdered, too. They have so much in common now."

"Mr. Farmer, Mr. Goodwin," said John Lloyd, breaking into the conversation. "Your keys, please."

Darrell Farmer appeared to stand even straighter. "I'm the security chief. I can't turn over my keys."

Schroder snapped his fingers. "Until we figure out who played video games with your security system, you might as well take a vacation. You won't need them anyway. I'm closing down the museum."

"You can't do that!" exclaimed Bill Whitney.

"Can't have the public trampling over the crime scene like cattle in a wheat pasture."

"Dr. Applebaum, ma'am, I won't have this man accusing me of being a slacker," complained Farmer.

Walter Goodwin put his keys on the table. "What else can

you expect, Darrell? Somebody sneaked in, killed one of our people, and sneaked back out like they were playing hide-and-seek and we were *it*. More my fault than yours 'cause I was on duty at the time, but it don't give the sergeant a lot of confidence in either one of us, does it? Dr. Applebaum, I'm real sorry."

Rachel Applebaum patted his arm. "Don't worry. I have faith in you and Darrell." She handed Schroder her keys and sat down across the table from Lydia. "I'm ready if you are, Miss Fairchild. The sooner Sergeant Schroder has a record of our alibis, the sooner he can turn his attention away from the people in this room. Despite the misleading appearances, I'd stake my life and reputation that no one on this staff committed this unkindness."

Lydia thought unkindness seemed a trifling word for the act of caving in Brad Hemphill's skull with a blunt instrument, but then, perhaps murder wasn't in Rachel Applebaum's lexicon. Homicide became an administrative problem that she handled by absolving her staff; after all, murder was not in anyone's job description. Nice people didn't kill.

An hour later by Lydia's Timex (on sale at Wal-Mart for twenty-five percent off), she conceded that Rachel was right about appearances being misleading. At least they were, according to Schroder's summation during the council of war in Darrell Farmer's tiny office.

Schroder leaned back in a wooden chair behind Farmer's desk and faced Lydia and John Lloyd. "According to what Farmer and Goodwin told me before you showed up, Branson, everybody left the museum by six P.M. Goodwin and the cleaning crew came in at six. Hemphill was dead *before* six, when Goodwin made his rounds. That murder was choreographed like a damn Broadway musical by somebody who knew the routine. Somebody on staff has to be guilty, but they're all cooperating like innocent little lambs."

John Lloyd looked relaxed, almost sleepy. "Tell me about your interview with Farmer and Goodwin, Sergeant. At present I know nothing of their accounts, except for a few cryptic remarks concerning the video system.''

Lydia slid into a chair and sipped coffee while Schroder related a tale of unlocked doors, false alarms, and two security guards who apparently didn't agree as to what a glitch was or wasn't. She took another sip of coffee and decided that caffeine had to rank next to four deep breaths as a restorative. She wouldn't mention her conclusion to John Lloyd, though. He might possibly accept therapeutic advice from her about the time hell froze over.

If anything, John Lloyd looked even more relaxed after Schroder's long recitation. ''Interesting,'' he murmured.

Schroder, on the other hand, looked about as relaxed as a constipated badger. ''Is that all you've got to say? Jesus Christ, Branson, this ain't much of a marriage. I'm doing all the talking and you're just sitting there on your behind looking like you're about to go to sleep in the middle of a kiss. What the hell have you got to contribute?''

John Lloyd leaned over and picked up a plastic bag that Schroder had dropped on the desk. ''Keys, Sergeant Schroder. This contains Rachel Applebaum's keys, which I noticed were all carefully labeled, a sensible precaution in view of the number of locks in this building. I suggest you compare her keys to those of the other staff members. That will at least tell us exactly who has what keys and to which doors. A useful contribution, I should think—and achieved without the necessity of search warrants or other unpleasant obstacles.''

Schroder looked only slightly mollified. ''I could've gotten the keys, Branson, without your help.''

''I am certain you could, Sergeant,'' agreed John Lloyd, watching as the detective compared keys.

''I'll be goddamned!'' exclaimed Schroder when he'd finished. ''Every son of a bitch on the staff, including that cleaning lady who looks like Lucy Ricardo in a Texas Tech sweatshirt, has a key to the front door. All of them have a key to the side door. All of them but Margaret Clark have a key to the back door. Everybody but Margaret Clark and the cleaning lady has keys to the major display areas. Their office keys are damn near interchangeable, and besides, a kid with a baseball card could pop those locks. I know; I looked. Everybody but the cleaning lady has keys to something called the stacks."

He dropped the bags in one side pocket and pulled a fistful of lined notebook paper from the other and waved it at John Lloyd. "These mini-statements, or alibis, you tricked those poor suckers into making—you know what they prove?"

"I am certain you will tell me."

"Other than they all agree Brad Hemphill wore white shirts with button-down collars and that he kept a spare shirt in his office, they prove exactly nothing!" said Schroder. "Not a damn thing except that everybody except Goodwin and the cleaning lady's got an alibi of sorts until at least ten-thirty or later, and who is the one person who can verify the biggest chunk of those alibis?"

"I am sure you will tell me that also, Sergeant."

"John Lloyd Branson, that's who. They all attended the party at the Whitney house. You were there, weren't you? You and Miss Fairchild? Unless your law partner here just likes to gallivant around dressed like a clown."

"Margaret Clark was with me until somebody called Bill Whitney to report the murder," said Lydia.

"Mrs. Bancroft Whitney mentioned that Dr. Applebaum, Darrell Farmer, and a conquistador whom I presume was Roberto Ortiz all left at the same time," said John Lloyd.

"What about the male chauvinist piglet? Abe Yates?" asked Lydia.

Schroder checked a sheet of notebook paper. "According to this, he left the museum about a quarter to six, went to the Halloween party until around midnight, and drove home. When he passed the building, he saw the patrol cars and lights, and stopped."

"I never saw him at the party," said John Lloyd, tapping his finger on the silver head of his cane. "However, that means nothing. There were two hundred guests, the main room was dark, and many people were outside on the terrace. Enjoying the moat, I believe, this being the season in which it smells the least stagnant."

"A moat?" asked Schroder, one side of his mouth curling up in either a smirk or a sneer. Lydia couldn't determine which.

John Lloyd shrugged. "Mrs. Monique Bancroft Whitney exhibits her ethnic heritage by adopting the worst features of its culture. It is an eccentricity I have noticed among many with her affliction."

Schroder lit a cigarette, exhaled a cloud of smoke, and watched it dissipate as it floated toward the ceiling. "I ain't interested in Bill Whitney's moat unless Abe Yates happened to be pulled out of it between eleven o'clock and midnight. Which he wasn't. But nothing says he was at this museum. Nothing says he wasn't. Hell, nothing says any of them were here or weren't here. The way I see it, anyone could've moved that body except Margaret Clark. And Abe Yates, if you believe him. Hell, Branson, if I hadn't seen that body myself, I'd be wondering if Brad Hemphill was dead at all. Give me some whys, because I'm fresh out of facts, not that any of them prove a damn thing. Worthless as tits on a boar."

John Lloyd smiled. "Not quite, Sergeant. I found some of your revelations most informative. But you did ask for one of my whys. Since you have the keys, why not lock the museum so none of our suspects can leave without our knowledge?"

"I can't keep those people prisoners. One of them would sue my ass."

"I doubt that very much, Sergeant. In fact, I think you will be unable to force them to leave after the next five minutes."

"And what the hell is going to happen in the next five minutes, Branson?" demanded Schroder, his eyebrows drawing together like two fighting fuzzy caterpillars.

"You are going to ask for suggestions from the staff as to where to begin your search?"

"Why the hell should I do that?"

John Lloyd arched an eyebrow. "Why, to hear what they have to say. Or perhaps to note what they do not say."

CHAPTER TWELVE

IT WAS ALL SCHRODER'S FAULT, JENNER DECIDED. IT WAS that son of a bitch's fault that he was still dressed head to foot in disposable clothing, including goggles, mask, and cap. It was Schroder's fault that he was standing in the morgue at Northwest Texas Hospital. It was probably even Schroder's fault that the morgue and the hospital kitchen evidently shared a common ventilation system. Jenner gagged as the odor of grilled onions and ground beef floated through the air vent to mix with the smell of formaldehyde and blood. He seriously considered throwing up.

That would be Schroder's fault, too.

Jenner swallowed several times to combat this nausea and stared at Brad Hemphill's nude body on the metal autopsy table. He concluded that while a man could die with dignity, he couldn't be dead with dignity—not if he was a murder victim. There was not a damn thing dignified about being the subject of an autopsy.

And that was about the only thing that wasn't Schroder's fault.

"Anybody mention that you look like a walking roll of toilet paper?"

Jenner glared through his goggles at Dr. Patrick T. MacElvoy, the Panhandle's only forensic pathologist. "Yeah, twice."

"No need to get surly." The pathologist pulled on his surgical gloves, humming under his breath. Dr. Patrick T. MacElvoy stood five feet six in his elevator shoes, wore his red hair in a flat top, smoked cheap black cigars, and favored classical music over country and western. He frequently entertained the cadavers with his own renditions of operatic arias because, he explained on numerous occasions, "They can't walk out on my performance." He intimidated lawyers and awed juries.

The cops loved him.

Jenner cleared his throat. "I've been at Special Crimes—" he stopped and took a deep breath "—up on the second floor, processing the body."

"First time?" asked Dr. MacElvoy.

Jenner blinked at the note of sympathy in the pathologist's voice. "Yeah."

MacElvoy nodded. "That explains why you look a little peaked. I thought maybe it was the fluorescent lights turning you the color of Limburger cheese. Takes some getting used to, processing a body. I remember my first cadaver. It was in medical school—gross anatomy class. My lab partners and I called him Ernest. We used to say we were working in dead Ernest."

Jenner gagged.

Dr. MacElvoy raised his eyebrows. "If you're going to lose your dinner, son, there's basins out in the hall."

Jenner breathed shallowly through his mouth. "I didn't eat dinner."

"Just as well." He turned on his recorder and started dictating. "Body is that of a young, white, well-nourished male approximately twenty-five to thirty—"

"He's twenty-six, Doc," said Jenner.

Dr. MacElvoy looked over his bifocals at Jenner, but continued dictating. "Twenty-six years of age, and identified as Brad Hemphill. No wound apparent to the naked eye—"

"We found a bruise on his rib cage, on the left side, when

we examined the body at Special Crimes,'' interrupted Jenner.

''I'm getting to it, son,'' said MacElvoy impatiently. ''A bruise isn't exactly the same thing as a wound. We don't want to confuse the damn lawyers. A bruise from a blow received just prior to death resulting in''—the pathologist poked Hemphill's side—''the fifth vertebro-sternal or true rib being broken to hell and back again.'' He looked at Jenner. ''Hell of a blow, son. Ribs can withstand great force. Just like a spring, they yield and then snap back. This one was broken by direct violence. The bone gave way and was driven inward at the point struck. That's just an educated guess from feel. Won't be able to swear on a Bible until I open him up, but my educated guess is worth more than most.''

Jenner pressed his own rib in sympathy. ''What hit him, Doc?''

''Hell, I don't know. I didn't see him being hit,'' replied the pathologist. ''But if you want an educated guess, I'd say it was something long and thin like a poker. He could have fallen, but I doubt it. Usually there's an abrasion when you fall, because you're trying to catch yourself, don't you see, and you tend to scrape the point of impact.'' He turned back to the body.

''Doc?''

''Yes?''

''There's a wound on his head, too. Sergeant Schroder found it. Above his right ear on the, uh . . .''

''Squamous portion of the right temporal ridge just above the mastoid,'' finished MacElvoy. ''I feel it. Bone's thin there, you know.''

Jenner didn't, but he'd take the pathologist's word for it. ''Scale-like in form and thin and translucent.''

Jenner thought MacElvoy sounded as if he were describing a seashell. ''Schroder said a blood clot probably killed him.''

MacElvoy looked at Jenner. ''Is that what Sergeant Schroder said? Well, maybe he's right. Probably is. He's a pretty good jake-leg pathologist—comes from attending so many autopsies—but he's not the one that has to testify as to the cause and mechanics of death, young man. He's not the one that gets reamed by some snot-nosed defense attorney who mispronounces all the parts of the body—''

''Like John Lloyd Branson?'' asked Jenner.

''No, not like John Lloyd Branson. Branson corrects *my* pronunciation. And the son of a bitch is right every time. Anyway, what I'm saying is, I can't swear that a subdural hematoma killed this boy or not until I open up his skull. I can tell you that what caved in his skull isn't the same hypothetical long and skinny weapon that caved in his rib. Look for something rounder and bigger, like a baseball bat.''

Jenner hoped it didn't have a ten-year-old boy on one end of it.

''That's odd,'' continued MacElvoy, leaning over to peer at the corpse's face. ''No bleeding from the nose or ears from the head injury. Blunt force trauma like that usually causes some. Not this time, though, and I wonder why. And no blood on the hair covering the wound, or any on the side of the neck. Curiouser and curiouser.''

''Is it important?''

''Might be,'' said the pathologist. ''Might not be. But damn near everything is in a homicide.'' He turned the corpse over and touched the liverish red patches that covered portions of the back and legs. ''Marked lividity on shoulders, hips, thighs, calves''—he lifted one foot—''heels. This body's been lying flat on its back.''

''Actually, we found it sitting up on a dinosaur,'' said Jenner.

Dr. MacElvoy's head snapped up and he stared at Jenner. ''That so? Well, where you found him and where he'd been are two different things.'' He turned Hemphill's body on its back again. ''I don't like it when a killer starts moving a corpse around. Makes my job harder. Besides, it's disrespectful.''

''Pretty cold-blooded, too,'' said Jenner. ''Let's face it, Doc. Most people don't like messing around with dead bodies.''

''Never bothered me,'' said MacElvoy, peeling the

wrapper off a cigar and lighting it. "At least my patients don't complain. And they don't lie. Remember that, son. The dead don't lie. How they lived and how they died is all laid out for me to read like a book. This fellow, for example, never exercised much. Poor muscle tone. He was nervous, too. Chewed his fingernails to the bone."

"Uh, Doc, what does he say about *when* he died?" asked Jenner. "You know, exact time of death."

"How the hell would I know that?" asked MacElvoy. "I wasn't there the second he died."

Jenner scratched his head and wondered why life was so damn difficult lately. Probably Schroder's fault. "But we've got to know, Doc."

MacElvoy sighed and picked up a scalpel. "Son, I can't tell you the exact time of death, and neither can any other forensic pathologist that's honest. Too many factors to consider. Temperature, humidity, body weight, whether there's ventilation or not, if the victim was indoors or outdoors. I can take the corpse's temperature. I can check the stomach contents for progress of digestion—which won't help a lot if I don't know when he last ate. A lot of things affect digestion, you know—physical activity, stress, sleep. I can check progress of rigor mortis. I can flip a coin. In other words, I can't tell you exactly when this young man died. But I can tell you approximately." He checked his watch, closed one eye, and looked at the ceiling, his lips moving silently. "My best educated guess is that he died between five and seven tonight."

"Schroder figured between six and eight," began Jenner.

"Tell the sergeant that I'll split the difference. This man died between five-thirty and seven-thirty—give or take thirty minutes on each side—but probably very close to the earlier mark, according to my best guess. How's that for an exact time?" He puffed his cigar for a moment, then flourished his scalpel. "Are you ready to open him up, Sergeant?"

Jenner nodded his head. The fluorescent light reflected off MacElvoy's scalpel, and Jenner felt sweat collect beneath his goggles. His face mask seemed to choke him, and he jerked it off to suck in lungfuls of cool, sweetish-smelling air faintly tainted by the odor of onions.

He leaned back against the wall and closed his eyes. No way would he watch; he'd witnessed enough indignities heaped upon Brad Hemphill. "I'm sorry," he whispered, then realized he was apologizing to an empty husk. Whatever presence he'd sensed at the museum was gone.

Brad Hemphill was truly dead.

"Sergeant."

"Yeah, Doc."

"This rib broke all to hell just like I figured. Snapped in two cleaner than a piece of crisp bacon. Want to see?"

God, but he wished MacElvoy wouldn't talk about food. "You're the doc. I'll take your word for it."

"Sergeant."

"Yeah, Doc."

"Keep your eyes closed, son. And you might want to cover your ears, too. I'm fixing to take off the sternum so I can see the heart and lungs. When I cut through those ribs, it sounds just like I'm snapping beans. I lose a lot of green cops about this time."

Jenner gulped, put his hands over his ears, and resolutely recited the multiplication tables. He was at eleven times seven when he heard the doctor calling.

"Sergeant."

The pathologist's voice sounded odd, and Jenner uncovered his ears and opened his eyes to see MacElvoy staring into the open cavity of Hemphill's chest. "Yeah, Doc, what is it?"

"Water."

Jenner pushed himself away from the wall, feeling disoriented. "You want a drink of water, Doc? Jesus, how can you stand to put anything in your stomach?"

Macelvoy shook his head violently. "No, you young idiot, I don't want a drink, but somebody sure as hell gave one to Brad Hemphill."

"What are you talking about?"

The pathologist looked at Jenner, his expression a blend of surprise and chagrin. "Tell Schroder he was wrong, and so was I. That's what I get for being a smartass with my educated guesses. This man didn't die of blunt force trauma from a blow to the right temporal ridge. The son of a bitch drowned."

CHAPTER THIRTEEN

"WHERE WOULD YOU LIKE TO BEGIN YOUR SEARCH, SERgeant, or do you have a preference?" Rachel Applebaum stood straight, shoulders back, looking both feminine and professional. Her long-sleeved white blouse was crisp, her navy skirt and blazer were unwrinkled, her low-heeled pumps were unscuffed. She did have a narrow run in one leg of her panty hose, which saved Lydia from feeling completely inferior.

"We've already searched paleontology, since that's where the body was found. Where do you suggest next, Dr. Applebaum?" asked Schroder, lighting a cigarette with a Zippo lighter so old, Lydia thought he should donate it to the museum.

"The Horror of Horrors," said an old woman in a high voice just short of a screech. Maude Young, head custodian, *did* look very much like the late Lucille Ball. Her hair was the same improbable orange color—if one ignored the gray roots—and her large, round eyes fringed with two-inch false lashes had the same look of perpetual surprise. Unless one looked closely, thought Lydia. Lucy's eyes never contained such an expression of cynical resignation.

"What the hell's that?" asked Schroder. "A freak house?"

Rachel Applebaum shook her head, a slight frown marring what had been up to then a perfectly flawless complexion. "It's an expression the staff uses to describe a room in the stacks area of the annex where we, uh, store donations to the museum that are not appropriate to the collection."

"She means, it's where we hide gifts like the stuffed two-headed calf," explained Bill Whitney. "People sometimes think that the museum will welcome whatever they happen to find in their attics as long as it's old. But age doesn't necessarily mean value. The rarity of an artifact, who owned it, where it was found, and sometimes the romantic connotations are what gives an artifact value. An old fence post is just a piece of wood—unless we know it was a fence post on the old XIT ranch. Then it's a collector's item. That's a slight exaggeration, but not much."

"That ain't why we need to look down there," said Maude, scooting to the edge of the couch, spreading her legs, and resting a hand on each knee. "It's because of Sarah Jane. She might have something to say, but she ain't gonna come outside the stacks with all these strange people around."

"Who's Sarah Jane?" asked Schroder.

Either Lydia had suddenly gone deaf or everyone in the lounge had gone into a state of suspended animation. Even John Lloyd sat silent and brooding, his black eyes hidden behind half-closed lids. The silence lengthened until she caught herself holding her own breath, afraid to break the perfect silence with an unsolicited sound.

Schroder had no such compunction. "Don't everybody talk at once."

Rachel Applebaum laughed, but it was a nervous sound, as if she were just discovering her staff was refusing to follow her agenda. "No one," she said, choosing her words as carefully as a bride chooses a trousseau. "Sarah Jane does not exist. Maude, don't waste the sergeant's time with superstitious tales."

"She ain't superstition, Dr. Applebaum. I seen her one night by that old World War I ambulance there on the second floor. She had on what my grandma used to call a Mother Hubbard dress, pale blue with little white flowers, and wore a sunbonnet tied around her neck and hanging down her back. Walter's seen her, too. Haven't you, Walter?''

Walter Goodwin looked like a man locked in a cage with an angry skunk. No matter how he wiggled, he was going to come out stinking. ''I, uh, have heard some stories.''

''Who's Sarah Jane?'' asked Schroder, his voice a little louder.

Maude leaned over, braced an elbow on one knee, and shook her finger at Goodwin. ''You told me she stole your flashlight one night and hid it on top the oil derrick. If she hadn't turned it on, you never would've found it. We didn't do it, and you didn't do it 'cause you got scared out of a year's growth when you had to climb up that derrick and get it down. And how about the time I found my mop leaning up against the side of that Plains Indian teepee? What about your lunch, Walter? You remember that? How did your apple get into that allosaurus's mouth? And the Pioneer Town exhibit? There's always something moved around there. A poker hand dealt out on the table in the saloon, or the bed turned back in the hotel room, or that pair of long johns we found hanging on the buffalo-horn chair in the sheriff's office, the ones with the back flap pinned shut with a badge. All them exhibits is built like real buildings, and they're all locked up. Nobody was in the museum except you and me and my cleaning ladies. We didn't do it, and you didn't do it. Who did all those things, Walter?''

''Who's Sarah Jane?'' asked Schroder, his voice an octave higher.

''That's enough!'' ordered Darrell Farmer in such a parade-ground voice that Lydia nearly saluted. ''Somebody on the cleaning crew was playing practical jokes.''

''Not my ladies,'' stated Maude, straightening up to glare at the security chief. ''You think anybody that scrubs floors and cleans toilets for a living has enough good nature left at the end of a night to play a joke? And they'd all sooner mop a floor twice as to climb up that oil derrick with Walter's flashlight. That thing's two stories tall!''

''Who the hell is Sarah Jane?'' shouted Schroder. Lydia

noticed the sergeant was sweating and one eyelid was jerking.

"Why, she's a ghost," said Maude.

"A ghost?" asked Schroder, pulling a wrinkled handkerchief out of his pocket and wiping his face.

"Not really," said Rachel Applebaum.

"Peasant superstition," stated Roberto Ortiz. "One finds the same thing in my native country." Lydia wondered which country that was since the art curator had a Texas drawl thick enough to chop and make a fire over which to cook a chicken-fried steak.

"Peasant!" screeched Maude, catapulting off the couch. "Just because I don't know who my granddaddy was four hundred years ago, like you do, don't make me a peasant. He coulda been a king for all you know, and I'm a princess who ought to be sitting around on her behind wearing a crown instead of cleaning the ladies' rooms. But one thing I'm not, and that's stupid! Something walks these halls at night, and it ain't me and my ladies or Walter. It's Sarah Jane!"

Maude Young flounced back down on the couch. Her lips were squeezed shut, and her chapped hands with their swollen, cracked knuckles were clenched. Lydia felt a chill that began in her belly and spread out to her extremities, like rigor mortis, that left her stiff and cold. Maude Young believed absolutely in Sarah Jane, and Lydia wondered which came first: the belief or the ghost.

Schroder sat at one end of the conference table, his faded blue eyes moving from one face to another. "A ghost," he repeated. "Why the hell not? Makes as much sense as anything else. What do you think, Branson? Shall I arrest the ghost or the dinosaur?"

Lydia heard the chair next to her squeak as John Lloyd leaned back. "Might I suggest we suspend judgment on the guilt or innocence of either party, Sergeant, until we hear the testimony of Sarah Jane."

Schroder's mouth gaped open, then snapped shut to the accompanying sound of teeth grinding together. "Are you crazy, Branson?" he finally asked, studying John Lloyd as though measuring him for a straitjacket.

"I am simply suggesting that we begin our search in the Horror of Horrors, Sergeant. That is where Sarah Jane is most frequently found, madam?" John Lloyd asked Maude.

Maude sat up straight and nodded. "That's right. There or anywhere else in the annex, close to the door to the stacks. Sometimes she's in Pioneer Town, sometimes in the wagon display. But mostly she stays in the annex. And she never goes up to the petroleum exhibit. Too new for her, I think. She prefers old things, like she had when she was alive."

"When was that?" asked Lydia.

"In the 1880s or 1890s," said Maude. "Leastwise that's when they wore them Mother Hubbards. I'm guessing, of course, 'cause she never told me exactly. Just that she died of pneumonia when she was young, eighteen, I think. They used to die of that pretty regular. And she wasn't ready to die. Well, who would be at eighteen? Just because somebody's a ghost don't mean they had a bad death; sometimes it just means they ain't ready to let go."

"And you've seen her?" asked Schroder. Lydia noticed him studying Maude as if he were measuring her for a strait-jacket, too.

"Yeah, like a bright light where there wasn't no light. And I feel her. Mostly I feel her, like she's there right beside me but I can't see her. She's real." Maude nodded again, her eyes darting between Schroder and John Lloyd.

Lydia rubbed her arms again where Maude's words had raised goose bumps. She knew exactly what the custodian meant. She felt the Butcher sometimes. He was real, too.

"You're not going to listen to that crazy old woman, are you?" demanded Darrell Farmer.

"Certainly," said John Lloyd, bowing to Maude. "Mrs. Young is a singularly honest person. Sergeant Schroder, shall we find this Horror of Horrors?"

"I'll show you," said Farmer.

"I believe not, Mr. Farmer," said John Lloyd. "Sergeant Schroder and I can manage. I am very familiar with the museum. I know where the stacks are, and I believe the room in question is on the west side of the lower level." He looked around the room. "Please remain with Officer Evans. We will return shortly."

"The hell you will, John Lloyd," said Bill Whitney. "We store artifacts in the stacks. You could be down there until the middle of next month looking for a blunt object."

An expression flashed across John Lloyd's face too quickly for Lydia to decipher. "I very much doubt we will take quite so long, Bill." He hooked his cane over his arm and walked through the door. Schroder looked at Lydia, shrugged his shoulders, and followed.

Lydia hesitated. She could feel her heart beating faster and her stomach beginning to twist and cramp with nausea. She clenched her fists and forced herself to walk through the door. Maude's ghost had nothing to do with her own ghost. The Butcher would not be in the stacks.

As she walked past the large oil derrick, Lydia looked up toward its top. "John Lloyd," she whispered. "Do you believe in ghosts?"

John Lloyd glanced at her impatiently. "Miss Fairchild, the frequently reported cold spots and inexplicably slamming doors attributed to supernatural visitations can be more accurately explained by an overactive imagination combined with an inadequate heating system and the normal shrinking of wood found in old buildings."

"I guess an inadequate heating system put Walter Goodwin's flashlight on top the derrick," she retorted.

"Of course not. Really, Miss Fairchild, you indulge in the most ridiculous flights of fancy."

"Branson, if you don't believe in ghosts, what the hell are we looking for?" asked Schroder.

John Lloyd stopped by a plain, unobtrusive door near an old elevator on the first floor of the annex. "Key, please."

Schroder fumbled through his collection of plastic bags until he found Rachel Applebaum's labeled keys. "You going to answer me or not?"

John Lloyd unlocked the door and flipped a light switch as he stepped through. Lydia followed him, glanced over his shoulder—and screamed. Two figures, their arms outstretched, loomed out of the shadows.

"What the hell!" shouted Schroder as Lydia careened into him as she tried to push her way back out the door.

"Lydia! They are mannequins!"

Lydia felt John Lloyd grab her shoulders and whirl her around into his arms. She burrowed her face into his shoulder, hanging on to his waistcoat and shaking so hard that her teeth chattered. "Mannequins?"

"Yes," he whispered, grasping her arms and forcing her around to face the two plaster figures.

"What the hell is wrong with her, Branson?" asked Schroder, his square, hard face looking surprisingly sympathetic.

John Lloyd hesitated and looked down at Lydia. She swallowed and shook her head. "Miss Fairchild was startled by the mannequins."

Schroder nodded. "They did kind of jump out of the darkness, didn't they, Miss Fairchild? Like they were alive?"

Lydia took a deep breath. "Yes."

Schroder nodded again. "Don't want to make a habit of imagining people who aren't there, Miss Fairchild. It's not healthy."

"Yes, I know."

"Figured you did." He patted her shoulder awkwardly, as if it weren't something he did often enough to remember how, and looked up at John Lloyd. "You want to tell me what we're looking for?"

John Lloyd clasped Lydia's hand and turned toward a narrow cement stairway. "In your interview with Farmer and Goodwin, they made several references to unusual occurrences in the annex. Video cameras blinked, sound and motion alarms went off unexpectedly. Fire alarms sounded. When Maude Young vehemently defended her ghost story, she also mentioned the annex, specifically the stacks area. I concluded that the sabotage of the security system had been planned for at least as long as the disturbances had been occurring. The annex was a testing ground, and Brad Hemphill had been under sentence of death for at least six months. He was executed tonight in what you rightly referred to as a choreographed performance. It was an absolutely brilliant crime planned to the last meticulous detail. It was also the cold-blooded act of a ruthless beast. Somewhere in this dark, silent place that beast has left his spoor, Sergeant."

Schroder looked around. "The murder weapon you mean?"

"I doubt it, Sergeant. Such a careful murderer is not likely to leave a bloody club behind. But perhaps he left something else."

"Like what, Branson?"

John Lloyd frowned. "Cigarette butts, a footprint on a dusty floor, a button from his coat perhaps, but some reference to his identity. No one can spend so much time in a confined area without leaving a trace. I certainly expect to find some evidence of tampering with the electrical system. It is the logical place after all. It is out of the public view and is not frequented by the staff except when a particular item is needed to refurbish a display. We begin by looking in the Horror of Horrors because Maude mentioned it as the place her ghost frequented. I believe her ghost and our murderer are one and the same."

"But Maude said she saw the ghost," said Lydia.

"She saw a bright light and a figure in a long, loose dress, Miss Fairchild. Looking into a bright light temporarily blinds you, and anything behind the light is indistinct. It was a clever trick, an optical illusion perhaps, but cruel. A woman less strong than Maude Young might easily have panicked and injured herself." He clasped her hand tighter. "Shall we go, Miss Fairchild, Sergeant?"

John Lloyd descended the open cement stairway through three levels of dimly lit, shadow-infested spaces filled with shelves of artifacts of every kind. Lydia hung on to his hand and tried to concentrate on something besides her fear. As they stepped onto the fourth and lowest level of the stacks, she noticed that the north wall was hung with bridles. She lifted one of the dangling reins and held it under her nose. She inhaled and thought of school shoes and Western-wear stores. An uneasy impression of something alien nudged her mind, and she shivered again.

"Let go of the artifacts, Miss Fairchild, and come along," said John Lloyd, tugging her hand. "We are here."

Here was a small room with no door and filled with junk, including the two-headed calf mentioned by Bill Whitney, a broken sofa, a marbletop table with no legs, a trunk with no lid, a cracked wooden churn, and many other equally antiquated objects, discards from countless attics and cellars. Lydia peered over the back of the sofa and saw several branding irons, a braided leather quirt, and a china doll, all scattered as if dropped by a careless hand. Impulsively she released John Lloyd's hand and edged around the sofa. She had to pick up the doll. It was lonely and it didn't belong in a junk room.

"Schroder!"

Lydia jerked back and crouched against the wall.

"Schroder, you son of a bitch, are you down there? Come on up. I got the autopsy results, but I want to be able to see your face when I tell you, and this cellar's darker than the inside of a whale's belly."

"Quit yelling, Jenner. You're loud enough to wake the dead," grumbled Schroder.

Lydia wished he hadn't used that expression.

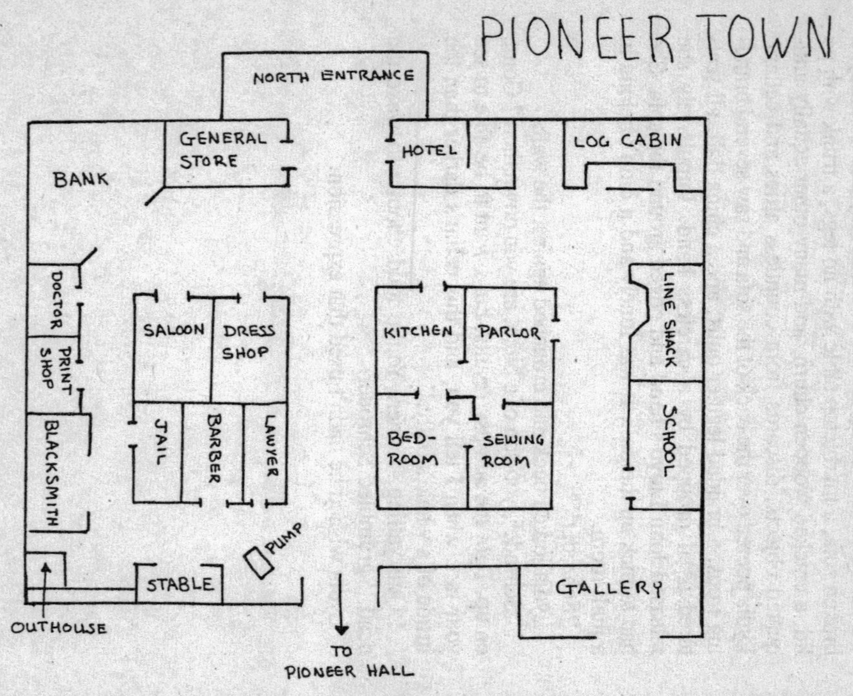
PIONEER TOWN
NORTH ENTRANCE
GENERAL STORE
BANK
HOTEL
LOG CABIN
DOCTOR
PRINT SHOP
BLACKSMITH
SALOON
DRESS SHOP
JAIL
BARBER
LAWYER
KITCHEN
PARLOR
BED-ROOM
SEWING ROOM
LINE SHACK
SCHOOL
PUMP
STABLE
OUTHOUSE
TO PIONEER HALL
GALLERY

CHAPTER FOURTEEN

JENNER WAS ENJOYING HIMSELF. IT WASN'T OFTEN HE'D HAD the privilege of telling Schroder he was misguided. It wasn't often he'd had the privilege of seeing Schroder flounder like a beached whale when the tide goes out. He leaned one shoulder (casually) against the wall, crossed his arms (casually) over his chest, crossed one leg over the other (casually) to rest the toe of his boot on the floor, glanced to make sure Lydia Fairchild was in a position to observe (and admire) his pose, and waited for Schroder to regain his composure. He hoped it took a long time.

"He drowned?" asked Schroder, an incredulous expression on his face. "The son of a bitch drowned in a museum in the middle of the Texas Panhandle, nearly a thousand miles from the nearest ocean?"

"He didn't drown in sea water, Schroder. Doc MacElvoy eyeballed a sample under the microscope and said it was fresh water. Well, not exactly fresh, but water from a tap. Stuff was full of chlorine," explained Jenner.

"He drowned in a sink?" asked Schroder.

"There is another source of fresh water in the museum," said John Lloyd.

Schroder swung around to the lawyer. "You're gonna tell me he drowned in a toilet bowl?"

"In this case anything is possible, but I very much doubt that scenario," said the lawyer. "A murderer who deposits his victim's remains on a dinosaur is hardly likely to commit his crime in a public toilet. The location does not match his macabre sense of drama. However, there is the watering trough next to the replica of a livery stable in Pioneer Town, an exhibit of which Brad Hemphill was curator. Need I mention that said livery stable contains numerous items, none of which are replicas, and most of which can be considered blunt instruments?"

"I want to look at that trough and that stable," said Schroder, rushing headlong toward the windmill exhibit and thus to the rest of the museum.

Jenner strolled after him and timed his second revelation to coincide with the detective's reaching the first windmill. After all, he didn't often gain the psychological advantage of Schroder. "There were two blunt instruments."

He heard John Lloyd Branson murmur "interesting" at about the same time he heard Schroder giving his imitation of an enraged bear bellowing. "Get your ass over here and explain, Jenner!"

Jenner speeded up his stroll to a gallop and arrived at the windmill before Schroder finished his sentence. "MacElvoy said one of the victim's ribs on the left side was broken all to hell before he died, and that the weapon that broke Hemphill's rib wasn't the same weapon that crushed his skull. One was round and skinny, and one was round and fat. Best educated guess, he said."

"You describing Cinderella's two stepsisters, or are you describing weapons?"

Jenner felt his face turn as red as the polka dots on Lydia Fairchild's clown costume. "Like maybe a poker and a baseball bat. Or that size anyway. And something else, Schroder. The lividity proves that the body was tucked away somewhere flat on its back."

"And the shirt, Sergeant Jenner?" asked John Lloyd, his black eyes intent.

"I was getting to that. We found white cotton fibers mixed with dust on his pants and caught in the hair on the back of his head, but none on his shirt."

"That's better. Why didn't you tell me all this in the first place?" demanded Schroder.

"If you could delay reprimanding Sergeant Jenner until another time," said Branson. "I want to examine the murder scene. Given these new facts, something is not right. Either the references to the murderer's behavior are contradictory, or I have misread them." Without waiting for the detective, Branson disappeared into the windmill exhibit hall on his way through the maze of rooms to Pioneer Town.

"Wait just a damn minute, Branson!" shouted Schroder as he hurried after the lawyer.

Jenner wandered back to where Lydia still waited and shrugged his shoulders. "I guess we ought to follow our two fearless leaders."

Lydia glanced toward an open door leading to what Jenner privately called the black hole from hell. "Would you go back into the stacks with me, Jenner?"

"You mean that basement junkyard where I found you and Schroder and our Panhandle Perry Mason? What for?"

Lydia hesitated, and Jenner noticed that she looked worried. Then he changed his mind. She didn't look worried; she looked scared—like a first offender who suddenly discovers he's up to his eyebrows in trouble; he can't make bail, his lawyer's out of town, and he's sharing a cell with a three-hundred-pound biker in a bad mood.

"There's something down there," she finally said.

"Like what? Did you see somebody?"

"No, but I had a feeling that there was something I should've noticed, something out of place." She shook her head, and Jenner watched the long blonde hair whip around her face. "Did you ever have a feeling that you missed some important connection, Jenner, that if you could go back and look at a situation all over again, then everything would be clear? It's like a mental itch."

Jenner rubbed his jaw. "Yeah, I have that feeling sometimes, usually because Schroder tells me how many connections I've missed. And I'm going to miss another one if I don't get myself to the crime scene before he realizes I'm not there. I can do without another ass-chewing. I tell you what, though. You go ahead and look for whatever it is that's giving you an itch. Just don't touch anything, because technically that area is part of the crime scene, too."

"I can't go down there," said Lydia abruptly.

"Why not? You afraid of ghosts?"

She laughed, an odd, humorous sound that Jenner didn't like. "There's supposed to be one, a girl named Sarah Jane, but that's not why."

Jenner waited, but Lydia didn't say anything more, just kept staring at the open door, as if it were the entrance to her own private spook house. He decided there was something out of place about the beautiful Miss Fairchild, too, as though she'd misplaced some important part of herself and couldn't remember where she'd left it. Unfortunately he couldn't help, not with a psycho running around swinging blunt instruments and drowning curators in watering troughs.

"Jenner! Get your ass in here!" Schroder's voice was a faraway bellow, but sounded nonetheless deadly.

"Come on, Lydia. It sounds like Papa Bear is getting to the pissed-off stage. Forget the museum's black hole for now. Maybe later I can go with you. Okay?" God, he sounded as if he were talking to a seven-year-old, but Lydia Fairchild reminded him more of an abused child than an adult. Something or someone had broken her, and she hadn't picked up all the pieces yet.

The Butcher?

Maybe. Probably even was. But that had nothing to do with a murder in a museum. The Butcher was dead, for Christ's sake.

"Jenner!"

He took a step, then turned toward Lydia. "You coming?"

Lydia Fairchild looked for a moment as if she despised herself, then nodded. "There's nothing else I can do." She laughed again, and Jenner wished she hadn't. Her laugh sounded worse than odd; it sounded . . . hollow. Like Jenner always imagined a ghost's laughter might sound. He shivered and looked over his shoulder as he took Lydia's arm and hurried her out of the annex.

Pioneer Town was exactly that—a replica of an early Texas Panhandle settlement with examples of a private home, a bank, ladies' emporium, hotel and saloon, jail, general store, barber shop, print shop, lawyer's office, an outhouse, a school, a blacksmith's shop and stable, plus two reconstructions: an actual cabin belonging to an early pioneer and a line shack from an old ranch. Each building was constructed of weathered planks and furnished with artifacts from the period. With a little imagination, one could feel the hot sun beating down on the uninsulated roofs, hear the clop of boots on the wooden sidewalks, and smell the dust of unpaved streets.

Jenner had a lot of imagination. He could imagine sitting in the sheriff's office on the buffalo-horn chair beside the pot-bellied stove, searing one side of his body while the other side froze; he could imagine going home to the four-room house, a mansion for that time and place, and sleeping on the uncomfortable bed, with its lumpy mattress, next to a wife wearing a flannel nightgown, whose number of pregnancies was frequently equal to the number of wedding anniversaries celebrated, and who wished to avoid or at least delay another exposure to the joys of motherhood; he could imagine shaving with a straight razor and cutting the hell out of his chin.

Jenner respected the pioneers, if for no other reason than that they survived being pioneers. He had no desire to bring back the good old days of outdoor plumbing, four-legged transportation, buffalo-chip heating, pneumonia in the winter and food poisoning from no refrigeration in the summer, long johns and corsets, horsehair sofas and coal oil lamps, diphtheria and smallpox, measles and tetanus.

The late-twentieth-century Panhandle was an improvement over its nineteenth-century counterpart in every respect but one.

Men still killed one another.

Schroder squatted by the watering trough glaring at its

hand-lettered sign: LIVESTOCK ONLY! DON'T DRINK THIS WATER! "I guess nobody told Brad Hemphill," he said.

Rachel Applebaum stood in the middle of the group of staff members wringing her hands. "Perhaps he slipped."

"The doc said no," Jenner replied. "There would've been some sign that he tried to catch himself."

"For God's sake, Rachel," interrupted Bill Whitney. "Don't even suggest it was an accident! Imagine the insurance company."

"You sound like you'd rather have somebody murdered," said a tall young man Jenner recognized from the video as Abe Yates. "Cold-blooded bastard, aren't you?"

"That's enough, Abe," snapped Rachel. "We have Sergeant Schroder to misinterpret every word we say. We don't need to pick at one another."

Bill Whitney wiped his forehead on the sleeve of his coat. "I didn't mean to sound as if I don't care what happened to Hemphill. I knew him when he was a kid. So did Rachel—Dr. Applebaum—and Margaret and even John Lloyd."

"Where is our friendly shyster?" interrupted Schroder, gazing at the crowd that included suspects, Canyon cops, Special Crimes, campus security forces, and Lydia Fairchild, who, Jenner noticed, was staring avidly in the windows of the pioneer home. "And who the hell let you people out of the lounge?"

"I apologize for the temporary absence, Sergeant," said the attorney, threading his way through the crowd. "I needed to make a phone call and also to instruct Officer Evans to escort the staff to the scene. I presume your stalwart crew acted upon my suggestion as to where the body might have been hidden?"

"Yeah, from the signs of disturbance in the dust, we figure it was hidden under the bed in the hotel display, just like you guessed."

"It wasn't a guess, but a deduction from Sergeant Jenner's reference to white cotton fibers mixed with dust. The hotel bed has a white bedspread, and one expects to find dust underneath a bed. Adding those facts to the hotel exhibit's close proximity to the location of the actual crime, the hiding place becomes not a puzzle but an easily solved logistic problem."

Schroder's expression said that he wouldn't mind finding Branson's remains stuffed under a bed somewhere.

"Which leaves us with two possible explanations as to why the murderer changed the victim's shirt," continued the attorney before Schroder could interrupt. "The first is that a dusty white shirt would immediately cause a search for flat, dusty places, which would inevitably lead to Pioneer Town, the hotel, and the blood on the pump, and he wished to delay the discovery as long as possible. However, that is inconsistent with his deliberate exhibition of the body, which insured the same results. The second explanation . . ."

The attorney's voice trailed off, and Jenner prodded him. "So what is the second reason?"

Branson looked at him and shook his head. "He wanted to delay discovery until after the autopsy. In other words, he was buying time. But why?"

"Or maybe he just wanted a tidy corpse," said Schroder, his face the dusty-red color of a weathered brick—which meant he was at the end of what little patience he had. "And maybe we need to discuss our spheres of influence, Branson. I don't recall turning over the investigation to you."

"Of course not, Sergeant. Collecting your bits and pieces of evidence holds little interest for me. The fact that the evidence points in two different directions is, however, of great interest to me."

"What are you talking about, Branson? Nothing's pointing in any direction except at one of your brilliant staff members."

Branson held up one hand. "Careful, Sergeant Schroder. If you have a particular suspect in mind, then you must inform him or her of his or her rights. Until that time, keep an open mind."

"Whose side are you on? I didn't ask for your help; you offered, remember?"

"You're helping the cops, John Lloyd?" asked Bill Whitney. "I thought you were my lawyer, and everybody else's lawyer for that matter."

"I want another attorney," announced Roberto Ortiz.

"I haven't arrested you yet, Ortiz, so you don't need a mouthpiece," said Schroder, sticking an unlit Camel in his mouth. "I got the right to question material witnesses, ain't that right, Lawyer Branson?"

"I don't think we can trust your tame lawyer, Schroder," said Yates, hooking his thumbs through his belt loops and leaning casually against the entrance to Pioneer Town.

"Don't be nasty, Abe," said Margaret Clark. "It's not good manners. I trust you, John Lloyd." Jenner decided the archivist did look a little dotty. He also thought she looked like somebody he ought to know.

John Lloyd pounded his cane on the tile floor. "Quiet, please. I had you brought here so that you might confront the reality of death. Brad Hemphill drowned after being struck in the ribs—which I believe caused him to stumble and hit his head against the pump at one end of the trough, inducing unconsciousness. He then rolled facedown in the water. As I'm sure you've already noticed, Sergeant Schroder, there is hair and traces of tissue and blood on the pump. I assume they are Brad Hemphill's."

Schroder nodded, his face grim. "We'll have to run them by the lab, but unless the murderer's setting up another diorama, I figure you're telling it the way it probably happened."

Branson looked at the staff again, his black eyes assuming that same mesmerizing expression that Jenner had seen before. Except it probably wasn't assumed. John Lloyd Branson had the most compelling eyes of any man Jenner had ever known. It was a wonder that the murderer didn't babble out a confession just to avoid having to look into them.

"These facts describe a murder committed as a result of a sudden impulse. Would anyone care to verify that?"

Jenner looked around. All the suspects were staring at the lawyer. For that matter, so was everyone else except Lydia Fairchild. She was captivated by the replica of a stable.

Branson glanced down at the watering trough as if considering what to say next, but not before Jenner saw his eyes change from mesmerizing to bleak, as if the lawyer had encountered something he didn't want to face. "However, if the murder is a result of sudden impulse, why does the murderer coldly hide the body, then move it? The usual response is to flee, not to initiate an elaborate cover-up. Also, death by drowning is not instantaneous. Particularly not this death. As I am sure you all know, there is a wire frame consisting of narrow rectangles roughly the width of a horse's muzzle covering the top of the trough. Unfortunately, Brad Hemphill had a narrow skull and the trough was full. I believe his face became wedged in one of the wire rectangles and he inhaled water until he died. The murderer would have had to wait several minutes at the crime scene for the victim to be beyond resuscitation. That fact also fails to support sudden passion. Lastly, there is the sabotaged security system, which indicates not a crime of sudden impulse, but one carefully thought out and executed."

"My God!" exclaimed Bill Whitney, his face the pasty color of stone-ground flour. "And you believe one of us did that deliberately?"

"I do not yet know what I believe. Until I know why Brad Hemphill died, I cannot reconcile the conflicting evidence of how he died. Was his death the result of a sudden impulse or a deliberate act? If it was the former, now is the time for the one responsible to step forward. If it was the latter, as an attorney I must caution you to say nothing."

"You're going to help the bastard get away with it?" demanded Abe Yates.

"I want to hear you answer that one, Branson," said Schroder.

Branson pounded his cane again. "If I might be allowed to finish." He looked at the silent faces. "As the attorney for this museum, I will assist Sergeant Schroder in stripping each of you to the bare bones if that is what is required to discover the—"he hesitated"—bastard who did this. If you are innocent of this crime, you have nothing to fear from me. If you are guilty, then I recommend you consult another attorney."

Jenner was awed by Branson's audacity. The son of a bitch as much as dared the murderer to stand pat. If anybody did demand another lawyer, his colleagues would assume he was guilty even if he wasn't. On the other hand, if the murderer didn't demand another lawyer, he was betting that Branson and Schroder couldn't uncover his identity and couldn't prove anything if they did.

Jenner wouldn't take that bet.

"I never did nothing like that," stated Maude Young. "I didn't come to work till nearly six o'clock, and I was gone by eleven. There wasn't no body here when I mopped the floor at seven, and even if there had of been, I didn't have nothing to do with it. I work at night, and he worked in the daytime. I just met him a couple of times when I had to run by for a few minutes. He seemed like a real nice boy. At least he wasn't no snob"—she bobbed her head toward Roberto Ortiz—"like some people I could name if I wasn't a lady. Us would-be princesses gotta be polite. But not too polite. So you tell me, Mr. Branson and Sergeant Schroder, what am I doing here?"

Jenner grinned. He didn't know what kind of princess Maude Young was, but as an American junkyard dog, she was Grade A Prime. Step on her tail, and she'd bite your balls.

Neither Branson nor Schroder winced, but Jenner had always figured the deadly duo wore cast-iron jockey shorts. Nip at their balls, and you'd break your teeth off at the gum line. "You're here, Mrs. Young," said Schroder, "because you were in the museum after five o'clock. So were the rest of you except Mr. Whitney, who's here because Dr. Applebaum called him, and I'm tolerating him unless he starts irritating me. Then I'll kick him out on the street, and I don't care who he represents. Everybody else on staff, including all the guards, was gone between five and a quarter after—except you seven, and I don't think fifteen minutes is long enough to kill Hemphill, hide his body, and sabotage the security system. But you could've done it at six, Mrs. Young, while your crew was cleaning offices and Goodwin and Farmer were at the front desk."

"That's impossible, Sergeant." Walter Goodwin stepped up beside the custodian and put his hand on her shoulder. "I was making my rounds a little after six, and I saw Maude near the derrick, so you just back off."

Maude patted his hand. "You're a good man, Walter, but I don't need no help. I'm an innocent woman."

Schroder looked frustrated, a condition Jenner knew always worsened the detective's disposition—a disposition that no one could describe as pleasant even when a case was going well, which this one wasn't. In Jenner's opinion, Goodwin's defense of Maude Young had just crossed two suspects off the list. If they were both near the derrick at just after six, neither one could have been in Pioneer Town killing Hemphill because, according to MacElvoy, he was probably already dead. He didn't think they did it before six, because there just wasn't time to wait until Hemphill died, then hide him, then screw with the security system, which brought up another interesting point.

"Schroder, who was watching the video monitors between five and six-thirty if all the other guards were gone, Farmer was at the front desk, and Goodwin was doing his walk-through?"

Goodwin and Farmer looked at each other, then at Jenner. "No one," said Farmer.

CHAPTER FIFTEEN

"THE WAY I SEE IT, BRANSON, WITH THE TIMES DOC MacElvoy gave us and the fact the body wasn't there at five and wasn't there at six, any one of them could've done it." Schroder leaned his elbows on Darrell Farmer's desk and stared down at a piece of paper. "I made up a list of who, when, where, and how. I believe that's what you told me I was responsible for. Well, here are the facts. Let's hear whys from you."

Lydia scooted her chair closer to John Lloyd's and glanced at the paper while Jenner looked over her shoulder.

Rachel Applebaum—In her office until signing out at 5:25. Attended Whitney party 7:30–10:30. Returned to Canyon with Farmer and Ortiz. Called back to museum by Darrell Farmer at approximately 1:00. Familiar with security system and daily schedule. Had keys to all doors and to the alarm system. Unmarried—no witnesses to verify missing hours.

Margaret Clark—In archives until signing out at 5:20. Attended Whitney party 8:00–12:30, as witnessed by Lydia Fairchild and John Lloyd Branson. Returned to museum approximately 1:15. Familiar with security system and daily schedule. Had keys to south and east doors and to alarm system but no key to hotel display area. Divorced—no witnesses to verify hours between 5:20–8:00.

Darrell Farmer—At front desk until signing out at 6:10. Attended Whitney party 7:30–10:30. Returned to Canyon with Applebaum and Ortiz. Called to museum by Walter Goodwin approximately 12:20. Security chief, capable of sabotaging the system, and is responsible for assigning daily schedule. Had keys to all doors and to alarm systems. Married, but wife is out of town. No witnesses to missing hours.

Walter Goodwin—Signed in at 5:55. Let cleaning crew in at 6:00. Walked through museum 6:00–6:30. Saw Maude Young near oil derrick "a little after 6:00." Watched monitors 6:30–11:30, when he took a thirty-minute dinner break. Discovered body at 12:05, informed campus security and Canyon police at 12:08, turned off alarms, and called Darrell Farmer 12:10. Familiar with security system, was alone in museum 11:00–12:00, knew daily schedule. Had keys to all doors and to alarm systems. Denies hearing or seeing anyone except cleaning crew. Married. No witnesses 11:00–12:00.

Roberto Ortiz—In his office in annex until signing out at 5:40. Attended Whitney party from 7:30–10:30. Returned to Canyon with Rachel Applebaum and Darrell Farmer. Called to the museum by Rachel Applebaum approximately 1:00. Familiar with security system, knew daily schedule. Had keys to all doors and to alarm systems. Married—wife out of town awaiting birth of first grandchild. No witnesses 10:30–1:00.

Abe Yates—Working in guns and saddles exhibit until signing out at 5:45. Attended Whitney party 7:00–12:00. No witnesses. Stopped at museum upon seeing lights and cars at approximately 1:00. Familiar with security system, knew daily schedule. Had keys to all doors and to alarm systems. Unmarried—no witness to verify missing hours.

Maude Young—Signed in at 6:00. Saw Walter Goodwin shortly after 6:00 at oil derrick. Mopped floor in Pioneer

Town 7:00–8:00. Did not see Hemphill's body. Mopped floor in paleontology exhibit 10:00–10:30. Did not see Hemphill's body. Signed out at 11:00. Had keys to all doors and to alarm systems, but not to hotel display area. Called back to the museum at approximately 1:00. Widowed.

John Lloyd hooked his cane on the edge of the desk, leaned back, and rested his arm on the back of Lydia's chair. She could smell the faint scent of his bay rum after-shave lotion. She wondered why John Lloyd Branson smelled as if he'd just stepped out of the shower. Didn't the man ever sweat? For that matter, did Schroder? Maybe in his case all that nicotine he inhaled had shriveled his sweat glands. She and Jenner certainly didn't have that problem. She was beginning to smell musty, as if she'd worn her clothes an hour too long. And Jenner? The kindest thing she could say about Jenner was that the lingering odor of formaldehyde didn't make her sick.

"You have the who, the when, and the where, Sergeant Schroder; but I fail to see that you have specified the how—or which of the whos is responsible," said John Lloyd, crossing one elegantly clad leg over the other. Lydia noticed that even the crease in his slacks still looked razor sharp.

"I figure twenty-five minutes maximum, Branson. I did a little dry run on the sabotage. I changed tapes in the recorder in under four minutes and that included unlocking doors and cabinets and pulling tapes from storage. The alarm board? Its back was held on with only two screws, and the murderer used alligator clips and a wire stripper to deactivate the motion and sound detectors. Five or six minutes if you know what you're doing, and he knew. Hell, Darrell Farmer could've done it all when he changed tapes, then killed Hemphill after six."

"Why deactivate the sound and motion detectors, Sergeant? If Maude Young and her ladies were here, the alarms were not on. Correct me if I am wrong, but I believe a vacuum cleaner would activate a sound detector."

"So they wouldn't go off when he came back after eleven

to move the body.'' Schroder had the answers for everything. ''Or Goodwin could've done it. Did you notice how many things were going on at around six o'clock? Walter checks in, Maude Young checks in, Walter starts his walk through and sees Maude. Unless Maude came into the museum carrying her mop, she had to spend a little time collecting her equipment, cleaning materials, and so on. I'm not saying either one of them is lying about their timetables. I'm just saying I don't think all those events took place as quickly as they think.''

He scratched his head. ''I don't think Maude Young did it, because she doesn't have keys to the display area, and it's stretching things to believe she picked the lock, shoved Hemphill's body under the bed, got over to the derrick, came back to the museum after eleven, picked the lock again, and hauled the body over to paleontology. Somebody would've had to help her, and the logical somebody was Walter Goodwin, and that's stretching things even further.''

He pinched the bridge of his nose, and Lydia sensed that Schroder was more fatigued than she had thought. He slumped in his chair. His thick shoulders had a rounded hunch, like those of an old man. He opened his eyes and looked at John Lloyd. ''Rachel Applebaum had time to do it, and so did Ortiz and Yates. Margaret Clark, maybe. But she couldn't have moved the body unless somebody did it for her, like Walter Goodwin, and I believe that about as much as I believe he helped Maude Young, so I'm excluding our archivist, at least for the time being. Yates, I don't know. If he was at that party, then he couldn't be here helping Brad Hemphill take a ride on that skull. Ortiz? He's a pretentious shit, but that doesn't make him a murderer.''

''What about fingerprints, hairs, and fibers, and so on?'' asked Lydia. She heard John Lloyd sigh and knew immediately she had asked a stupid question, but she couldn't seem to concentrate on why. Her mind felt sluggish, and her mental itch was worse.

''Miss Fairchild, I got more fingerprints than the FBI, and they all prove nothing. Any half-assed defense attorney right out of law school would point out to a jury that museum staff members' fingerprints in the museum are about as surprising as bird shit on a roller coaster."

Lydia's eyes stung and she blinked away tears. John Lloyd was right. Not only was she losing her strength and her spirit, she was also in danger of losing her mental faculties. If she wanted to avoid becoming an apathetic mental case with her emotions curled into a fetal ball, she had to act against her fear. Any of her fears would do.

"I got the facts, Branson, and they don't prove a damn thing, just like you said."

"Can you verify these sign-out times, Sergeant?" asked John Lloyd.

Schroder lit a cigarette and squinted one eye against the ribbon of smoke that lazily rose from its tip. "That's an interesting question, Branson. We have the checkout sheet, but it shows that Brad Hemphill signed out at five-thirty-five, which is an admirable trick for a man probably in the process of drowning. It does tally with what the suspects told Miss Fairchild, but that means shit, too. If you're gonna kill somebody, you try to be consistent with your lies."

"Perhaps we could discuss the situation with Mr. Farmer," suggested John Lloyd. "It's possible he would notice a discrepancy."

"It's possible he might notice his head if he looked in a mirror, but I wouldn't depend on it. Him and his control of access. If access to this museum was any more controlled, the whole population of Canyon could march through here at midnight." Schroder exhaled a cloud of smoke and gestured at Jenner. "Go get Colonel Blimp."

"I figured him for a sergeant," remarked Jenner as he left the security chief's office.

Schroder rolled his eyes toward the ceiling, then back toward John Lloyd. "These kids don't even recognize common expressions."

"Colonel Blimp is dated, Sergeant. You should modernize your vernacular."

"That's the pot calling the kettle black, isn't it, Branson? You've haven't modernized the way you talk since Teddy charged up San Juan Hill. Besides, I like being dated if it means I'm not like that freeze-dried bunch in there.'' He pointed his thumb toward the volunteer's lounge. ''The only ones that show any kind of feelings about Brad Hemphill's murder are Abe Yates, who's pissed as hell, and Walter Goodwin, who at least has the decency to express sorrow. Rachel Applebaum's worried about covering her staff's ass, which I guess is her job; but it doesn't make me like her much. Whitney keeps jabbering about the museum's insurance policy, and Ortiz is scared he's going to embarrass some great-granddaddy that's been dead for four hundred years. Farmer's more upset about his security system than he is about Hemphill's dying, and Maude Young's too busy telling ghost stories to think about anybody else.''

''What about Margaret Clark, Sergeant?'' asked Lydia. ''She was crying.''

Schroder's faded blue eyes held a mingled expression of cynicism and anger. ''Mostly because of Brad Hemphill's connection with her daughter, Miss Fairchild. For Margaret, everything comes back to her daughter. Even when she's being an informed source for the grand jury, she's always hoping that one of the bastards she's tracking is the one who killed her daughter.''

He glanced at John Lloyd. ''Oh, yeah, I know she's the informed source, and I got a pretty good idea how she gets some of her information, but I don't rock the boat. Hell, you couldn't live in this fucking world if you didn't compromise. I don't like it, but I do it. I reckon Margaret does, too.''

''Don't you have any sympathy for her, Sergeant? Her daughter was murdered.''

He nodded. ''Knocked unconscious and smothered with a pillow. Happened up in Canadian. No suspects, no witnesses. Somebody's spent the last twenty years walking free while Lindsey Clark's spent them in a coffin. That ain't going to happen here.''

Jenner opened the door and Darrell Farmer walked in. Lydia decided fatigue must be getting to the security chief, because his back didn't look nearly as straight and stiff, and his eyes looked sunken. Probably no worse than her own.

She felt as if her eyeballs must be resting on the back of her skull. Right next to the mental itch.

Schroder handed him the checkout sheet. "Can you verify these times, Farmer? Anybody fudging about when they signed out?"

Farmer took the sheet and glanced at it quickly. "It's correct."

"Anybody act a little different? Nervous, maybe?"

"Not that I noticed."

"Then you'll swear that everybody is telling the truth?"

Farmer's tongue flickered out and licked his thin lips. "Of course."

"Then who signed out for Brad Hemphill?"

"I don't know!"

"Did you know everybody in the lounge had keys?"

Farmer's mouth twisted, as if he was making a valiant effort not to curse. "Damn bastards!" So much for valiant efforts, thought Lydia. "Security is some kind of a goddamn game to them, like all that crap with the ghost. I talked to Dr. Applebaum about it, but she just said it was all my imagination. Like I had one."

"So which one of your damn bastards hated Brad Hemphill enough to kill him?"

Farmer looked astonished. "How could anybody hate a mouse like him? You might as well hate one of those dummies on display in Pioneer Hall. He just didn't have much of a personality."

"Might I ask, Mr. Farmer, when you saw Brad Hemphill last?" asked John Lloyd.

"About four-thirty, up in the archives," replied Farmer. "Same place he was every afternoon."

"Of course he was in the archives," said Margaret Clark after Jenner had escorted her into the tiny office, and she had seated herself in the chair John Lloyd had politely offered her. "He usually is in the afternoon. He's researching a Panhandle history book. Or he has been the last two months. Should I have mentioned that?" She looked at Schroder's slowly purpling face and nodded. "Yes, I can see I should have. I don't have my head on straight tonight. The anniversary, you know. Then poor Brad, and you were so busy asking what we were doing and where we were, and then, of course, you caught us with our keys showing. I can just imagine what Darrell Farmer will have to say about that at the next staff meeting. We were supposed to turn in our keys to the outside doors when he was hired two years ago, but my heavens, some of us have been here longer than God, and we resented him and his security system. Having to check in and out and be grilled if we stayed a minute later than five. It was like nobody trusted us anymore. So we all kept our keys. I suppose he'll blame us for every hiccup his precious security system had, like we were responsible."

"Were you?" asked Schroder.

"Of course not. We never used the keys. We just kept them as a gesture."

"Including Maude Young?"

"My, yes. Maude's worked for the museum nearly as long as I have. If she'd been helping herself to the collection, it would've turned up long before now."

"When did you last see Brad Hemphill, Margaret?" asked John Lloyd.

"At five-fifteen, when I told him I was ready to lock up the archives."

"You're certain of the time?"

Margaret Clark pursed her lips and frowned. "John Lloyd, I wouldn't have said it if I hadn't been certain. Some people may say I'm crazy, but I can tell time. The reason I remember so clearly is because I was flabbergasted. Brad never stayed past a quarter to five. Not ever. He marked his place in the book he was studying, tucked his notes in a file folder, and asked if he could leave it on my desk overnight. He said he didn't have time to walk across the museum to his office in the annex."

Schroder leaned forward, and Lydia saw John Lloyd stiffen. "He said he didn't have time?" asked the detective.

"Really, Sergeant, you should have your hearing checked. Yes, that's what he said. But then he dithered around, as if he really didn't want to leave, until I finally had to push him out. Even then he followed me downstairs to the first floor and all the way to Pioneer Hall before he stopped.'' She hesitated a minute and rubbed her hands together. ''Sergeant, are you absolutely sure he didn't faint and hit his head on the pump? He was looking like such a wrung-out dishrag last evening, I thought he might be sick. His hands were shaking; he was sweating and looked absolutely colorless. But then, he was so pale anyway.''

Lydia clutched the edge of the desk. She recognized Brad's symptoms. He hadn't been sick; he had been scared to death.

CHAPTER SIXTEEN

JENNER RESTED ONE HIP ON THE CORNER OF THE DESK AND watched Margaret Clark depart in a cloud of black silk, leaving behind a dejected Schroder studying his timetable and scratching the gray-and-red stubble on his chin. "So Hemphill was alive after five-fifteen. That eliminates Rachel Applebaum. No way she could've done it all in five minutes or so."

"Interesting," murmured John Lloyd, stroking his own chin, which, in contrast to Schroder's, looked freshly showered, shaved, and lotioned.

Jenner wondered how the attorney did it. Nobody should look that goddamn good at nearly six in the morning. It was unnatural. The man must be a machine. On the other hand he, Sergeant Larry Jenner, felt like hammered shit. But if he felt it, Lydia Fairchild looked it. She was hanging on to the desk so hard that her fingernails were turning white. Her face was already white, and even her lips were colorless. She looked as if her blood was slowly draining away, leaving her translucent. If she turned much paler, she'd be invisible except for her brilliant blue eyes, and even they looked glassy and faded.

"Hey, Lydia, how about another cup of coffee?" he asked, leaning down to touch her shoulder.

She jerked backward, stumbled out of her chair, and half fell against Branson. The lawyer wrapped his arms around her waist and pulled her back against his chest.

"What the hell!" exclaimed Schroder, pushing himself out of his chair and resting his fists on the top of the desk.

Jenner didn't remember catapulting off the desk to reach Lydia, but he must have, or else he wouldn't have found himself standing up with Branson's hand planted in the middle of his chest.

"Back," ordered the attorney.

"Hey, I was just trying to be polite," protested Jenner. He stepped back anyway. No way would he argue with John Lloyd Branson when the man's eyes looked as if they belonged to a seriously pissed-off rattlesnake.

"You startled her," said Branson.

"If that's startled, what does she do when she's scared?" asked Jenner.

Lydia brushed her hair away from her face and struggled upright. "I act like an even bigger fool." She turned and rested her hands on Branson's shoulders, tilting her face up toward his. Jenner wondered if Lydia even realized what she was doing, or if the lawyer did when he clasped her around the waist. There was something so commonplace about their pose, as if they always stood just like that.

"John Lloyd, he was afraid of something," said Lydia urgently.

"Of course he was," said Schroder as he sat back down. "He was going to meet a killer."

"But how would he know that?" demanded Lydia, turning to face Schroder. "Think about what everyone's said about him. A nerd, a mouse, quiet, scared, a good boy. That isn't the kind of person who deliberately meets someone he knows might hurt him. That means it wasn't the killer he was afraid of. It was something else."

"Like what? Maude Young's ghost?" asked Schroder.

"I don't know. Maybe. But I think it's important to find out." She gazed over her shoulder at Branson. "It's one of those references you're always talking about, John Lloyd. It's significant if we look at it in the right context."

Schroder ground out his cigarette butt on the tile floor and dropped it into his pocket. "Hell, Branson, we got dinosaurs and ghosts; we might as well chase a wild goose or two. Just as long as you don't suggest a seance, Miss Fairchild, I'm willing to try anything."

"Occasionally your humor is enlightening, Sergeant," said Branson, releasing Lydia and picking up his cane. "I suggest we conduct a seance of a sort and ask Brad Hemphill to reveal himself."

Jenner started to laugh, but shivered instead when he looked at the lawyer's face. Branson was serious.

"You want to explain that?" said Schroder.

Branson turned and opened the door. "It occurs to me that we have neglected the victim, Sergeant. We know how he died, but we know only what others have told us of how he lived and nothing whatsoever of the whys. You accused our suspects of being unfeeling, Sergeant, but you and I are no less guilty, I more than you, since I knew Brad when he was a young boy. In your search for facts and my concentration on the murderer's motives, we forgot Brad Hemphill. He became a piece in a puzzle instead of its heart. This was not a random crime, but an act of violence occurring within a closed circle. The victim's motivations are at least as important as the murderer's. Until we know Brad Hemphill, we cannot hope to meet his murderer. Might I suggest you begin your relationship and I renew mine with young Brad by examining his effects? In other words, why not search his office?"

"Holy shit!"

Jenner silently echoed Schroder's comment as he stepped into Brad Hemphill's office. Small—no more than ten by ten—the room held an old gray metal desk in front of a locked and barred window, a filing cabinet in one corner, a wooden bookcase, and narrow work tables along two walls.

And candles.

Fat ones, skinny ones, tall ones, short ones; green, yellow, pink, orange, white, lavender; a kaleidoscope of sizes and colors of candles filled Brad Hemphill's office. A candelabrum stood on his desk next to an old manual typewriter; candles lined the windowsill; candles shared space with small artifacts on the work tables; candles served as bookends in the bookcase; and a candle sat atop the filing cabinet.

"Fascinating," said Branson, looking around the room.

"I can understand a candle or two for decoration," said Bill Whitney, turning slowly in a circle to look at the room. "But this is . . . is strange."

Jenner thought Whitney's comment was a little closer to the mark than Branson's but not by much. Both of them ought to be honest: the room was damn weird. If it was indicative of Brad Hemphill's personality, then the young curator must have had so many screws loose, he rattled when he walked.

"Brad was eccentric," said Rachel Applebaum, blotting her forehead with a lace-trimmed handkerchief.

The room wasn't hot, so Jenner decided the tension must be activating the director's sweat glands. That was okay with him. In his opinion Rachel Applebaum was nailed down too tightly. Nothing slipped through her cracks; no impulsive words or actions, no spontaneous emotions. Maybe a little tension would melt her self-control. Maybe that's what Branson hoped when he insisted she and Whitney observe the search. It sure as shit wasn't for the reason he gave: that Applebaum and Whitney had known the victim since childhood and they might interpret some of the references to Hemphill's behavior to be found in his office. Jenner didn't consider *strange* and *eccentric* much of an interpretation.

"Did you know about all this, Rachel?" asked Whitney.

The director nodded. "I knew, but he promised not to light them."

"Did the fire marshall know about this? God, did the insurance company?" Whitney raked his fingers through his hair. "A pyromaniac on staff, and you never said anything? Jesus, Rachel!"

"He wasn't a pyromaniac. He had a fixation about the electricity's failing, and he wanted to be prepared. He even carried one of those fountain pen–size flashlights clipped on his shirt pocket. And when he went into the stacks, he always took two big flashlights with him. He asked my permission to take a Coleman lantern, but I refused. We store too many valuable artifacts there. I couldn't risk his spilling any of the fuel."

"Why was he afraid the electricity would fail?" asked Lydia, staring at the candelabrum and shivering.

Rachel tugged at the lace on her handkerchief. "There was an electrical storm the night Margaret Clark's daughter died, and all the lights went out. He lived next door, and I think he always associated the electricity's failing with Lindsey's death."

Schroder pulled open the center drawer of the desk. "More candles and matches. And two flashlights. Even the Boy Scouts aren't this prepared. Hemphill wasn't playing with a full deck, Dr. Applebaum."

"Don't slander him!" Her voice sounded thick, as though she was screaming through a gag. "He was a wonderful curator. He knew more about the history of this region than anyone else on the staff, myself included. And he was always so careful, constantly verifying his facts because he was afraid of making a mistake. He was afraid of everything. He was another Lindsey Clark cripple—just like Margaret is." There was a ripping sound as Rachel Applebaum tore the lace from her handkerchief.

Whitney wrapped his arms around her. "It's all right, Rachel. I felt sorry for him, too, but all this"—he gestured at the room—"says he wasn't very stable."

"Who hated him, Rachel?" demanded John Lloyd.

"I don't know! No one. Who could hate someone as harmless as Brad?"

"That is what I am asking you, Rachel. You know your staff. Who had argued with him lately? Who had reason to resent him? Had anyone complained about him recently? Think! Had you noticed anyone watching him?"

Branson threw his questions at her like body blows until she cowered in Whitney's arms and covered her ears. "Stop! Stop it, please!"

"Goddamn it, John Lloyd!" shouted Whitney. "What the hell are you trying to do to her?"

"Break through her denial," answered the attorney, his eyes focused on Rachel Applebaum. "This is not an error to be corrected by submitting the proper report to some state agency. It is not a public relations problem to be solved by distributing optimistic press releases. It is not a crisis in morale to be resolved by a show of confidence in your staff. It is murder!"

Branson swallowed and rubbed a knuckle across the top of his eyebrows. "Rachel, it was little Brad Hemphill from Canadian who died. If you know anything, or have sensed anything about any member of your staff, please tell us. Not because it is your duty to society, but because it is your duty to the little boy who lived in the two-story house with the white cupola and grew up to work with you."

Rachel Applebaum lifted her head from Whitney's shoulder. Her face was gaunt from strain, and Jenner felt an eye-prickling surge of pity. "It's happening all over again, isn't it, John Lloyd? All the suspicion, all the doubts, all the wondering about each other. It's just like Lindsey. Someone she knew killed her, and someone Brad knew killed him. Somebody on this staff killed him. We'll all be cripples because we'll never be able to trust one another again. We'll always want to ask one another that single question: Did you kill Brad Hemphill?"

"Did you, Rachel?" asked Branson.

She shook her head. "No, and I refuse to stand in moral judgment of anyone else by making wild accusations against my staff."

Jenner watched the lawyer looming over Rachel Applebaum like an inquisitor and remembered Branson saying that he'd strip everyone to the bare bones. He had already shredded his first victim and learned nothing except that Rachel Applebaum wouldn't be telling tales out of school.

"He didn't have any red candles," said Lydia suddenly.

Branson's eyes flashed about the room. "Bravo, Miss Fairchild, an astute observation. Would you care to speculate as to why?"

"There you go with your whys again, Branson," said Schroder, searching through another desk drawer. "Maybe he just didn't like red."

Lydia glanced around the room. "If he didn't, he was as obsessive about that as he was about the candles. There's no red anywhere. Even his books don't have red dust jackets."

"So maybe he threw them away," Schroder suggested. "I don't keep dust jackets, either."

"No, he didn't, because some of his books have them." She knelt down and pulled a book off the shelf. "Oh, God," she whispered, staring down at its front cover. "I have a copy of this book: *A Little Class on Murder* by Carolyn G. Hart."

"Miss Fairchild, your taste in literature is improving."

She ignored him. "There's a big red apple in the center of the jacket, but Brad Hemphill cut it out. Sergeant, this is important."

"If this was one of those cop shows on TV, we could figure somebody killed Brad Hemphill with a candle because he didn't like red," exclaimed Schroder, leaning forward to look at Lydia. "Then we'd search for somebody wearing a red shirt and with wax under his fingernails, and we'd wrap this case up in time for the closing commercials. But this is the real world, and every murder victim leaves a mess behind he probably wouldn't have left if he'd had any choice. Nobody wants strangers rooting around in his life like hogs in a trough, but a murder victim doesn't have any choice. So now we know a couple of strange facts about Brad Hemphill that maybe he didn't want anybody to know, but that doesn't mean those facts have anything to do with his murder."

"Rachel, do you have an explanation for this facet of Brad's behavior?" asked John Lloyd.

The director's eyes were filled with puzzlement overlaid with distaste. "No, and I refuse to speculate. This is disgusting! Picking over a man's belongings and dissecting him as if he were diseased."

Schroder pulled a file folder out of Hemphill's desk drawer and flipped it open with a pen. "Cops do a lot of disgusting things. It's one of the perks of working with drug dealers, rapists, and murderers."

"We cannot disregard the candles and his apparent hatred of red. Both facts reveal character, Rachel, and a victim's character is often the motive for murder."

Schroder looked up at the lawyer. "Branson, I wonder how much of the time you're right by accident instead of on purpose. Brad Hemphill's character damn sure set him up for murder. The little son of a bitch was a tattletale."

"What?" demanded Rachel Applebaum, outrage sharpening her voice.

Schroder smiled at the director, and Jenner felt cold, as if the room's temperature had dropped below the freezing mark, and Schroder wasn't even smiling at him. Rachel Applebaum ought to have frost on her cheekbones.

Schroder tapped an open file folder. "You ain't exactly sitting on moral bedrock yourself when it comes to judging your staff, are you, Dr. Applebaum?" Schroder rose and leaned over the desk to stare at her. "Or are you going to tell me that Brad Hemphill was full of shit when he wrote this letter?"

"What letter?"

Schroder pushed a piece of museum stationery across the desk with the end of his pen. "This one, Dr. Applebaum, that accuses you of sleeping with Bill Whitney and threatens to inform the museum committee of your so-called improper relationship. That wouldn't do you any good at all, would it? Whitney here might have to put up with a little public disapproval and some private jabs, a few winks and nudges from the boys at the country club, maybe sleep on the couch at home until his wife figures he's been punished enough, but you wouldn't get off that easy. It doesn't matter what the courts say about equal treatment of the sexes. It doesn't matter that it takes two people to have an affair. You're the one who's going to get the shit kicked out of you."

"That's not fair," protested Lydia, stepping over to take Rachel's hand.

"I didn't say anything about fair, and I never said I agreed with it, but I am saying that Rachel Applebaum had a reputation and maybe a job to lose if Brad Hemphill went to the committee. People have killed for a lot less reason than that."

Rachel Applebaum licked her lips. "I never saw that letter."

"This is a carbon, Dr. Applebaum. The original went somewhere."

"Are you going to believe anything that little shit wrote, Sergeant?" exclaimed Whitney. "The kid was crazy, certifiable. Look at this office. Would a sane person live like this?"

"That doesn't make him a liar, does it, Dr. Applebaum?" asked Schroder.

Rachel Applebaum didn't reply, but then, she didn't need to, thought Jenner. Her face said it all.

CHAPTER SEVENTEEN

"MISS FAIRCHILD."

Lydia pressed her forehead against the window of the private-home replica in Pioneer Town. She stared through the glass at a nineteenth-century living room, a room that less than an hour ago she would have said matched John Lloyd Branson. Both were solid and old-fashioned, occasionally uncomfortable but always dependable. That was before the revelation in Brad Hemphill's office, and she'd realized that her hero attorney had size twelve feet of clay.

"Miss Fairchild." She heard the wooden bench by the home's front door creak under his weight. "Miss Fairchild, this silent treatment is quite out of character for you. I would much prefer a verbal or even physical attack."

"You knew about Bill Whitney and Rachel Applebaum, didn't you?" she demanded, looking down at him as he sat on the bench. "They were the ones you were trying to protect."

He braced his back against the outside wall of the replica, deposited his Stetson and cane on the bench, and stretched out his legs, crossing his ankles. "Rachel, certainly."

Lydia considered his answer and decided she didn't like it

for reasons that had nothing to do with the case. "That's an interesting reference. How should I read it, that you condone her behavior, or that you support the double standard that condemns her and excuses your friend, Bill Whitney, or that—" She stopped and looked away.

"Or because I would behave in exactly the same manner?" he asked.

She could feel his eyes on her and refused to look at him. "It had occurred to me," she admitted.

"I assumed as much from your expression just before you bolted from Brad Hemphill's office." He caught her hand and pulled her down on the bench beside him. "In spite of the fact that Monique Whitney has all the lovable qualities of a black widow spider after mating, I find Bill Whitney's behavior reprehensible. I consider marriage a moral and legal contract, binding in both respects. If he is unable to meet the terms of the contract, in other words, if he cannot remain faithful, then he should terminate it in the properly proscribed manner."

"Meaning?"

"Meaning, if he cannot live with that woman, a task which I suspect requires saintly attributes Bill Whitney does not possess, then he should divorce her. He and Rachel are behaving in a most dishonorable fashion."

"But you are covering it up," Lydia pointed out. "Isn't that the same as condoning it?"

"I am not covering it up! I simply condone murder less than I condone adultery. A choice between two evils, Miss Fairchild. Sex is a wonderful red herring in a murder case because it frequently obscures less obvious but no less strong motives. I had hoped to discover the truth and prevent a public scandal, but I failed. When this case comes to trial, it will be difficult to bar that letter from being introduced as evidence."

"But she's not guilty. She didn't have enough time to kill Hemphill."

John Lloyd shot her an impatient glance, and she wondered what stupid observation she'd made this time. "Of course she is not guilty. I never assumed she was, but the attorney for whomever is finally tried for the murder will certainly accuse her. It is an inevitable and excellent defense strategy. One always offers the jury alternate suspects. I do so myself.'' He pounded his fist on the bench. ''Damn it, if she had only been frank with me.''

Lydia swallowed. John Lloyd Branson never pounded benches. Or tables, walls, or doors for that matter. He considered it uncivilized. And he rarely cursed. Usually, then, she was the target. This time she was innocent, or she thought she was. However, given her diminishing mental capabilities, she might have committed some gigantic indiscretion and failed to notice. She'd certainly missed whatever point John Lloyd was making about Rachel's lack of frankness.

''I don't understand. What did you expect Rachel to do? Confess her affair before Schroder learned about it?''

He rubbed his eyes and looked at her. ''Had she been truthful about the staff's interrelationships, her own irregular liaison might not have been revealed. Conflicts occur even among the compatible, Miss Fairchild, and that disparate group of egocentrics are not compatible.''

''But Schroder would've found the letter anyway.''

''I might have uncovered the guilty party before Schroder searched that office if Rachel had admitted to receiving the other memos from Brad Hemphill.''

''What memos?''

''In your haste to escape my hypocritical presence, Miss Fairchild, you missed Sergeant Schroder's further examination of the infamous file folder and his discovery of Brad Hemphill's legacy of goodwill: a series of memos directed to Rachel Applebaum accusing other staff members of every imaginable dereliction of duty from incompetence to burglary. His scurrilous communiqués demonstrated such a gift for innuendo, imputation, insinuation, if not actual slander, that any supermarket tabloid would have immediately hired him as a gossip columnist at a six-figure salary. Sergeant Schroder is elated by the revelations. I actually saw him smile—twice.'' He ran his fingers through his hair.

''Are you saying the memos are lies?''

''I do not know what to believe, Miss Fairchild. Nothing

is logical. A murder seemingly committed in sudden passion, yet cleverly concealed. Then, for no rational reason that I can see, it is revealed. Sergeant Schroder's team reports there is no evidence of tampering with electrical wiring in the stacks, yet alarms went off in that area.''

''They didn't find anything in the Horror of Horrors?'' asked Lydia, her unease returning.

''They found Brad Hemphill's fountain-pen flashlight, which only proves he was there and nothing else.''

''But that can't be all. I felt something down there, John Lloyd. Maybe there are ghosts. Maybe Sarah Jane was trying to tell us something.''

He looked at her as if she'd lost her last tenuous grip on reality. ''Miss Fairchild, I trust you will not repeat that statement in front of Sergeant Schroder. While I may be tolerant of your sudden fascination with psychic phenomena, he already doubts your mental stability. Do not confirm his suspicions.''

''I am not crazy, John Lloyd! You're the one who said time was linear.''

''Please, Miss Fairchild, I do not wish to debate opposing philosophical theories of time in relation to the physical universe. At present, I am interested only in facts, and there are too many facts, too many references to behavior that is inconsistent. Everyone speaks of Brad Hemphill as a shy young man afraid of confrontation. Yet the memos give the opposite impression.''

Lydia forced herself to concentrate on what John Lloyd was saying. ''What did he say in the memos?''

''He accused Darrell Farmer of losing keys to the outer doors and of being lax about demanding that staff members check in with security when staying after hours. Yet Margaret Clark speaks of Farmer's questioning the staff if anyone stayed later than five, and she admits the staff kept the keys in defiance of Farmer's orders, a fact that Hemphill must surely have known.''

''What was his motive for making an accusation like that? It's so easy to disprove.''

''Is it, Miss Fairchild?'' he asked. ''The memo does contain a half truth. Farmer did lose track of several keys in the sense that he did not have control of them. The other memos are much more damaging and less easy to disprove. In fact, I am afraid that it will be a case of the individual staff member's word against that of a dead man's. It is as if Brad Hemphill knew he would be murdered and left those memos to deliberately provide everyone with a motive and to insure that every staff member was scrutinized by the police regardless of his or her alibi."

Lydia felt the fine hairs at the nape of her neck spring erect. For somebody who didn't believe in psychic phenomena, John Lloyd could make a convincing case for precognition. She glanced toward the watering trough and closed her eyes, trying to reconcile the terrified Brad Hemphill who cowered in the archives until Margaret Clark shooed him out with the malicious Brad Hemphill who wrote those memos. She opened her eyes. She couldn't; they weren't the same man at all.

"What will you and Schroder do now, John Lloyd, apply thumb screws and try to break everyone's alibi? Arrest the person with the strongest motive?"

John Lloyd rose and smoothed his hair. "We shall attend the sergeant's interrogation of the last three subjects of Brad Hemphill's memos to hear their explanations of that young man's accusations. Then, Miss Fairchild, we shall attempt to fit all our references into a single context. And if we cannot . . ."

"Go on, if we can't?"

He shrugged his shoulders and picked up his hat and cane. "We may have to arrest the dinosaur after all." He held out his hand. "Come along, Miss Fairchild. Faint heart never catches the dastardly villain."

She took his hand and let him pull her up. "I thought that was, faint heart never caught fair maiden."

He turned her hand over and kissed her palm, then folded her fingers over the spot. "That is another subject we must debate at a later time, my dear Miss Fairchild. For now, in the words of another Victorian gentleman, the game's afoot."

She clenched her fist and noticed that her thighs were tingling again. "Then, I suggest you get on with the hunt. This fair maiden needs to rest her faint heart. I'm not up to witnessing another of your and Schroder's bone-stripping interviews." She closed her eyes and rubbed her forehead.

"You do have rather attractive circles under your eyes, Miss Fairchild. Perhaps you should lie down in the lounge."

She opened her eyes and shook her head. "I don't think I want to wait with the condemned. I'll just sit here on the bench, or look around a little. It's a wonderful museum."

He hesitated a moment longer, his black eyes looking at her speculatively. "I would rather you stayed close by, Miss Fairchild. Remember, there is still a murderer loose in the museum."

"According to you and Schroder, he or she is in the lounge under the watchful eye of Officer Evans. Besides, there must be about a hundred cops in this building, John Lloyd."

"I have not seen an officer since we have been talking. I believe those who have not returned to their regular duties are searching the staff's offices or are outside keeping the public away from the doors."

She darted a quick glance at him. Concern had replaced the speculative look in his black eyes, and she felt guilty for lying to him. Almost. "I'll be fine."

"And if you are startled again, Miss Fairchild?"

"Oh, for God's sake, John Lloyd. I'm not an emotional cripple yet, and even if I were, what can you do about it? Graft me to your side?"

He glanced down the hall toward the security area and sighed. "All right, Miss Fairchild, you may have a few minutes' respite, but remember, observing and listening to these interrogations is part of your job. I will expect you to join me shortly." With a last glance in her direction, he left.

She waited until he disappeared into the security area, before she whipped around the corner of the home exhibit and peered through the window into what was obviously a child's bedroom and studied the toys on the floor. She wasn't an expert in antiques, but she did remember her American history. The assembly line method of mass production of goods had been a fairly late development in the nineteenth century, and she didn't believe that china dolls had been among the first items manufactured and assembled. Therefore, the china doll in the bedroom and the china doll in the Horror of Horrors shouldn't be identical in every detail. Even if both had been made by the same doll maker, there should be subtle differences. She'd noticed the similarities while John Lloyd propounded his theory of how Brad Hemphill had died, but the significance hadn't occurred to her then. Not until she'd run back to Pioneer Town to escape her doubts about John Lloyd's motives in concealing his knowledge of Rachel and Bill's affair, seen the doll again, and learned that instead of evidence of tampering with the wiring system, the police found only Brad Hemphill's little flashlight, did she make the connection between Pioneer Town and the Horror of Horrors. If she was right, then she knew why Brad Hemphill died and she had a good idea who killed him.

But she had to be certain, and that meant going back into the stacks—alone. If she was wrong, she could avoid making a fool out of herself by explaining her theory to John Lloyd and Schroder. But if she was right, then she would prove to herself that she was John Lloyd's equal, that she was also capable of answering those whys of a murder.

It would prove something else.

It would prove that she had conquered at least one of her fears. Because she was terrified of going back to that musty, shadow-infested, haunted place where the past was stored.

But she had no choice.

Drawing a deep breath, she wiped her hands on her clown suit and pulled a museum visitors' guide from her shoulder bag. Studying it for a moment, she located herself, then walked rapidly through the gallery on the east side of Pioneer Town and into the guns and saddles exhibit. She got as far as the oil derrick before she stopped to control her shaking. Her heart was pounding, but it was full daylight now, and the sun pouring through the huge expanse of glass gave her courage. Nothing could happen in the daytime. Ghosts and other related horrors only happened at night.

She quickly walked through the windmill exhibit, through the door into the annex, and down a hall to the door beside the old elevator. She heard policemen's voices talking and joking as they searched the annex offices and felt better. She wasn't alone. She stared at the closed door to the stacks and wanted to scream with frustration. She was sure it was locked. Of course it was. The police had already searched that area and they wouldn't leave an unlocked door, not in a museum. She tasted defeat as if it were literally ashes in her mouth.

Lydia reached out to touch the locked barrier—and the door swung open. The stacks beyond were dark as night. Feeling her heart pounding, she tried to control her breathing. It was too loud; she sounded like a bellows with each breath whistling through her lungs and coming out her mouth in a whoosh. She might disturb something—or someone.

Reaching inside the door, she groped for the light switch, and bulbs glowed with anemic illumination. The two mannequins, male and female, waited just beyond the door like two wild creatures whose movement ceased only when the lights came on.

"You're not really alive," Lydia whispered as she sidled past them toward the cement stairs. Their plastic smiles mocked her, and she ran down the stairs to the next level, her legs trembling so badly, she tripped on the last step and sprawled on the landing. "They're not alive," she gasped. "Don't be such a scared wimp, Lydia."

Grabbing the metal pipe that served as a bannister, she pulled herself up. Her eyes stung and she wiped away the hot tears, feeling the deepest shame she'd experienced since she was a child. She was twenty-four years old—a woman—and she was crying because she was afraid.

She swallowed, straightened her shoulders, and walked down to the fourth level. She took another deep breath and felt choked. The air was thick and heavy and oppressive with the scent of old leather and wood and fabric, the past stored on shelves, hanging on nails, stacked in corners. She stopped to finger the bridles, feeling the stiffness of the leather, inhaled their odor, and smelled the newness of the tanning. She examined several braided leather quirts, noticed the cheap quality of mass-produced goods, and her certainty grew.

Giving the hanging leather tack a last glance, she walked through the door into the Horror of Horrors. The stuffed, two-headed calf gazed at her from its four glassy eyes. Something clicked behind her and she whirled around, smothering a scream. There was nothing there. She searched the shadows and thought vaguely how endless the stacks seemed, when really the area was not that large, perhaps a hundred or more feet in length, less in width. It was the darkness, the four different levels, that gave the area its feeling of vastness. She listened but the clicking sound was not repeated, only the indistinct creaks and groans of an old building.

Feeling her heartbeat and respiration settle down to a steady thunder and roar, she turned back and walked around the broken old sofa, leaning down to pick up the china doll. It felt warm and comforting in her hands, as if it were grateful to be rescued. "It's okay," she whispered. "I won't let them throw you out."

She thought she heard a sigh and whirled around again, clutching the doll. Emptiness and shadows greeted her, and she blew out her pent-up breath. Time to leave before her overwrought imagination conjured up something more substantial than fancied sighs. She had what she came for; better not push her courage. She smiled as she started up the stairs. She had proof of the motive, and she had conquered her fear of being alone in a dark place. Not bad for a few minutes of effort. Tomorrow she'd take the next step down her private dark passage and remember the Butcher.

She shuddered and felt her heart pound harder. She could sense him at the outermost edges of her imagination and took the stairs two at a time. She was at the landing of the second level when she heard the door close, and the lights went out. The darkness rushed in and surrounded her.

"Help me!" she screamed. But it wasn't a scream; her throat was paralyzed, and the only sound that escaped her was a breathy moan. It was like being caught in a nightmare and finding it impossible to cry out. She tried to swallow, but her mouth was completely dry. She felt herself slipping away into the past and tried to force herself to move. She couldn't do that, either. You can't escape in a nightmare, she reflected; you can only wake up, and even that's impossible if the nightmare's real. Like this one.

She curled up on the floor in a fetal position and hugged the doll.

She heard his breathing before she felt him. As his hands pawed at her shoulders, she screamed again and kicked out viciously. She thought her foot touched someone, but she didn't wait to find out. She scrambled away in the darkness, her body bent in a crouch, holding the doll in one hand, with the other outstretched in front of her, feeling for obstacles. It was odd, but the air was thick, almost tangible, and she sensed something ahead. She froze and held her breath. The Butcher! He was still alive and had trapped her again!

"Lydia."

She drew a sobbing breath. He was calling her and she was defenseless. She didn't even have her can of Mace in her shoulder bag.

"Lydia."

The voice was insistent. And different from her memories, lighter, higher, distant. But the Butcher had a hundred voices; that's how he'd fooled her in the first place. She sniffed the air for his odor of brimstone and human filth but smelled sagebrush instead—sagebrush and sunshine and wildflowers. She peered through the darkness and saw a flicker of light dance across a door. Glancing wildly around and seeing nothing, she scuttled toward the door, pushed it open, and slammed it behind her.

She felt something brush against her leg, and, as she stumbled back against the door and flung out her hand, she screamed. Her fingers brushed against a wall switch and she sank to the floor in relief as the lights flashed on. She looked around and laughed hysterically. The room was empty—empty except for five racks of guns of every conceivable length, vintage, caliber, and size. At least she wouldn't have to worry about being defenseless.

She pushed herself to her feet and glanced at a workbench. On it lay the longest, heaviest, most deadly looking rifle she'd ever seen. Enormous cartridges lay scattered next to it. Impulsively Lydia touched the rifle. Its barrel was old and nicked, and the wooden stock was scratched and gouged, but like the china doll, it felt comforting. She rubbed her hand along its barrel, felt the cool metal beneath her fingers, inhaled the greasy scent of gun oil.

Hesitantly she picked up one of the cartridges and loaded the gun. She'd never loaded a gun before, any kind of a gun, and wondered why she felt so sure she was doing it correctly, wondered, too, why she was doing it at all. She would never fire this rifle, would never fire any rifle. She couldn't. She hated guns. She was an educated, civilized woman. No way would she commit an act of violence with a gun.

Leaving the gun on the workbench, she picked up the doll and reached for the doorknob. She twisted it and pushed, but the door remained closed—closed and locked. "Oh, God, no," she whispered and pounded her fist against its wooden panels. "John Lloyd!" she screamed. "John Lloyd, help me!"

She heard a chuckle from the other side of the door and felt cold chills dance up and down her back. The Butcher had fooled her, tricked her into another locked room, and this time she would die. She knew it!

She took a step backward, smelled the filthy scent of the Butcher, and saw him materialize in front of her. "You're dead," she whispered.

He smiled. "You won't let me die, Lydia, because I'm part of you."

His lips moved but his voice originated inside her own mind, and Lydia knew she was insane—or soon would be. "You don't exist. You're a ghost."

He smiled again, that spastic stretching of his lips that never quite reached his dead, dead eyes. "But I'm your ghost, Lydia. You created me because you need me."

"Why should I do that? You were evil, and I don't feel one damn bit guilty about killing you."

She heard his laughter beating inside her head. "That's not why you feel guilty, Lydia. Don't you remember?"

Remember? Remember? Remember?

"No!"

"Then we'll live together until you die, just the two of us. I am that which you cannot remember but cannot forget."

She took another step back, and he moved forward in an unearthly choreography. "Is that a riddle? If I guess the answer, do you disappear in a puff of smoke and a dash of sulphur?"

"Only you would be flippant when you're on the verge of madness."

"Then I don't have anything to lose, do I?"

"Only John Lloyd."

"No!"

"Yes, Lydia, because you can't have us both, and you need me. As long as you have me, you'll never have to face the truth, but John Lloyd won't let you hide, will he?"

The Butcher's face took on a menacing, three-dimensional clarity it had lacked, as if the ghost she only half believed in had suddenly taken on flesh. She heard him breathing—like the panting of a wild beast—felt her scars burn as if they were fresh cuts, smelled the pungent odor of his body and hers, and knew that whether this was her imagination, or whether time had folded in upon itself, she was reliving her confrontation with the Butcher, and it was real. Reality was what the mind perceived, and she needed this reality to mend the broken places in her spirit.

She lifted her head and met the Butcher's eyes, saw herself in their opaque depths, and remembered what she'd fought so hard to forget. With a ragged sigh she accepted the truth about her own nature: given sufficient provocation, she could kill without regret, but worse than that, be glad she did it.

"I remember," she told the Butcher. "Now go back to whatever fiery furnace you were stoking."

"It isn't that easy, Lydia," said the Butcher, his words resounding in her head. "When you create a ghost, it takes on powers of its own." He stepped closer, his hands reaching for her.

With a scream she stepped sideways, hitting her side against the workbench. Dropping the china doll she'd held like a talisman, she grabbed for the rifle.

"It's too late, Lydia," he panted, his fingers curled like talons around her arm.

"No, it's not," she gasped out, jerking away and struggling to lift the heavy gun to her shoulder. She felt a draft of air flow past her and looked up to see the Butcher stumble backward against the door. His figure was less distinct, as though a shadow stood between them.

Lydia sighted down the rifle. "Burn in hell, you devil!" she screamed and pulled the trigger. The recoil slammed her backward into the wall, and just before she lost consciousness—when time lay furled layer upon layer and the past coexisted with the present—she thought she saw an indistinct figure in a long, loose blue-flowered dress leaning over her.

"Sarah Jane?" she asked, and smelled sage and sunshine and wildflowers again.

CHAPTER EIGHTEEN

"SO WHERE'S YOUR SWEET YOUNG THING, BRANSON?" asked Abe Yates.

Jenner took two giant steps sideways to get away from the battlefield when he saw Branson's face take on that intent look that preceded his really serious bone-stripping. He thought Yates was lucky to be sitting on the floor already. Otherwise the lawyer might kick the curator's ass up between his shoulder blades and tell God he slipped. As it was, Branson looked down at Yates, as if trying to decide between skewering him with the blunt end of his cane or merely re-arranging his teeth with the toe of his boot.

"You are fortunate, Mr. Yates, in two respects. The first is that Miss Fairchild is temporarily occupied in examining Pioneer Town's many attractions. Otherwise the necessity for restraining her from committing assault and battery upon your person would seriously interfere with this investigation. Secondly, you are fortunate that I am more civilized and therefore less likely to administer the caning you so richly deserve. However, do not provoke me further. Miss Fairchild is *not* my sweet young thing, nor is she anyone else's.

She is very much her own woman, and sweet is not the proper adjective unless one uses it to modify tart."

"You better listen to him, Yates," said Jenner. "I saw her lay out the meanest pimp in Amarillo—" He ran unexpectedly out of breath, mainly because the end of John Lloyd Branson's cane was compressing his diaphragm.

"That will be enough, Sergeant," said Branson, his voice as sharp as the look in his eyes. "Miss Fairchild's past activities are hardly germane to the conversation."

"Yeah, sure," agreed Jenner, thinking that Lydia Fairchild's past activities were very germane. Sort of like posting a sign warning trespassers that you owned a pit bull.

Yates held up both hands in supplication. "Hey, I'm sorry. It's just when a broad's as foxy as she is, you figure she's used to men coming on to her."

"I suggest you remember that foxes bite and are occasionally rabid," said John Lloyd, a peculiar expression in his eyes.

And that particular fox had already bitten John Lloyd Branson, Jenner decided. There was no other explanation for the way the lawyer practically foamed at the mouth whenever another man came within sniffing distance of Lydia Fairchild.

Schroder interrupted before the lawyer could administer another verbal blow. "If you can get your mind off your assistant, Branson, we got a few people we need to talk to."

"You've already talked to Rachel all you're going to, Sergeant," said Whitney, sitting on the couch with his arm around Dr. Applebaum. He looked tired and dispirited, which Jenner figured he ought to be. No man wants his extramarital tomcatting made public, much less have it figure in a murder case. Still, the way he was holding on to the museum director made Jenner wonder if Whitney's feeling didn't run a little deeper than just friendly concern for the woman he'd been sleeping with.

"I just got one more question, Whitney," said Schroder. "Dr. Applebaum, do you still deny ever receiving that letter or those memos?"

She looked up at him, her green eyes dull. "I swear to God, I never saw that letter or those memos before."

Schroder lit a Camel and exhaled a cloud of smoke. "Then how come one of my men found the originals tucked away in your desk drawer?"

Her face went slack, as if all the muscles had suddenly failed. "I don't know," she said, her voice a monotone. "I never put them there."

Schroder didn't look convinced, but Jenner noticed John Lloyd was frowning, as if he'd just heard something he didn't like, but couldn't decide why he didn't like it. It was that kind of frown.

"What memos are we talking about?" asked Abe Yates.

"It seems that you folks underestimated Brad Hemphill. All the time you thought he was a harmless pup afraid of his own shadow, he was busy digging up enough dirt on this staff to bury you all ass-deep to a buffalo. He missed his calling. He should've been a reporter for the *National Enquirer*."

Schroder studied the assembled staff, all of whom Jenner thought looked a little peaked after the long night. Of course, no sleep and having to look at Schroder's face had that effect on people. Actually, Schroder's face alone would do it. Probably had something to do with the detective's habitual expression. Like a vulture's on short rations.

"I don't believe it," stated Margaret Clark. "If it were true, we'd all know. Brad was the curator of history, you know. He was a fact-checker. If he saw Roberto walking out with one of those Oriental vases tucked under his coat, Brad wouldn't yell 'Stop, thief!' He'd first ask if it were a real vase; then he'd ask if it were from the collection. Then he'd check the answers fourteen ways from Sunday, and by that time everyone in the museum would know what was happening."

"I'm not a thief! Don't call me a thief!" Roberto Ortiz's face was slowly turning the rich orange-red of a wild plum.

"Oh, for heaven's sake, Roberto, I was using a hypothetical example. Don't be so quick to jump at what a person says. It's bad for your blood pressure." Having subdued the art curator, she faced Schroder again. "Besides, even if Brad Hemphill found out something nasty about somebody, he'd be too afraid to tell."

"Maybe somebody was counting on that," said Schroder. "Otherwise the murderer would've searched Hemphill's office and destroyed those memos. But he didn't, and now I want to do a little fact-checking of my own." He gestured toward the door. "Mrs. Clark, you first. Come in to Mr. Farmer's office."

Margaret Clark leaned back in the armchair and shook her head. "I don't believe so, Sergeant. If you have anything to say to me, you can say it here. I'm not guilty of murder, and I'm not ashamed of anything else I've ever done, either."

"Then maybe you'll tell me what accession records are?" asked Schroder.

"Basically it's a list of every gift donated to the museum. A card is made for every item with donor's name, description of the gift, and a number." Margaret Clark tapped the side of her nose like jolly old Saint Nick in the Christmas poem. Jenner wondered if that meant something magic was about to happen. With ghosts and oddball murders, a little magic wouldn't be out of place.

"So you have a card for every single item in the archives?"

"Yes. I have to know what we own, Sergeant. I'm not flighty when it comes to records."

"Brad Hemphill thought so. His memo accuses you of falsifying your accession records." Schroder's head poked forward like a vulture's as he watched the archivist.

Margaret Clark's pursed her mouth. "Isn't that strange? I haven't done a thing to my accession records. What on earth was that boy talking about?" She clapped her hands over her mouth and giggled. Schroder raised both eyebrows, while Branson raised one. A giggle from somebody who looked as if she just left a funeral was worth a raised eyebrow or two, decided Jenner.

"Oh, my," said the archivist. "Oh, my. I know now what Brad is—was—talking about. But it's still strange. Why would he mention that? It was certainly nothing I did." She waggled her finger at Schroder. "Not that everybody would believe what happened. It was naughty, of course, but not ugly. She's never done an ugly thing—if she did it, of course. And I'm not saying she did. . . . "

"Mrs. Clark!" Schroder's voice sounded like the hoarse bark of a fat Great Dane. Or maybe the despairing cry of a hungry vulture.

"Sergeant, you needn't raise your voice. This is a museum, you know. Not quite the same thing as a library as far as quiet goes, but still, no one wants to hear loud voices."

Schroder's mouth snapped closed. The detective didn't have a cigarette in the corner of his mouth, or he'd have bitten it in two. As it was, Jenner heard his teeth grinding together. "Mrs. Clark, who's *she*, and what did she do?"

"Why, Sarah Jane, of course," answered the archivist.

"The ghost?"

Margaret shrugged her shoulders impatiently. "That's the only Sarah Jane I know, Sergeant." She leaned over and nudged Maude Young. "You remember my accession cards, don't you, Maude? I unlocked the archives one morning and found a stack of accession cards listing acquisitions neither the museum nor the archives own—including a Spanish marching band. I didn't even know the Spanish had marching bands. And the carousel. There's supposed to be a carousel in the middle of Pioneer Town, and that's just ridiculous. The whole thing cheered me up, and it being an anniversary day, I needed cheering up. Anyway, I told Brad about it, and we giggled over some of the items. Actually, we didn't giggle. Brad wasn't much for giggling."

Schroder rubbed his hand over his face. "You're telling me that you told Brad Hemphill about the cards?"

"I just said so, Sergeant. Have you had your hearing checked recently? Men your age begin to lose their ability to hear the upper ranges of voices."

"Believe me, Mrs. Clark, I can hear you."

"If I might interrupt, Sergeant," said John Lloyd, depositing his hat and cane on the conference table and pulling out a chair. After turning it around to face the couch and Margaret Clark, he seated himself and braced one elbow on the table. It was all done with a casual elegance that Jenner could only admire. And envy.

"Margaret, to summarize, Brad knew about the false accession cards, and he also knew that you believed the ghost—"

"Sarah Jane," interrupted Margaret Clark.

"—Sarah Jane was responsible."

"I never said that. I don't know whether she was or not, so I'm not about to accuse someone who is possibly supernatural and possibly might have supernatural powers, because that's foolish."

"For God's sake, do you believe in the ghost or not?" demanded Schroder.

"Possibly," replied Margaret Clark.

"If I might continue, please," said John Lloyd, looking as casual as before. Which only proved to Jenner that the lawyer wasn't normal. Or else Margaret Clark really didn't bother him. Which was a possibility, given the fact that John Lloyd Branson's secretary was an axe murderess—acquitted—so maybe his definition of loony was a little looser than the ordinary person's.

Margaret Clark leaned over and patted his knee. "You go right ahead, John Lloyd. Don't mind me. But then, you don't, do you?"

"As I was saying, Brad Hemphill knew the truth, yet he deliberately wrote a memo giving a false impression. Do you have an explanation as to why he might have done so, Margaret?"

Margaret Clark patted her eyes with a handkerchief. "No, I don't, John Lloyd. It's out of character for Brad."

"I agree with you, Margaret," Branson said, rubbing his jaw.

"Sergeant, Mr. Branson." Walter Goodwin stood up and cleared his throat. "Mrs. Clark told everybody about those accession records. It wasn't no secret. And another thing. Before you go thinking that Maude and Mrs. Clark are crazy, sometimes I think I see that ghost, too."

"Goodwin!" exclaimed Farmer.

"About time you told the truth, Walter, instead of being a mealymouth," said Maude Young, patting her orange hair.

Schroder slammed his fist down on the conference table. "I don't want to hear any more about any goddamn ghost! No ghost killed Brad Hemphill and toted his remains all over hell and back again."

"She sure didn't," said Maude and gave a quick nod. "She plays a joke now and then, but she wouldn't hurt nobody."

"Mrs. Young!" exclaimed Schroder in what Jenner thought sounded more like a growl than a voice. "While we're on the subject of truth, I want to know about the rare artifacts you broke in the Pioneer Town exhibit, the ones Brad Hemphill wrote about in his memo."

"I never done it. I been working in this museum for nearly eighteen years, and I never broke anything. I'm always real careful. That's why Dr. Applebaum lets me clean the displays. Usually it's the assistant curators or the exhibit staff that does it, but she said she trusted me, so I get to do the special ones like Pioneer Town. I'm a good custodian. There was never a cobweb or a speck of dust when I finished."

Schroder exchanged glances with Branson, then reached in his coat pocket and pulled out a small manila envelope that Jenner recognized. It was Brad Hemphill's personal effects. "You didn't have any keys to the Pioneer Town exhibit, Mrs. Young." He tipped the contents of the envelope on the table. "But Brad Hemphill had two sets, and one of them had your name on them. Did Hemphill take your keys away when you started breaking artifacts?"

"I told you I never broke nothing, and Mr. Hemphill didn't take my keys. I gave them to him. I got ready to clean the private home in Pioneer Town one night about three weeks ago, and there was glass all over the kitchen floor. Now, long johns in the sheriff's office and a poker hand in the saloon are one thing, but broken plates in the kitchen are something else again. I was real upset and called Mr. Hemphill. He asked me to come in the next day, and I did. He was a nice young man, Sergeant, had a lot of gumption but not much grit. He was scareder of me than I was of him. He kept saying that accidents happen, but I said it weren't no accident and that I didn't do it. I said I figured Sarah Jane was unhappy about something and this was her way of telling us. Ghosts aren't much at carrying on conversations, you know. They mostly talk inside your head, and you have to listen real close."

She ignored Schroder's puffed-up face and continued unfazed. Which was just as well in Jenner's opinion because Schroder's eyelid was jerking, and that meant that anything he said would include some four-letter words, and that might give this group of genteel killers a bad impression of the police.

"But Mr. Hemphill looked real unhappy himself. I guess he didn't know what to believe, so I gave him my keys and told him to watch the exhibit. If something else turned up broke or moved or any other kind of funny business happened, then he knew it was Sarah Jane and not me."

"Tell me, Mrs. Young, did anything happen?" asked John Lloyd courteously.

Maude shook her head, her face both sad and solemn. "I guess it was me Sarah Jane was mad at, because once I gave up my keys, nothing else happened that I heard. I feel real bad about it, too, like I done something wrong. But I didn't, Mr. Branson. I didn't do anything except what I was supposed to."

"That's right, Mr. Branson," said Walter Goodwin earnestly. "Maude told me all about it."

"What are you, Goodwin, a professional witness?" Schroder inquired. "You jump in and alibi Margaret Clark, and now you're saving Mrs. Young's bacon. Any reason I should believe you?"

"I've never known Walter to lie," interjected Rachel Applebaum. "Nor Margaret and Maude, either."

"I'm an honest man, Sergeant," said Goodwin, straightening his shoulders and sucking in his belly.

"The last serial killer I arrested told me the same thing," said Schroder. "And if you look at it one way, I guess he was; at least he never stole anything off the bodies of his victims."

"Are you comparing us with a psychopath, Sergeant?" asked Roberto Ortiz, his head tilted upward at such an angle that Jenner decided the curator risked drowning if he went outside in a hard rain—unless he wore a clothespin on his nose.

"That's the wrong word, Ortiz. We call them sociopaths or say they have a personality disorder. And they ain't all killers, either. I read where one psychiatrist said that the most successful sociopaths are politicians and bankers. Of course, he never met this bunch. He might have added museum curators to his list. And speaking of curators, you want to talk in here, or would you rather have a little privacy?"

"Talk about what, Sergeant?"

"Hemphill wrote a short memo about you, Ortiz. A pretty nasty one, as a matter of fact. You might want to take a run at explaining it and hope Goodwin here backs up *your* alibi, too."

"I told you everything I'm legally required to. You have my keys, and I gave the young lady my schedule."

"You don't want to say anything about a journal you deliberately lost, one written by a member of Coronado's expedition?" Schroder stared at the curator from under his bushy eyebrows.

Ortiz's head snapped down to a more normal position. "Alleged journal. We're not absolutely certain it's authentic."

"Who's not?" demanded Margaret Clark. "Who's the archivist here? Me—and I say it's authentic. The paper's been tested, the ink, and according to the rare book specialists I consulted, it couldn't be more authentic if Coronado himself had written it in blood."

"Somebody on Coronado's expedition kept a diary?" asked Jenner, thinking what a pain in the ass that must have been before the invention of spiral notebooks and ballpoint pens.

"Not exactly," replied the archivist. "It was a journal written by one of the expedition's survivors after Coronado returned to Mexico in disgrace. Brad said it was more exciting than reading an adventure novel. I never knew he was interested in that kind of book—men's adventure, I mean. But you never know, do you? Anyway, I guess the journal was a sort of tabloid of its time, full of not very nice comments about all the men and women on the expedition. Brad promised to let me read the translation when he finished. I couldn't read the journal itself—written in a very archaic Spanish, you know, and the handwriting and grammar of that day make translating old documents a chore. We were so pleased when Roberto's grandmother donated it to the museum. It's been in his family hundreds of years."

"So did you steal back the family heirloom, Ortiz?" asked Schroder.

Ortiz licked his lips and looked as if he wished he could burn Schroder at the stake, just as Coronado had arranged for a few Pueblo Indians who showed a regrettable lack of appreciation for Spanish culture and religion. "My grandmother was old and senile and did not consult with the family before donating the journal."

"I'm sorry about your grandmother, but that doesn't answer my question. Did you steal the journal?"

"No, he didn't."

Everyone in the room turned to look at Rachel Applebaum. The director was rubbing her temples. She, Jenner decided, was another victim of whoever killed Brad Hemphill. Murder investigations were just plain hell on skeletons in the closet, even when those skeletons had nothing to do with the crime. A detective never knew which one did and which one didn't until he lined them all up.

"You know something about this, Dr. Applebaum?" asked Schroder.

"At Roberto's request, I did not publicize it in any manner, but the museum returned the journal to him."

"What!" exclaimed Margaret Clark in an outraged voice. "When? And why wasn't I told? The journal is the responsibility of the archivist."

Rachel Applebaum spread her hands in a gesture of helplessness. "Roberto pointed out that his grandmother was not mentally competent at the time she made the gift. The situation could have become quite ugly. Mr. Whitney and I felt that it was best to return the journal to avoid any litigation."

"You were going to sue the museum? Roberto Ortiz, you are sneaky and underhanded!" Margaret Clark's formidable bosom heaved with several indignant breaths. "No, you're worse than that. You're a sneaky, underhanded little shit!"

Branson looked at the archivist. If he was shocked by her use of profanity, he didn't show it. But then, Jenner suspected that not much shocked the lawyer. "So this memo, like the others, contains truth that is falsely represented. I find all this information fascinating."

"So do I, Branson," said Schroder. "It's just fascinating as hell the way this little group covers one another's asses."

"Have those memos been fingerprinted, Sergeant Schroder?" asked the attorney.

"I got the fingerprint man on it now. Why, you want to make sure Hemphill's fingerprints are on them?"

"No, I want to make certain that Rachel Applebaum's are not," replied Branson.

Schroder's face went blank for a second like a computer screen whose program crashes without warning. "What the hell?"

"I suspect our clever murderer has prepared another diorama, Sergeant, one I find even more puzzling than the first."

"What are you talking about, Branson?" Schroder's voice was a lot calmer than his face.

"All the memos concern affairs that are somewhat less damaging than they first appear."

"I wouldn't find one particular *affair* innocent," said Schroder, looking at Bill Whitney and the director.

Branson waved away the comment as if he were swatting a pesky fly. "That affair was also well known to the committee, if not a subject for casual conversation. Had we felt it interfered with the operation of this museum, the committee would have terminated the employment of one party and asked the other to resign his responsibilities. No, Sergeant, the murderer wants us to look more closely at certain people, but is uncertain upon whom he wants to cast the most suspicion. It is almost as if he is presenting us a list of possible suspects whose apparent motives may be dismissed in the hope that we will uncover a more dangerous secret during the investigation. I find such behavior inconsistent. Why not deliberately implicate another person with an accusation that could not be readily disproved? An even more puzzling question is, why should the murderer do anything at all? Had he left well enough alone, we might possibly never have proved anything. As it is, I am more suspicious of unwritten memos than am I of those discovered.''

''What unwritten memos? If they weren't written, then they don't exist,'' said Schroder.

''Exactly, Sergeant,'' said Branson, standing up. ''Why are Walter Goodwin and Abe Yates not the subject of misleading documents?''

''Me?'' asked Goodwin, his face looking puzzled. ''But I haven't done anything to give Brad Hemphill any reason to write nothing to Dr. Applebaum.''

''Neither had anyone else, Mr. Goodwin, yet they find themselves main characters in a memo. Why not you? Why not Abe Yates?''

Jenner looked toward the door, wondering why the assistant curator was keeping his mouth shut for once. ''Holy shit! Where is Abe Yates?''

There was a distant loud boom, followed by a splintering sound, and John Lloyd Branson turned not white, but gray, as if he had aged a hundred years in a second. ''My God! Lydia!''

CHAPTER NINETEEN

LYDIA FELT SOMETHING TOUCH HER FACE, SWUNG HER FIST wildly, then gasped and clutched her right shoulder just above her breast. "You can't hurt me, you son of a bitch. You're a ghost."

"Lydia! You're safe! It's John Lloyd!"

Lydia opened her eyes to see John Lloyd bending over her, holding a wet cloth in one hand and gingerly touching his jaw with the other. "What happened?"

"You mean other than you just rocked Branson's head back on his neck with a right hook?" asked Schroder, standing at the end of a couch striped in some kind of gold-toned material.

Couch? Lydia looked around an unfamiliar room, saw a desk, two armchairs, a round coffee table, and everyone she'd met at the museum so far, all standing in a circle around the couch staring at her as if she were the subject for a biology-class dissection. "Where am I?"

"In my office, Miss Fairchild," said Rachel Applebaum.

"How'd I get here?"

"Branson carried you," said Jenner, his face looking solemn and less boyishly handsome than usual. "I offered to help, but he just cussed me out and told me to move out of his way.''

''John Lloyd never curses,'' she said, looking at her uptight attorney who was sitting on the couch, his hip firmly pressed against her waist as if to keep her from falling off.

''Since most of what he said had one syllable and four letters, it sounded that way to me. I think he was a little upset. We found you lying on the floor of the gun room, with the door all blasted to hell and a buffalo rifle beside you.''

''That will be enough on the subject of my language and comportment, Sergeant Jenner,'' said John Lloyd firmly. ''Miss Fairchild, if you can refrain from administering more blows, I will finish cleaning the gunpowder off your face.''

''Gunpowder?''

''Your weapon used a cartridge loaded with a substantial amount of black gunpowder, Miss Fairchild. Your face resembles a lightly smoked turkey breast.''

''You're lucky you didn't blow yourself up with the door,'' said Bill Whitney. ''That was a Sharps Big 50 buffalo gun, and I bet it hadn't been fired in a hundred years.'' He turned to the director. ''About that door, Rachel . . .''

''If you mention the museum's insurance policy, I'll pinch your head off, Bill Whitney,'' said Rachel, handing John Lloyd a fresh cloth.

''Did you see anyone else?'' asked Lydia, her words muffled by John Lloyd's scrubbing.

''Like who, dear?'' asked Margaret Clark, hovering just behind John Lloyd.

''Who were you shooting at, Miss Fairchild?'' asked Schroder, his face as grim-looking as Lydia's felt.

''At the—'' She stopped. Who would believe her? Who would believe that a sane person held an extended conversation inside her head with a man who wasn't there. God, but that had been the granddaddy of all flashbacks. ''My imagination,'' she finished. ''The lights went out, and I thought I felt someone pulling at me. Then I saw the door to that room and rushed in to escape. Then somebody locked me in, and I imagined that someone was coming after me, so I shot him.''

Walter Goodwin looked puzzled. ''But that door wasn't locked, Miss Fairchild. Mr. Branson here pulled it right open. Of course there wasn't much of it left—a Big 50 does a lot of damage—but the doorknob was still there. The door was closed, but it wasn't locked.''

Lydia tried to sit up, but John Lloyd pushed her back. ''But I couldn't get out.''

''How did you see the door if the lights were out?'' asked Jenner. ''That place is darker than a pissant's butt.''

''There was a beam of sunlight that hit the door.''

''But all the windows are boarded up,'' said Rachel Applebaum, a frown wrinkling her forehead.

Lydia felt her mouth dry out again. Where had that beam of light come from? And who had called her name? Sarah Jane? Or the Butcher? She glanced at all the faces curiously staring back at her and swallowed. Was she mad? Or sane? Or were all dark passages haunted?

''Shall we leave the discussion of how Miss Fairchild managed to get into the gun room, but failed to get out again? There is the more important question of why you went back to the stacks.''

Lydia grabbed at the question like a lifeline. At least it didn't require a supernatural answer. ''John Lloyd, I know why Brad Hemphill was killed. I knew it last night, but didn't know I knew it.''

''Perhaps you could be a little more coherent, Miss Fairchild,'' suggested John Lloyd. ''What did you know?''

''I saw a china doll on the floor of the Horror of Horrors. I saw the identical doll in Pioneer Town. China dolls weren't mass-produced in the nineteenth century, so how could two be absolutely identical? Then there was the smell.''

''What smell?'' asked Schroder impatiently.

''The bridles and all that other riding tack in the stacks smelled like a Western-wear store, when they shouldn't have. Old bridles shouldn't smell like new leather—unless they are. And some of the tack hanging in the stables display upstairs looks old, but smells new. So I went back in the stacks to test my theory.''

''What theory?'' demanded Whitney.

"Somebody has been replacing artifacts with replicas. Several of the bridles hanging in the stacks are cheap reproductions. I'll bet they even have MADE IN HONG KONG stamped on them."

"Oh, my God," breathed Rachel.

"Excellent reasoning, Miss Fairchild," said John Lloyd. "Cowboy collectibles are the newest fad on the art market. Old leather quirts and bridles, not to mention such items as saddles, handguns, hats, spurs, badges, blankets, branding irons, and grass ropes are worth thousands of dollars. Such items have the added advantage of not being easily identified. It is much safer for the thief to steal a pair of Ed Hulbert spurs worth six hundred dollars than to steal the painting of Hogarth's mother, also owned by the museum. Ed Hulbert made many pairs of spurs, but Hogarth only painted one portrait of his mother. A thief who knew his market could filch a hundred thousand dollars' worth of cowboy artifacts in a few hours, load them in the trunk of his car, and drive away with no one the wiser. Rachel, I would suggest an immediate inventory of the museum's holdings to ascertain exactly what and how much Abe Yates stole."

"Abe Yates?" Rachel exclaimed. "I'm sorry, John Lloyd, but I can't automatically assume he is guilty just because he left the lounge without anyone's noticing."

Bill Whitney took her hand. "Rachel, I think there's more to it than that. Am I right, John Lloyd?"

"Abe Yates is assistant curator of history, with keys to all the display areas. He is not mentioned in any of the memos. He was the last one to sign out of the museum—"

"But he was at the party," objected Rachel. "He couldn't have moved the body."

"But none of you saw him," said Schroder. "And I don't trust that alibi anyway. One stranger in a mask and costume looks a whole lot like another." He slapped Jenner's shoulder. "Now that we know Miss Fairchild's not dead, son, let's go help the Canyon cops find that little son of a bitch. He'd have been better off giving himself up before we found out he was pilfering artifacts. Anybody who murders while in the process of committing another felony is guilty of capital murder in this state, and I'm going to see that he takes a short ride on a gurney for a legally administered lethal injection."

Lydia tried to push herself up. "The state of Texas won't get a chance if I find him first. That bastard is responsible for nearly scaring me out of my mind—literally."

John Lloyd pinned her shoulders down. "Miss Fairchild, your language is deplorable, and your thirst for revenge is uncivilized. Besides, I am not altogether certain that Abe Yates is the unconscionable lout that circumstances make him appear. There is the fact that someone placed a worn sofa cushion under Miss Fairchild's head. Since every other suspect was in the lounge, I have to assume it was Abe Yates. That is hardly the action of a merciless killer."

"Don't you dare defend him, John Lloyd!" exclaimed Lydia, tears running from the corners of her eyes.

"My dear Miss Fairchild, I am not defending his terrifying you. I will have a few words to say to the young man on that subject. But I am questioning the other charge. Still, that is no reason for you to cry."

"I'm not crying over that," she said, pushing against his wrists. "I'm crying because my right shoulder is in agony and your shoving on it isn't helping."

John Lloyd jerked his hands away, then gently caressed her shoulder. "There?" he asked, an unnecessary question in her opinion, considering the grimace his touch inspired.

He lifted his head to look at the crowd. "Out," he ordered.

"I want to know what you meant, Branson, about questioning the other charge," said Schroder, giving Jenner a shove toward the door.

"Later, when you apprehend Yates. I must attend to Miss Fairchild now." He looked around the circle of faces. "Out, I said."

Lydia saw Schroder hesitate at the door, as though debating whether to stay and argue, but John Lloyd turned his head and glared at the detective. Schroder left, pushing a reluctant Jenner. Lydia didn't blame him. The look on John Lloyd's face was enough to daunt even Special Crimes' finest cop.

The rest of the crowd nearly trampled each other in the exodus. Margaret Clark was the last one out. "Do you think she's badly hurt, John Lloyd? Those old buffalo guns have a recoil like a mule's kick. Do you want me to stay?"

The face he turned toward the archivist would have quailed a lesser woman. However, Margaret Clark was not a lesser woman. She giggled. "No, I guess you don't."

"Interfering old busybody," muttered John Lloyd as Margaret closed the door. "How do I get you out of this disreputable costume?"

"What?"

"Miss Fairchild, I am not Superman, and I do not have X-ray vision. The recoil from a rifle the weight and caliber of the one you fired can easily fracture a bone. I want to see your shoulder."

Lydia gestured. "Velcro down the back."

Slipping one arm under her back, he eased her up and ripped the costume open from neckline to waist. Releasing her, he pulled the bodice down to bare both shoulders. "God!" he breathed.

Lydia twisted her head to look and gasped. A huge bruise that was already turning purple covered the right half of her chest down to the upper slope of her breast. "No wonder it hurt. I guess I didn't hold the gun right. I don't have much experience, and I was in a hurry. . . . " She stopped on another gasp as John Lloyd lowered his head and gently outlined her bruise in kisses. She turned her own head and blindly kissed whatever part of his face her lips could reach.

His head came up, his black eyes glowing with a hot, sweet light she'd seen only once before. He hadn't kissed her then, but she didn't intend giving him an option this time. She burrowed her fingers into his thick blond hair and tugged gently. "Kiss me, damn it!"

"Who could resist such a sweet invitation?" he murmured. And accepted.

By the time the kiss ended, Lydia had learned two things: first, John Lloyd was fully as good at kissing as he was at cross-examining a witness and, second, he'd obviously had a lot of practice. She briefly considered whether or not she ought to feel jealous, but decided to feel grateful instead. She was the ultimate beneficiary of all that experience. It beat kissing somebody who was still working on his learner's permit.

John Lloyd lifted his head and stared down at her. His eyes widened and glowed again with that hot light before he grabbed the bodice of her costume and jerked it up over her bare breasts. "Miss Fairchild, your disdain for foundation garments may someday soon tempt me into making improper advances we shall both regret."

"How soon, how improper, and what makes you think I'll regret it?"

He swallowed and looked momentarily disconcerted. She felt pleased. She'd managed to both strike him speechless and disconcert him in a single night. John Lloyd Branson had cracks in the dam of his self-control that he didn't even know about yet. She intended to widen them until the dam broke. She felt his equal now; she'd walked down her dark passage and conquered fear. She wanted all that strength and passion he'd offered earlier and she'd rejected. Actually, given how hot and hungry she felt, she'd take the passion and forget the strength temporarily.

"Miss Fairchild, as a result of your experience, neither one of us is behaving normally."

She arched her eyebrows. "I spent the time talking to a ghost—which is a good reason for acting abnormally. What's your excuse?"

"I heard the gunshot, knew your stubborn, impulsive behavior had led you into trouble again, and thought that this time you were dead!"

His voice rose to a shout, the murmur of voices in the outer office quieted, and someone knocked on the door. "Go away!" he roared and the knocking abruptly ceased.

"I didn't act impulsively—this time—and I don't know why you should automatically assume that a gunshot means I'm in trouble."

He braced a hand on either side of her head and leaned over, his face inches above hers. "In the less than six months you have worked for me, Miss Fairchild, you have been shot, knocked unconscious in an elevator, insulted, threatened, and very nearly butchered by a serial killer. My group health insurance carrier has hired a clerk just to process the claims I have filed on your behalf. And you wonder why I think every gunshot means you are in trouble. Every time you leave my side, utter chaos results. You have disrupted my life, inspired me to acts of idiocy I would never have believed myself capable of performing, and tempted me into taking liberties inappropriate to our relationship.''

She looked up at him, saw the glow returning to his eyes, and smiled. ''So what do you plan to do?''

He sat up and straightened his waistcoat. ''Take four deep breaths.''

''What!''

''And ask what happened in the stacks.''

She shivered and hugged herself. ''I went insane—I think. I talked to the Butcher—except I was really talking to myself, I guess. But I remembered, John Lloyd. I lived my feelings all over again, and I discovered that the memory I feared wasn't of killing the Butcher; it was of remembering that I was glad I killed him. I was afraid of facing that fact about myself.''

He put his head over her lips when she tried to continue. ''Those without remorse hardly need to create ghosts, Miss Fairchild.''

She pushed his hand away. ''But I'm not sorry he's dead.''

''A sensible attitude on your part, since he was a monster in human form, and you doubtless saved dozens of lives by taking his. However, you are horrified to discover that not only do you not regret killing the Butcher, you are actually glad that you did, so you conjure up a ghost to punish yourself.''

''He was more than that,'' said Lydia slowly. ''He didn't disappear when I remembered. He threatened me instead.''

''So you shot him.''

''Yes. He, or my subconscious, or whomever I was talking to, said he was part of me. He was right. I share his ability to kill.''

''Possessing the ability to kill is not the same as possessing the desire to kill. That you will never have.''

''You're wrong, John Lloyd. That's why I had to kill him again. So that I would accept that I, or any of our suspects, will kill again and again if we feel the need, and need is not so far from desire.''

He shook his head. ''No, Lydia. You killed your ghost when he became the symbol of evil instead of a symbol of your guilty conscience. I hardly see that as meaning you are a serial killer in embryo. Rather, it demonstrates that you are a sensible young woman who does not intend to allow herself to be a victim, even metaphorically.''

She studied his eyes and saw only sincerity. Besides, he called her Lydia, and he never did that unless he was telling the truth. ''I'm telling you that I talked to a ghost and that I am glad I killed a man, and you don't think I'm crazy?''

''My dear Miss Fairchild, since you never do anything halfway, I should have expected your flashbacks to go beyond the ordinary. I never expected a ghost and a buffalo gun, but then, you seldom do the expected. That does not mean you are crazy.''

She glanced away. ''What if I told you I think I met Sarah Jane down there, that I think she told me how to load the gun, and that she pushed the Butcher away when he would've grabbed me? Do you still think I'm not crazy?'' When he didn't answer, she looked up to find him studying her.

''What do you believe you saw, Miss Fairchild?'' he asked quietly, his drawl less noticeable.

''I don't know! That's why I'm asking you! Did I have a hallucination, or is Sarah Jane's spirit haunting the stacks?''

''I think perhaps we should stop with one ghost and a buffalo gun, Miss Fairchild. A spirit, when defined too closely, tends to vanish. Besides, you made a reference to our suspects I wish to discuss.''

She scrolled through her memory for comments she'd made. ''Yes, I said any of them would kill if they felt the need.''

''I think your recent revelation that you, too, were capable of taking a life has made you cynical, Miss Fairchild. Most individuals, such as our suspects, will kill only within a certain narrow range of circumstances such as self-defense or to protect a loved one, or in extreme cases, revenge.''

''Or greed, or money, or sex, or ghosts, John Lloyd.''

''Ghosts, Miss Fairchild? I think you are still unsettled.''

''If that's your euphemism for crazy, I'm not. You convinced me of that.''

''I may have been optimistic,'' he murmured.

''I don't mean figures in white sheets and wrapped in chains, or even hallucinations like mine. I mean secrets. Our suspects are your basic upscale middle class, John Lloyd. They are respectable, with good reputations. They care what the neighbors think. For that reason they would kill to hide a secret that might embarrass, humiliate, or make them in any way look like fools.''

''Which one would you consider the most likely to kill, Miss Fairchild? No, let me be more specific. Which one do you believe would be capable of killing Brad Hemphill?''

She frowned. His voice held a note of urgency as if the question were more than idle curiosity. ''But we know Abe Yates killed Hemphill.''

He waved his hand in irritation. ''Assume for a moment that he is innocent.''

She raked her teeth over her lower lip several times and considered. ''Margaret Clark would kill for revenge, but since Hemphill was a little boy when her daughter was murdered, I would have to exclude her. Unless, of course, it turns out Brad did it after all.''

''Doubtful, since he was home in bed at the time,'' said John Lloyd.

''Darrell Farmer would kill Hemphill for laughing at his security system, or maybe Brad knew a secret, such as Farmer got a dishonorable discharge or secretly drank. Maude Young would kill to keep her job, and Roberto Ortiz would kill to protect his image of himself. Rachel Applebaum would have killed to protect her affair. If it weren't for the fact that the times are wrong, I would certainly think she had the best motive.''

''The memos were faked, Miss Fairchild,'' said John Lloyd abruptly.

Lydia listened as he told her his conclusions about the memos. ''What a sleaze! It's bad enough to murder somebody without trying to blame it on someone else. Plus, the idea was so stupid. He must have known you wouldn't be fooled.''

''Abe Yates does not know me, Miss Fairchild, and he did not know I would involve myself in this investigation. Schroder would have believed those memos, would have examined every facet of those people's lives, at least until the fingerprint report. Perhaps even beyond that point. Eventually he would have dismissed the memos, but not before he knew everyone's secrets.''

''This whole conversation is superfluous. Abe Yates killed Brad Hemphill, period. But if he hadn't, any of the others could have.''

''However, one had the ability to kill but lacked the desire. Another had the desire but lacked the ability to do an adequate job.''

She levered herself up to a sitting position and clutched her costume over her breasts. ''What are you talking about?''

''Miss Fairchild, when confronted with conflicting accounts, always check your references.''

''What conflicting accounts?''

''Impulse versus deliberation. The murder seems too impulsive to fit the elaborate circumstances of the cover-up. Every action attributed to Abe Yates is contradictory. He moved the body to direct attention away from Pioneer Town, yet a more sensible course would have been to leave it hidden under the bed or hide it in another exhibit—not deliberately expose it. But the most noticeable contradiction, Miss Fairchild, is that Abe Yates did not immediately flee following the murder. Why did he take the risk of remaining? He must have known that the theft of artifacts would eventually be discovered.''

''So what are you saying, John Lloyd?''

''We have two opposing sets of references. They cannot fit into a single context.'' He pulled her costume over her shoulders and reached around to fasten the velcro tabs. "Therefore, we are going to the archives."

"You think Abe Yates is hiding in the archives, John Lloyd?"

"No, Miss Fairchild. I think the murderer is."

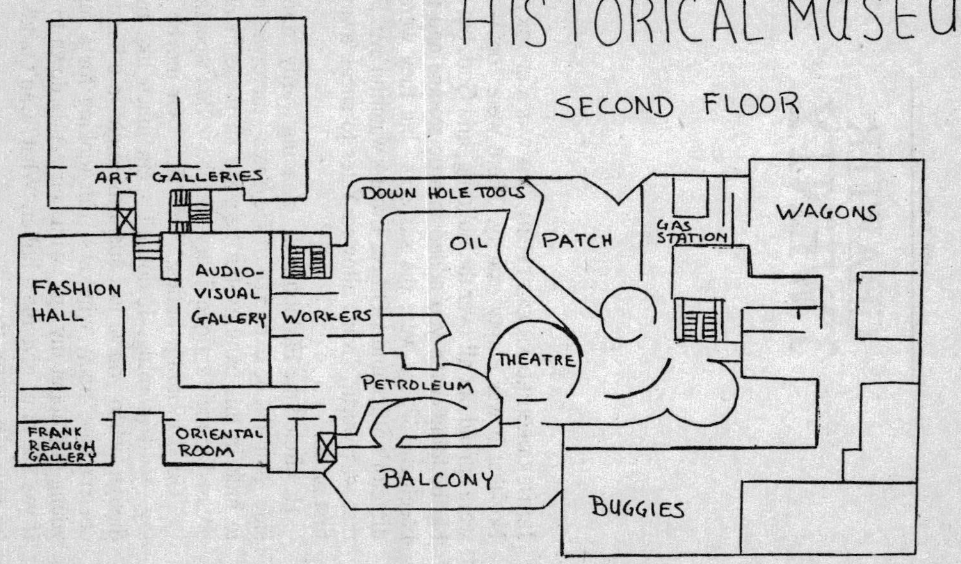
PANHANDLE-PLAINS
HISTORICAL MUSEUM
SECOND FLOOR
ART GALLERIES
DOWN HOLE TOOLS
OIL
PATCH
GAS STATION
WAGONS
FASHION HALL
AUDIO-VISUAL GALLERY
WORKERS
THEATRE
PETROLEUM
FRANK REAUGH GALLERY
ORIENTAL ROOM
BALCONY
BUGGIES

CHAPTER TWENTY

JENNER DECIDED AN EMPTY MUSEUM WAS A SPOOKY PLACE. Not that it was empty exactly. There were cops—but they were spread out all over the building, and God, but it was a big building when you added in attic storage and the sub-basement. There were the suspects—but they were in the director's office under Officer Evans's watchful eye. For what that was worth. Evans allowed Yates to sneak away in the first place.

He circled the Fashion Hall, glancing warily from side to side. Not that he expected to see Yates—there was no place to hide in this exhibit—but because all those mannequins dressed in their antique finery seemed to be inspecting him.

"Good evening, ladies," he said. "Or maybe I better say, good morning. It doesn't seem much like morning, though, when you've just spent the night in a building that doesn't have many windows. I'm looking for a fugitive—young guy about my age, with hair nearly down to his ass. If you see him, give me a holler. What? Can't talk? Just tap on your glass cases then."

He grinned and saluted one of the mannequins just as a powerful blow sent him staggering through the door, across the hall, and into the Frank Reaugh Gallery, where he finally lost his balance completely and slammed into the far wall at an unsafe speed for hitting immoveable objects like walls.

"Oof!" he said, or maybe it was "whoosh"; it was hard to tell when he was trying to find where he'd left his breath at the same time he was trying to get up, pull his gun, and shoot the bejesus out of whoever kicked him in the ass.

"When you're searching for a suspect, keep your goddamn mouth shut, Jenner," ordered Schroder.

"Damn it, Schroder, I could've shot you, sneaking up on me like that!"

"I wasn't worried. The way you were jerking around, you'd have shot yourself in the pecker before you ever got that gun out. Better your pecker than any of the exhibits, though. That damn Whitney never would've shut up about the insurance. Get your ass off the floor, and let's search the petroleum wing. I got men stationed at the elevators and all the stairs. Son of a bitch can't get away if he's on this floor."

Jenner got up, pride and behind both smarting. He wondered if one cop had ever filed on another cop for police brutality. He wondered if the ACLU would take his case. Then he wondered what a jury would think of a cop who talked to life-size Barbie dolls in period clothes and decided he'd keep his bruised back end out of the courtroom.

He followed Schroder down the hall and into the petroleum exhibit, a maze of displays and dioramas that fostered the illusion that one was standing in the middle of an oil field. It was a kid's dream of a place to play hide-and-seek, and a cop's nightmare of a place to search. "Hey, Schroder, what are we doing walking around these exhibits like we don't have good sense? The museum has a perfectly functional video system. Why don't we assign a cop with a walkie-talkie to watch the monitors and radio when he sees the whites of Yates's eyes? Hell, I'll volunteer."

"No video system," said Schroder. "Yates tore shit out of the monitors and did some terminal damage to some of the cameras. Farmer's working on it, but I think he's got the chances of a snowball in hell of fixing it. So it's left up to the cops, son, just like always."

"Jesus, Schroder, we need the whole department to search this maze."

"Shut up and search. Go across the balcony to the theatre, and I'll go through the tools exhibit. If he's here, we'll get him in a pincher."

Jenner circled around a curving wall and onto the balcony. Pincher, my ass, he thought. Yates wasn't here on the second floor; probably wasn't anywhere in the museum. Probably had six copies of every key and had sneaked out when everybody rushed to the stacks when Lydia Fairchild thought she was a buffalo hunter. Bastard was halfway to Albuquerque by now. Jenner sighed and listened to the echo of his boot heels on the tile floor.

Echo?

He stopped, held his breath, and listened. The clicking sound of heels continued. "Son of a bitch," he said under his breath.

He ran across the balcony on his toes, making as little noise as possible. Rounding the corner and running into the dark hall outside the theatre, he caught a glimpse of the slim, long-haired figure of Yates. He decided against ordering him to stop. All that would do was make the bastard run again, and Yates knew this museum better than Sergeant Larry Jenner, who admitted to himself that he got lost every time he left Pioneer Hall. Putting on an extra burst of speed, he ran into the shadows of the other side of a mock oil-storage tank, saw the denim-clad legs of his prey, and executed a beautiful flying tackle just like the one he made in the last game of his high school career, when he played for the Amarillo High Sandies against the Palo Duro Dons. He could hear the screaming of the fans just as if it were happening all over again at that very moment.

But the fans sounded different than he remembered.

"Help! Rape!"

And he didn't remember the running back he'd tackled then slamming a briefcase against his head.

"Let go of me, you peasant!"

And he definitely didn't remember any football player he knew in high school who wore lipstick.

Jenner let go of a youngish-looking woman with long black hair caught in a barrette at the back of her head, and scrambled up. "God, I'm sorry, ma'am. I thought you were Abe Yates, a dangerous murderer."

"Do—I—look—like—a—man?"

The woman asked the question with a heartbeat between each word, so the sentence became a series of blunt objects pounding at Jenner. "Well, no, but you look like him. I mean, you've got a ponytail, and you're wearing jeans, and it's dark. Here, let me help you up."

"Touch me again, you pervert, and I'll have you fired." She scrambled up and dusted off her denim jeans. "I may anyway. In fact, I think I will."

"Listen, lady, it was an honest mistake."

"I don't care to hear your excuses. Tell them to my attorney when he sues the police department."

"What's going on here, Jenner?"

Jenner had never been so glad to see Schroder. In fact, it was the first time he'd ever been glad to see the scruffy, overweight detective. "I tackled this lady. I saw her from behind and thought it was Yates."

"Ma'am, I'm Sergeant Ed Schroder, and this is Sergeant Jenner. I'm afraid you stumbled into the middle of a police search. We have a fugitive suspected of capital murder loose in the museum. I'll have to ask you to accompany Sergeant Jenner to a place of safety until I have an opportunity to ask you why you're in the museum."

The woman straightened her shoulders and tilted her chin up. "I have no intention of accompanying this man anywhere." She looked at Schroder and let her lip curl up slightly, just enough to piss Jenner off. So what if Schroder looked a little sloppy with his shirttail crawling out of his pants and last week's menu on his narrow tie. That was no reason to look at the homicide cop as if he were something a wino threw up in the gutter. Jenner was sorry he hadn't tackled her harder. He was sorry he hadn't stuck his elbow in her kidneys. He was sorry he hadn't broken at least three of those long fingernails she was waving around under Schroder's nose.

"I have no intention of answering your questions, either, Sergeant Schultz."

"That's Schroder, ma'am."

"My family has had very bad experiences with the Boches."

"Beg pardon, ma'am?"

"I think she means beet soup, Schroder. Maybe she's got gas. Maybe that's why she's in a bitchy mood," Jenner whispered to the older man.

"The Germans, you peasant. I'm French, you know."

"No, ma'am, I didn't, but unless you've got a diplomatic passport, Sergeant Jenner here's going to escort you down to the director's office. Come to think of it, even if you do have a diplomatic passport, Jenner's still going to escort you. We just won't arrest you first for interfering with an officer in the performance of his duty."

There was a gasp of outrage from the woman. "Do you know who I am?"

"No, and we don't give a pig's fart, either," said Jenner under his breath.

"What did you say?" demanded the woman.

Schroder nudged Jenner in the ribs.

She looked at both of them suspiciously, then tilted her head back a little farther. Jenner decided she needed to clip her nose hair. "I am Monique Bancroft Whitney, and my husband is president and sole stockholder of the Bancroft Whitney Land and Cattle Company."

"I'll be damned," said Jenner. "I thought he owned an insurance company."

"He is also president of the Panhandle-Plains Historical Society and is here in this very museum."

"He's in the director's office, ma'am. Sergeant Jenner will show you the way."

Monique Whitney's eyes narrowed. "He's in the director's office, is he? I know the way, and I don't need a guide."

Schroder gestured at Jenner. "You don't have a choice, ma'am. I told you, we're searching for a murderer. We don't want you taken hostage."

"We don't?" said Jenner, thinking Yates wasn't stupid

enough to kidnap this woman. "I mean, we sure don't. This way, ma'am."

Monique recoiled from Jenner. "You may follow me, but stay out of my way." She started toward the administrative wing. "Oh, Sergeant, carry my briefcase. I understand from my telephone conversation with John Lloyd Branson that it contains information that will solve your murder case."

"So you're the one he called this morning," said Schroder. "In that case, I think I'll go along with you. I'm interested in anything that interests Branson."

"I can't imagine that you'd have anything in common with John Lloyd," said Monique over her shoulder as she walked through the door and into the director's reception area. She stopped, glanced around the room, and saw the closed door to Rachel Applebaum's office. "I suppose they're in her office."

Officer Evans stood up. "Yes, ma'am, but you can't go in there."

Monique didn't bother to answer, merely pushed Evans out of the way and slammed open the door. "You slut!" she screamed.

Jenner looked over her shoulder to see John Lloyd Branson with his arms around Lydia Fairchild. The sergeant would have sworn under oath that the lawyer was busily fastening up his beautiful young assistant's costume.

Branson fastened the last tab, smoothed the red dotted material over Lydia's back, and finally looked up at Monique Whitney with eyes at least ten degrees colder than freezing. "You will, of course, explain your uncivilized and rude behavior."

"I thought my husband and Rachel Applebaum were in here."

"I see."

"Where are they?" demanded Monique.

"I'm here, Monique," replied Bill Whitney, pushing through the crowd and taking her arm.

"Where is she? Rachel Applebaum?"

"In the board room with several of the staff. What the hell are you doing here?"

"I called her."

"And I'd like to know why, Branson," said Schroder, parting the group in front of the door by simply walking through. Most got out of the way.

"Sergeant Schroder, have you met Mrs. Bancroft Whitney?"

Schroder looked as if he were suffering from indigestion.

"Ah, I see that you have," continued John Lloyd. "Come in, you and Sergeant Jenner, and close the door. Mrs. Whitney, please sit down and hand me the briefcase."

"I'm coming, too, John Lloyd. This is museum business," said Bill Whitney, looking at his wife with what Jenner recognized as vigorous dislike. If Mrs. Monique Bancroft Whitney ever turned up on the back of a dinosaur, Special Crimes wouldn't have to exert much effort to find her murderer.

Schroder dropped into one of the armchairs, his face still looking sour. Jenner didn't blame him. Monique Whitney gave him gas, too. He wondered what Bill Whitney's Maalox bill was every month.

Lydia Fairchild sat on the couch next to Branson, seldom looking anywhere else but at the lawyer, her eyes faintly predatory. Jenner wondered if John Lloyd Branson knew he was being stalked or cared if he did know.

Branson leaned comfortably back on the couch. "It occurred to me that the invitations to the Halloween party that figures so prominently in our suspects' alibis were unique in that each was done in calligraphy and included the guest's name. An examination of the invitations would reveal which staff member actually attended the party and which one did not. Monique graciously consented to drive down with your briefcase, Bill."

"How did you know to call Monique? The last thing you knew was that we thought Rachel had taken it with her to Canyon last night."

Branson nodded. "After you left, Monique indicated to Miss Fairchild and me that she might have been mistaken."

Whitney looked at his Monique, his face suddenly old and

desperate looking. "My wife and Dr. Applebaum often fail to communicate."

Monique Whitney smiled, or at least her lips twisted. Jenner had once seen a rattlesnake ready to strike that looked friendlier. "She and I have always had a conflict."

Branson glanced at his friend. "You understand, Bill, that I had to see those invitations."

Whitney nodded, and Jenner knew he understood more than that. He understood that John Lloyd Branson was apologizing for the necessity of bringing Monique Whitney to the museum.

Branson opened the briefcase and removed the invitations. Separating them into stacks, he passed one to everybody but Monique Whitney. "If you are ready, gentlemen, Miss Fairchild."

"Let me have some, John Lloyd," said Monique Whitney, holding out her hand and snapping her fingers.

Whitney looked horrified. "Monique!"

"Madam, you are not part of this investigation," said Branson.

"And I suppose Rachel Applebaum is."

Lydia carefully put her invitations on the table. "Monique, dear, are you always this unpleasant, or is this a benefit performance? If so, I'm going to cancel you for lack of interest. You are incredibly boring. If you don't shut up, I plan to call the health department and tell them that moat you're so proud of is full of Type A diphtheria germs."

Schroder sat in his chair and made snuffling noises that Jenner recognized as laughter. Branson reached over and squeezed his assistant's knee, while Bill Whitney sat with his mouth open. Lydia leaned over and picked up her stack of invitations, a flush on her cheeks. Jenner felt like saluting.

Monique Whitney turned white under her several layers of skillfully applied makeup and opened her mouth. Lydia raised her eyebrows and the other woman sank back in her chair, her face absolutely ugly with hatred. Jenner thought Lydia Fairchild would be wise to watch her back.

After several minutes five invitations lay in the middle of the coffee table. Branson stared at them for several minutes, then rubbed his forehead. "Abe Yates was at the party. Monique, do you remember what time he came?"

"I can't be bothered with keeping up with the museum staff," she said with a twisted look of victory.

Schroder leaned over and tapped her arm. "Can you be bothered with calling a bail bondsman? 'Cause I'm close to arresting you for interfering with a police investigation, and you won't like the jail. No privacy, and your cellmates will all be what you call peasants. Most of them don't smell very good, either."

"Bill, did you hear him threaten me? Did you, John Lloyd?"

Branson leaned back and stroked Lydia's hair. "I suffer from selective deafness. My physician is quite concerned about it."

Bill Whitney looked at her. "This isn't a game, Monique, and you don't earn any points for being a bitch. If the sergeant decides to arrest you, there is nothing I can do about it. You will be booked into jail, and imagine what the Junior League will say about that."

Monique looked even more horrified at the thought of being ostracized by the Junior League than she did of having the health department drain her moat. She cleared her throat. "I do remember Abe Yates because he was one of the first guests. He came at seven o'clock. Bill had been late coming home from the office and wasn't ready yet, so I had to greet the guests."

"Do you know when he left?" asked John Lloyd urgently.

"Of course not. Why should I? If he didn't have the manners to find his hostess and thank her, I certainly didn't have the time to dance attendance on him."

Schroder got up. "This doesn't change my mind, Branson. Abe Yates had plenty of time to kill Hemphill and hide his body before he went to that party. And he could've left in time to put it on top of that dinosaur. So if you were hoping for an alibi for him, then you're out of luck."

"But the murder is inconsistent with Abe Yates's behavior," insisted Branson. "And there are the memos."

"If Abe Yates was at that party at seven, then he didn't

have a lot of time to be typing memos, did he, Branson?" asked Schroder. "The fact is, Brad Hemphill caught Abe Yates stealing artifacts, and Yates knocked him into that pump and lèt him drown."

CHAPTER TWENTY-ONE

JOHN LLOYD REMAINED SITTING ON THE COUCH, SLOWLY running his fingertips along the edges of the invitations. Monique had bolted from her chair and rushed out of the office with Bill Whitney trailing her, the look of a desperate man facing ruin dragging his tall body into a round-shouldered slump. Lydia could hear Monique's shrill voice lashing out at everyone who got in her way, meaning everyone within her sight, and Lydia suspected the woman had good vision. Bill Whitney's deeper voice vibrated with conciliatory tones as he tried to smooth ruffled feelings, rather like pouring oil on troubled waters. In Lydia's opinion there wasn't enough oil in the world to calm those particular troubled waters.

Schroder and Jenner stood at the door, the older homicide cop hesitating, as if he dreaded facing the domestic battlefield on the other side. "Wouldn't know of another way out, would you, Branson?" he finally asked.

John Lloyd looked up, his expression distant, as though concentrating his mind on a problem having nothing to do with the potential bloodletting in progress on the other side of the door. "No, Sergeant, I do not. I have, however, thought of a possible solution to my own dilemma."

"What dilemma is that, Branson, that you don't believe Yates is guilty because he tucked a pillow under Miss Fairchild's head? Did it occur to you that maybe that was because he didn't have time enough to tuck it *over* her head? In other words, maybe we got there too fast?"

If he heard the sarcasm in Schroder's voice, he didn't react. That same distant look of concentration remained. "That is only the last in a series of references to Yates's character that make it impossible for me to believe he is the murderer. A methodical thief such as he would not indulge in such a clumsy murder."

Schroder assumed a patient expression, as if he were a coach trying to explain a football play to a not very bright player. "Your problem is that you want to make everything too complicated, and I went along with you for a while because that dinosaur bit threw me. I forgot murder generally isn't complicated, especially this kind of murder, which I'd call domestic just because we've got a circle of suspects who all know each other. It's a family situation, and what you get is one family member getting p.o.ed at another family member and picking up the nearest weapon and shooting, stabbing, or in this case, whacking him with it. Brad Hemphill walked in on Abe Yates while Yates was busy building up his retirement fund by collecting artifacts to sell. You got your typical family murder. Husband—Hemphill—catches wife—Yates—violating the family honor—stealing from the museum—and Yates grabs a blunt instrument from the livery stable and kills him. When Yates realizes what he's done, he hides the body and trots off to the Halloween party."

"Why does he return to type the memos and move the body?" asked John Lloyd.

Schroder looked around the room impatiently. "Shit if I know. I guess to throw suspicion on the rest of the family, and to make sure we don't look too closely at Pioneer Town."

"Then you admit he typed the memos."

Schroder glanced at the door, as if trying to decide if he'd rather face the quarrel outside or John Lloyd's questions. "I guess he had to; nobody else had a reason, and I heard from my fingerprint technician. There weren't any fingerprints on the stationery except a couple of Brad Hemphill's on one memo. So I'll give you the fact that the memos were fake."

"If he planned such an elaborate scenario, why use facts so easily checked?"

Schroder's patience gave out. "How the hell do I know, Branson? Why don't you ask him when we find the son of a bitch?"

"I intend to do just that, Sergeant, and might I suggest that you do not use excessive force to apprehend Yates. It is always so embarrassing when a suspect is injured during arrest, only to find out later that he was innocent of the crime."

"I never use excessive force, Branson, and you goddamn well know it."

John Lloyd wiped his hand over his face. "I do know it, and I apologize, Sergeant. My only excuse is the unpleasant prospect of uncovering an alternate suspect. These people are not strangers to me. I have known three of them since I was a young boy. I knew the victim and have tried to distance myself from the anger I feel whenever I remember exactly whose body is lying in the morgue."

Schroder's expression changed from outrage to sympathy. Jenner merely looked sick, as if he were remembering the corpse's last appearance. Lydia tried not to think about that.

"I'm sorry about Hemphill and the rest of your friends, Branson," said Schroder, his hoarse voice softening. "There's nothing nice about murder, either for the victim or for anybody he leaves behind. None of those people out there will be the same after this is over. But you don't need to worry about an alternate suspect. Once we knew about those artifacts, this became an easy murder, and you just don't like easy murders."

"In this particular situation, I am right to suspect the easy solution. As I pointed out once before, these are brilliant people, and one expects something more from them."

"Well, you don't have an alternate suspect, and that dinosaur is the extra trimming you seem to want. So forget it, take Miss Fairchild out to breakfast, then go home to Canadian."

"Earlier this morning Miss Fairchild pointed out to me

that anyone can kill, given the right need, anyone at all, even respectable, brilliant people. I only have to discover the need and I will know the murderer."

"You sit here and cogitate awhile on your alternate murderer, and I'll go catch the real one." Schroder waved his hand at Branson and opened the door. Quarreling voices poured in like water from a broken dam. The sergeant took a deep breath and dived in. "You people shut the fuck up. Didn't your mothers ever tell you it's not nice to yell in a museum?"

The door closed behind him, shutting out, or at least muting the verbal wounds being inflicted in the melee.

John Lloyd stood up and held out his hands to Lydia. "Come along, Miss Fairchild. The archives wait."

She took his hands and allowed herself to be pulled up, but when he released her and would have turned away, she put her arms around his waist and burrowed her head against his shoulder. "Why did he ever marry her, John Lloyd?"

She felt John Lloyd freeze and waited not only for his answer, but his reaction to the death grip she had on his waist. His grandmother would've called it forward behavior for a well-brought up young lady. On the other hand, John Lloyd's grandmother had owned a saloon until Canadian voted in temperance in 1903, so maybe her ideas of proper behavior were a little more lenient than her those of her peers. Or maybe they weren't. Lydia didn't give a damn either way.

John Lloyd sighed and locked his arms around her. "Miss Fairchild, are you upset at the sounds of domestic violence and in need of comforting, or should I interpret this embrace as a further sign of the deterioration of our professional relationship?"

She lifted her head to look at him. "Haven't you ever heard of professional growth?"

"I hardly think the bar association had this in mind, Miss Fairchild."

She rested her cheek against his chest. "They're all a bunch of stuffy lawyers anyway. So are you going to answer my question?"

He chuckled and stroked her back from shoulders to waist.

"If nothing else, you are tenacious, Miss Fairchild, but to reply, I doubt that Bill married Monique because she was endowed with a sweet nature."

"And I doubt she married him because he made her thighs tingle," said Lydia tartly, tipping her head back to look up at him.

John Lloyd cocked one eyebrow. "A singularly poor reason to marry, Miss Fairchild."

"But a singularly necessary reason, Mr. Branson, if one wants the domestic fires to continue burning."

He chuckled. "In that case, I suspect that any tingle Monique Whitney might feel would be attributed to an allergic reaction to laundry detergent, and any domestic conflagration would have her calling the fire department. In short, Miss Fairchild, I do not know why he married her. It was a mystery in Canadian. After Lindsey Clark's murder, we all assumed he would marry Rachel Applebaum after all."

"What do you mean, after all?"

"They had been engaged but had quarreled, and Bill had begun keeping company with Lindsey. To be frank, I think any tingle in his relationship with Lindsey was a misplaced hormonal response to her youth and beauty. Had she not been murdered, I believe they would have ended the engagement by mutual agreement, but of course it ended with her death. Bill and Rachel attempted to repair the frayed ends of their relationship, but apparently the mending failed to hold, and Bill married Monique, to his everlasting regret."

"So why doesn't he divorce her?"

John Lloyd frowned. "Miss Fairchild, I cannot begin to understand the nature of the glue that holds that marriage together, nor do I understand the reason for your curiosity."

Lydia shrugged. "I guess it's because of Schroder's comment about lives being ruined by this murder. Maybe I want to see something positive come out of the wreckage, like a flower growing on a garbage heap."

He hugged her and laughed, his face looking young, as if the twelve or so years between them didn't exist. "While I find your turn of phrase amusing, Miss Fairchild, please do not attempt any matchmaking. The utter chaos that might result from your interfering with Monique Whitney's life is too awful to contemplate. You may find her a contemptible woman, but I have always sensed that she resembles a sleeping cobra, and one had best not wake her. But to change the subject, do I make your thighs tingle?''

Lydia coughed and felt herself blushing clear to the hairline. ''That's an impertinent question.''

''But one essential to professional growth.''

She awkwardly freed herself from his arms and scooped up the invitations from the coffee table. ''Hadn't we better go to the archives now?''

He plucked his cane and hat from the couch, took her arm and escorted her to the door. Opening it, he looked down at her, his eyes harsh with warning. ''Lydia, did I not warn you that I am a dangerous man when aroused?''

She swallowed and ducked under his arm and into the reception area, wondering exactly how she should interpret that very ambiguous question.

''You want to see the file Brad left with me?'' asked Margaret Clark, seated across the table from John Lloyd and Lydia in the archives.

John Lloyd placed his hat and cane in an empty chair. ''If you please, Margaret.''

Lydia stirred uncomfortably on the hard wooden chair. Her shoulder was beginning to ache, her head hurt, and she noticed a slight ringing in her ears. From that buffalo gun, she thought resentfully. Which was all Abe Yates's fault. And John Lloyd was trying to get the little weasel off. ''I don't know why you're being so stubborn, John Lloyd. Schroder was right. You can't stand a cut-and-dried murder case. Or should I say a hit-and-drown case?''

He threw her an irritated look. ''Miss Fairchild, that turn of phrase was flippant and far from amusing. I suggest you keep an open mind. Abe Yates is our client.''

''Since when?''

''Since I decided that he must have changed Brad Hemphill's shirt.''

"That doesn't make any sense at all. Besides, you don't know if it's true or not."

"My dear Miss Fairchild, Abe Yates's changing Brad Hemphill's shirt is perfectly consistent with the actions of a man who placed a cushion under your head. He is a most complex individual and one who, in spite of his spurious and lewd remarks concerning your person—"

"What lewd remarks?"

"—seems to have some compassionate instincts."

"What lewd remarks?" Lydia repeated.

"I believe he called you *foxy*, and while I am not completely familiar with all the connotations of that expression, I do concur with his assessment—although I would not use that particular term. It reminds me of truck stops and garbage-strewn roadside parks."

She gasped. "What are you saying?"

He glanced at her, an amused and reckless smile on his face—exactly the kind of smile she imagined her pirate ancestor must have had just before he sacked a coastal village. "Do you not mean *why* am I saying such outrageous things, Miss Fairchild?"

"All right. Why?"

He leaned over and cupped her chin, tilting her face up. "Because you tossed down the gauntlet, my dear, when you demanded I kiss you, and again when you walked into my arms not ten minutes ago. Do not be surprised that I have accepted your challenge."

She looked into his eyes, feeling a recklessness of her own. "You make this sound like a duel."

He released her and leaned back in his chair. "You accuse me of being overbearing and dictatorial in our professional relationship, Miss Fairchild. Did you think I would be diffident and shy on a more personal level?"

She drew a deep breath and straightened her shoulders. "I won't be dominated—"

He interrupted, nodding. "Good. Submissive women bore me." He looked up. "Ah, Margaret, you have the file."

Lydia sat with her mouth hanging open, staring at him.

The archivist handed him the folder and a book. "I wish

you'd tell me why you're so interested in Brad Hemphill's notes for his Panhandle history."

John Lloyd opened the file, then glanced at Lydia. "Miss Fairchild, close your mouth. There are no flies in here to catch." Lydia snapped her mouth closed. He continued, looking up at Margaret. "Because I am convinced that somewhere in these notes is the reason Brad Hemphill was murdered. Why will tell us who." He picked up several call slips written in a tiny, crabbed handwriting. "If you will pull these items please, Margaret. My familiarity with the archives does not extend to the boxes of uncatalogued material you have locked away."

Margaret took the call slips and spread them out like a hand of playing cards. "So I'm following a paper trail again, John Lloyd? What fun! Oh, dear, I wish I hadn't left my deerstalker at home."

John Lloyd gave the archivist an affectionate glance as she rustled away, then turned his attention to Lydia. "Miss Fairchild, let us divide these pages of notes for perusal."

Lydia took several pages of notes written on yellow legal size paper and flipped through them, stopping at the last page. "John Lloyd, you can stop looking. Here's the motive, and it's exactly what Schroder said it was." She laid the page on the table and tapped it with her fingernail. "This is a list of stolen artifacts, or at least I think it is. See, here's the china doll and several bridles, quirts, spurs, badges, and so on. Brad knew Yates was stealing. He must have done an inventory of his own. That's why Schroder's men found the little flashlight in the stacks. Brad Hemphill had been down there inventorying the stored artifacts."

John Lloyd glanced at the list, then pointed at a notation at the top of the page. "He dated this, Miss Fairchild. I noticed he dated everything. He was a very methodical young man. According to this date, he had known about Yates's thievery for two weeks, yet he had done nothing—"

"He didn't get a chance to, John Lloyd. Yates killed him first."

John Lloyd toyed with the page for a moment. "I believe that explanation is too simple. Please note that there are only twenty-five items listed on this page, yet you speak as if you found a multitude of substituted artifacts. Did you?"

Lydia rubbed her forehead. "I found at least ten bridles in the blacksmith's exhibit that smelled new and at least that many more in the stacks, but there are only three listed here. I don't understand."

"Margaret said that Brad Hemphill always checked and re-checked his facts, Miss Fairchild. He had not finished his inventory, so he had not said anything to Rachel or to Yates. I doubt this list is the motive for his murder. If it were, Abe Yates had to know about it and would have destroyed it. No, the motive is something else."

Lydia glanced through the other papers. "There's nothing here but notes of historical events." She replaced them in the folder and picked up the book. "Why was Brad Hemphill reading this? It's a history of the Bancroft Whitneys, John Lloyd. I saw one just like it at the Norman Castle."

Margaret Clark returned carrying a dusty box. "Goodness gracious, my dear, the Bancroft Whitneys are a pioneer ranching family in the Panhandle. Very important. Knew Charlie Goodnight and all the men who were wheelers and dealers in the last century. Poor as dirt until oil was discovered on their ranch back in the 1930s. Brad was so excited about that book. We just received our gift copy last week. He was hoping to get a new slant on the early ranching industry."

Lydia opened the book and flipped to the page marked by a slip of paper. "If it's like most family histories, it's been sanitized of any scandal or underhanded dealing. A family history could make Aldolf Hitler look like a statesman with a bad press. . . ."

She stopped, losing her voice for a minute, which was probably just as well. When she was finally able to talk, she had her fury under control—almost. "Damn it! That bitch! That reconditioned bitch!"

"Miss Fairchild! Your language!" John Lloyd's face was a study in amused disapproval. "If you have gained control of your vocabulary, perhaps you could enlighten us on whom you are maligning."

Lydia stuck the Bancroft Whitney family history in his face and pointed one shaking finger at a photograph. "That person! Monique Bancroft Whitney! Except I guess she wasn't a Bancroft Whitney yet. Look at her, John Lloyd. If I'd seen this page when I was looking at the book in her moldy mausoleum, I'd have slammed the volume across her surgically corrected nose. She's wearing a clown suit—she and Rachel and Bill Whitney—but she and Bill Whitney even have on white clown makeup. And she sneered at me as if I was something her gardener fished out of that damn moat! She is a complete, unrefined, uncut, one hundred percent bitch, and I won't forget this."

John Lloyd closed the book and clasped both her shaking hands in his. "Miss Fairchild, petty social revenge is unbecoming for a lady."

She jerked her hands away. "Did I ever claim I was a lady, John Lloyd? Well, I'm not, and furthermore, I don't want to be if it means I have to keep a stiff upper lip and ignore people like Monique Whitney. I'd rather give her a stiff lip instead. She's overdue."

Margaret Clark shook her fist in the air. "Right on, my dear!"

John Lloyd looked at them as though they both had grown two heads. "Ladies, please. I agree, Monique Whitney is a most unpleasant woman, whose company is only slightly preferable to a rabid skunk's, *but* she is *not* a murderer!" His voice thundered in the quiet room, and Lydia gulped back her next comment. John Lloyd swallowed and patted his forehead with his handkerchief. "Please excuse my tone, but Monique Whitney did not kill Brad Hemphill, and at present, that is all that concerns me. Margaret, the box, please."

Subdued and, Lydia thought, even awed by John Lloyd's outburst, Margaret handed him the dusty box. "Whatever he'd been working on was in here, John Lloyd. Until a week ago, he'd been grubbing through these old papers every day."

"What are these papers?" asked John Lloyd, flipping open the box.

"Some of the papers from Roberto Ortiz's grandmother's estate," answered Margaret. "I guess when Rachel returned that journal to Roberto, she didn't know about these papers. The family was older than God, you know.''

''I wonder if they knew Monique Whitney's ancestor. To hear her talk, he *was* God.'' Lydia felt John Lloyd's glare and closed her mouth.

Margaret giggled, but sobered the second John Lloyd turned his five-thousand-watt glare in her direction. She cleared her throat. ''The first Ortiz came through Texas with Coronado. I guess he didn't think much of the area. All this open space scared the pants—or whatever they wore—right off those Spaniards. No landmarks, my dear,'' she explained to Lydia. ''Just grass. Very disorienting. Coronado's men didn't know if they were coming or going. Anyway, the Panhandle didn't see the family again until the 1870s when Roberto's great-grandfather built a plaza on the Canadian. That was really the time period that interested Brad, but he started translating the journal because—well, just because it was there.''

She put her hands on her hips, or where Lydia guessed Margaret's hips would be. It was hard to know the exact location, since the archivist wore a hoop skirt under her black dress. ''I'm really put out with that Roberto. All that history locked away where no one can learn from it.''

''It is his family's history,'' ventured Lydia.

''Poppycock!'' exclaimed Margaret. ''Coronado is history and belongs to everybody. Roberto could at least furnish a translation of the journal.''

''He did. Or someone did.'' John Lloyd's voice held a peculiar note that silenced Margaret's tirade. ''Here is a handwritten translation. The ink is faded, but still quite legible. It is in English, oddly enough. I would have expected it to be in modern, grammatically correct Spanish.''

''Nothing odd about that,'' said Margaret. ''Roberto's grandmother was English, as I recall. Very elegant old lady. Offered me tea when I visited with her about her gifts. I hate tea—unless it has ice in it. Sat in that stuffy living room and worried about balancing that teacup on my knee while I choked down one of those tiny sandwiches she served. Cream cheese and something green—I never inquired as to just what.

No wonder the English conquered most of the world. They were looking for something decent to eat. It was quite an experience, my dear,'' she said, looking at Lydia. ''Antimacassars on every surface where there wasn't a doily. Or are the two the same?'' The archivist shrugged her shoulders. ''Anyway, nothing senile about that old woman. Can't imagine why Roberto thought she was. He probably didn't like her calling him Bobby, and taking back the journal was his way of thumbing his nose. Futile gesture, since the old lady's been dead since summer.''

''Eureka!'' exclaimed John Lloyd, pushed back his chair, grabbed his cane and hat, then leaned over to swiftly kiss Lydia. ''Miss Fairchild, your dissertation on secrets and the middle class was psychologically indisputable.''

''What?'' said Lydia, disconcerted not only by John Lloyd's comment, but by his sudden reversal in personal tactics. From warning her off, he was now assaulting her breastworks—metaphorically speaking.

John Lloyd waved the translation at Margaret. ''I doubt that Roberto was as concerned with his grandmother's reputation for mental alertness as he was with his own reputation as one of the New World's bluebloods.''

CHAPTER TWENTY-TWO

THE DERRICK ROOM WAS SO NAMED BECAUSE OF THE REPLICA of a wooden oil derrick that covered a considerable amount of the available floor space. A vintage Ford pickup sat next to the rig's base to simulate the power source often used by wildcatters in the early days of oil exploration in Texas to operate the cable tool drilling rig. Situated in front of a two-story glass wall, the derrick towered dramatically toward the ceiling, an awesome display of man's ingenuity and a symbol of the black gold that transformed a windswept region of cattle ranchers and farmers into a national resource.

Sergeant Larry Jenner didn't consider the economic significance of the display. Nor did he particularly give a damn about the historical accuracy of the derrick. He did, however, care a great deal about its more mundane features, such as the strength of its timbers, the length of the nails holding those timbers together, and its general stability. In other words, how likely was it that the whole structure would collapse into a pile of creosoted toothpicks suitable for use by the Jolly Green Giant?

Jenner looked down at the museum floor, then wished he hadn't. Never look down when you're thirty or so feet up in the air hanging on to an oil derrick and wishing to hell you'd taken up another profession. Something safe—like being a reference librarian. He bet reference librarians had regular working hours, not to mention sanctioned coffee breaks. He bet reference librarians didn't have to handle dead bodies or attend autopsies. Most important off all, he bet reference librarians didn't have to crawl up two-story oil derricks. Of course, they didn't work for a bastard like Sergeant Ed Schroder, either.

"Jenner, you waiting for your hair to fall out?"

"No."

"Then start climbing. You've been hanging on to that same rung for the last ten minutes. That derrick ain't gonna get any shorter."

A couple of watching cops snickered, and Jenner thought he saw Schroder grin in acknowledgment. Son of a bitch probably thought he was funny. Special Crimes' own stand-up comic. "I'm taking a break, Schroder," he yelled down. "I got a muscle cramp."

He saw Schroder roll his cigarette to the other corner of his mouth. "You haven't climbed fast enough to get a cramp, Jenner. I've seen turtles with arthritis move faster than you. Now climb on up to the top and see if Yates is up there."

"He's not. He's got better sense than to trap himself up here where's there's no place to run."

"We don't know that for sure, do we? Besides, it's the only damn place we haven't looked. Now get your ass in gear and check it out before Yates dies of old age." The cops snickered again.

"Stuff it in your ear," muttered Jenner under his breath and climbed another three feet.

"What did you say?" demanded Schroder.

Jenner reached the top of the derrick and peered over the rim.

"Dr. Livingston, I presume," said Abe Yates with a grin as he emerged from under a grease-stained tarpaulin lying on top of one of the rig's thick wooden beams.

Jenner looped his arm around the top rung of the ladder and glared at the assistant curator. "You son of a bitch. Why the hell did you make me climb this bastard? You knew you'd have to come down anyway.''

Yates raised his hand—which unfortunately was holding a very deadly-looking revolver. An old .45, Jenner thought, although at a distance of eight inches caliber didn't matter a hell of a lot.

''Actually, it was a good bet,'' said Yates. ''You can't see the top of this derrick from anywhere in the museum, and I'd planned on staying up here until dark, then climbing down and finding another hidey hole. This museum has dozens of them, and I'll bet you cops didn't find half of them when you were searching. Nobody could unless you knew where to look, and I know. Eventually, I'd planned on leaving the building by whichever door had a sleepy cop in front of it. I didn't plan on that fat cop down there being such a damn bloodhound.''

Jenner had a sudden inspiration. ''You forgot, Yates, we've got video cameras. You can't get within ten feet of a door without showing up on camera.''

Yates laughed. ''I disabled the monitors and as many of the cameras as I had time to while everyone was hovering over the blonde Viking.''

''Darrell Farmer fixed them.''

Yates laughed again. ''Darrell Farmer couldn't fix his zipper if he caught his shirttail in it, Sergeant. He can operate that video system, can tell you the theory of how it works, but the stupid son of a bitch can't fix it. I found that out early on when I was doing a little experimenting on the best way to sabotage the cameras.''

''All the alarms going off in the stacks was you, huh?'' asked Jenner, wondering why his flashes of inspiration never worked.

Yates frowned. ''Only once—when I crossed two wires wrong. The rest of the time I don't know why the hell they went off. Caught me in a hell of a fix a couple of times. I had to hide in the stacks damn near all night while firemen were tramping around in their rubber boots, and I didn't like it. It's weird, you know. I'm not superstitious, but it got to the point I had to force myself to go down there at night. Felt like someone was living there. It's real crazy. You want to know something crazier? Brad Hemphill wasn't afraid of the stacks. He used to say they felt friendly. Hell, it even smelled different when he was there, like sunshine and empty places."

He shook his head. "Real crazy place. Anyway, as for the security system, you're going to have to call in the professionals, and the particular company that set up the museum's system is in Houston. It'll take awhile to get them here, and they won't repair that system in an hour. In fact, they won't be able to repair it for a week, and by that time, I'll be gone. So don't count on any electronic help in tracking me."

"Jenner! Are you talking to yourself, or did you find Yates?"

Yates sat up, keeping his revolver aimed at Jenner's head. "Sergeant Schroder, good morning. Jenner and I were having a pleasant conversation until you interrupted."

"Is that you, Yates?"

"In the flesh, Sergeant."

"Jenner, get his ass down here. I got a nice warrant for your arrest, Yates. Signed by a judge in the prescribed manner."

"Uh, Schroder, we got a problem up here."

"What the hell kind of problem, Jenner?"

"He's got a gun."

There was a long silence at the bottom of the derrick, and Jenner waited patiently while he wondered if the Amarillo Public Library had any openings for reference librarians.

Yates finally broke the silence. "While we're waiting for your boss to reevaluate his piss-poor tactical position, tell me how the blonde Viking is. She's all right, isn't she? The world doesn't have such an oversupply of sexy broads that it can afford to lose one."

"Lydia's fine."

"I figured she was, or that lean, mean bastard Branson would've burned this place to the ground if it meant getting me."

"You shouldn't have messed with Lydia."

"You're telling me? Jesus, that broad ought to have a

warning plastered across her forehead: THIS WOMAN IS HAZARDOUS TO YOUR HEALTH. I tried to grab that china doll she was clutching, and she kicked me in the balls. To be fair, I don't think she knew it, because she was going ape shit. I never saw anybody so scared. I felt sorry for her. I was going to turn the lights back on and get the hell out of there as soon as I could move without throwing up, but then she locked herself in the gun room."

"She said you locked her in there."

"Me? I never touched that door. It's a damn good thing, too, because about the time I got my feet under me, she blew hell out of that door and the wall opposite, which was nice in a way. That particular wall had the junction box I'd been messing around with. I appreciated her destroying all that evidence before the cops had a chance to take a second look. But if I'd been standing in front of that door, I'd have a hole in my belly the size of a baseball."

"Too bad you don't. Then I wouldn't have my ass hanging thirty feet in the air."

"Wasn't my idea to have you climb up here."

The man whose idea it was cleared his throat. Jenner was amazed the sound traveled so far. Actually, it wasn't all that far; it just seemed that way when you were hanging on to a ladder and your legs really were cramping.

"Yates, give your gun to Sergeant Jenner, and come on down. You're backed into a corner, and there's no need for anybody to get hurt. The chase is over, and you don't want a charge of resisting arrest added to the other charges."

"Schroder!" Yates raised his voice and his gun. He directed the voice toward the bottom of the derrick, but the gun barrel he rested firmly against Jenner's forehead. Jenner immediately began to sweat—and to plan his résumé for the library.

"I'm listening, Yates."

"I'm coming down, Schroder. I want you and all the other cops to drop your guns in the front seat of the old pickup at the base of the derrick, then back over to that corner between the little foyer and the glass wall."

"You're crazy, Yates! You don't have anywhere to run."

"I beg to differ, Sergeant. Now move it, and nobody gets hurt."

"Hey, Schroder, this asshole's got a revolver resting between my eyebrows."

"Won't do you any good to shoot Sergeant Jenner, Yates. One of us will get you."

"It won't do Sergeant Jenner a hell of a lot of good, either, Schroder, so let's not make this into a Mexican standoff. You leave your guns and back off, and Jenner and I will climb down—very slowly, so I don't miss a step and shoot him by mistake. Then he and I will walk away."

"You walk out of this museum, and the SWAT team will shoot you full of holes," shouted Schroder.

"Very unwise, Schroder, because I might have an involuntary muscle spasm and shoot the sergeant here. Besides, why do you think I plan on walking out of the building? I'm very bright; I know, statistically speaking, that my chances of escaping under the guns of a SWAT team are somewhere between slim to none. I expect to choose my own time when the odds are maybe a little better. All I'm asking is a fair chance. I come down, the sergeant and I walk into one of the displays, I handcuff the sergeant to an artifact—a heavy one—and I disappear. You release the sergeant and take up the chase again. Just think of this as a time-out, or maybe a temporary cease fire."

"This isn't a goddamn ball game, Yates!" yelled Schroder.

Jenner could hear the frustration in the detective's voice, and he tried to remember what the procedures were when a cop was taken hostage. Did the police negotiate, or was the risk of being snatched part of the job description? He couldn't remember. The problem was, no cop in Amarillo's history had ever found himself in a hostage situation. It was his damn luck to be the first.

"You heard my terms, Schroder," replied Yates.

"I can't agree to them," said Schroder.

Yates looked back at Jenner. "You ever wear earrings, Sergeant?"

"What kind of question is that?"

"Do you?"

"Once, when I was working undercover."

Yates moved his revolver to Jenner's earlobe. "Sergeant Schroder, I'm going to pierce Jenner's ears just so you'll know I'm serious. You understand I'm doing the piercing with a .45 revolver, so I can't guarantee the aesthetic effect."

"Jesus Christ, Schroder!" screamed Jenner. "He means it! How about you show a little cooperation and *get the fuck in that corner*!"

"All right, Jenner, take it easy, son!" Schroder might have intended to sound soothing, but Jenner picked up a definite tone of scared shitlessness. It made him feel better. At least the fat bastard wasn't going to trade Sergeant Larry Jenner's earlobe for an arrest.

"Do we have a deal, Sergeant Schroder?" asked Yates.

"We're moving, but you listen. If I don't find Sergeant Jenner in good shape—and that means breathing and without any man-made holes leaking blood—you're going to be the sorriest bastard on two feet."

Yates waited silently, and Jenner heard the clatter of metal against metal as the cops threw their guns in the pickup. "Thank you, Schroder, for that show of support for a fellow officer. Jenner, turn around so you're facing the windows, and start down, one step at a time, and don't be a hero. There have been more dead heroes than Congressional Medal of Honor winners, did you know that?"

"I'll remember the next time I play Trivial Pursuit and the question comes up." Jenner carefully turned around, plastered his spine against the rungs of the ladder, and felt Yates unsnap his holster and lift his gun out. Ten years as a cop, and no one had ever taken his gun away from him. He blinked his eyes. Damned if he wasn't tearing up with humiliation.

He took a cautious step down to the next rung and discovered why Yates wanted him to climb down facing outward. It was a damn dangerous way to get to the bottom. His arms were at an awkward angle behind him so he could grip the rungs with his sweaty hands. He stopped. If it took both hands to hang on, then Yates couldn't be holding a gun. Jenner looked over his shoulder—and into the barrel of the assistant curator's revolver.

"I'm a professional thief, Jenner, not a dopehead stealing somebody's video recorder to buy his next hit of crack. I work at it. I know how to dismantle security systems, or at least sabotage them. I know art and antiques as well as anyone in this museum, and I can damn near climb a brick wall using nothing but my fingers and toes. Like I said, I'm a professional, so don't expect me to climb down this ladder like some candy-ass kid, okay?"

"Some profession, Yates. It's immoral as hell."

"On the celestial chart of wrongdoing, I suspect an honest thief rates considerably higher than a congressman on the take or a savings and loan officer. I do have some principles." He nudged Jenner with the revolver. "Start climbing."

Jenner started down again. No point in arguing with a professional—particularly one with a gun.

His foot had barely touched the floor when Yates's arm circled his neck and jerked his head back to an uncomfortable angle. He felt the revolver's barrel gouging his ear and froze.

"We're going to do a little dance now, Jenner," said Yates. "I'll take a step back, and you follow my lead. Any questions?"

"When does the music stop?" asked Jenner in a croak.

Yates chuckled. "That's what I like about you, Jenner. You got a sense of humor. Some cops don't. They're the ones to watch. Dangerous bastards, most of them. Another bit of trivia for you. Did you know most of the world's real badasses don't have a sense of humor?"

"No kidding? Then maybe I better tell you that Schroder's got the sense of humor of a grizzly bear with piles. You're really going to regret screwing Sergeant Ed Schroder."

"Then I'll have to avoid Sergeant Schroder." Yates maneuvered his way to the door of the windmill exhibit. "Just a few more feet, Jenner, then I'll leave you for Schroder to claim."

"Yates!"

Jenner looked wildly around the room as best he could, considering his range of vision was mostly limited to the ceiling and walls. He heard footsteps—rapid footsteps—footsteps of a man running like hell.

"Shit! It's Farmer!" exclaimed Yates, tightening his grip on Jenner's neck. Jenner gagged.

"Yates, you son of a bitch, you ruined my video system!"

Jenner could see the security officer now. Farmer's eyes were round and furious and seemed to consist mostly of white, with the iris and pupil existing in miniature form purely for contrast. He looked like an actor in a horror film, one in which zombies with big staring eyes haunted the nights. Jenner wished somebody would tell this particular zombie that it was midmorning and order him back into one of his monitors until dark.

"Farmer!" shouted Schroder in a bullhorn roar. "Stop!"

He heard Yates curse, a standard four-letter profanity with which Jenner heartily concurred, then felt the assistant curator's arm slip from around his neck. Before Jenner could react, he felt a tremendous blow and he stumbled forward at Mach one—right into Farmer's outstretched arms. The two sprawled on the floor with Jenner's knee landing squarely in Farmer's groin. Farmer lost any immediate interest in monitors, cameras, or Abraham Yates. Rolling off the groaning, prostrate man, Jenner wished to hell people would stop kicking him in the ass.

CHAPTER TWENTY-THREE

"THE MEMBER OF CORONADO'S EXPEDITION WHO SUPPOSedly sired Roberto Ortiz's direct ancestor is revealed in the translation to have died without issue shortly after the expedition left Mexico City."

John Lloyd's nostrils quivered as if he were a bloodhound who had just caught the scent of his prey. In Lydia's opinion it was more likely his own odor of sanctity. He had a certain self-righteous gleam in his eyes that said he believed he had found the context in which all the inconsistent references had significance and that he believed he was right—without any question whatsoever. It only remained to chisel that context on two tablets of stone and present them to Sergeant Schroder.

"Miss Fairchild, get up. You are dawdling again."

Lydia conjured up a mental image of Roberto Ortiz and tried to imagine his picking up a blunt object and attacking Brad Hemphill. She pictured John Lloyd stripping Ortiz to the bone, then tossing what was left to the dogs of public humiliation. She could believe the second event, but not the first.

"Wait a minute!" said Lydia, clinging to her chair.

"What is it, Miss Fairchild?" asked John Lloyd, frowning down at her.

She frowned back in lieu of an answer because she didn't have one, other than a mental itch that said John Lloyd was moving too fast. And she couldn't seem to think at all. Her mind was on overload.

Margaret Clark looked from John Lloyd to Lydia and back again, tapping the side of her nose and pursing her lips. "Roberto Ortiz, a fake Spanish conquistador. I always thought he postured a little too much. He knew he wasn't the genuine article, so he worked twice as hard pretending he was. You know, like an actor who's unsure of his role, so he overacts. He's much worse around strangers. Like tonight. He had his head thrown back so far, I really thought he was going to dislocate his neck. But he's harmless, John Lloyd. Not like Monique Whitney. She takes herself seriously."

"You don't think Ortiz does?" asked Lydia, rubbing her forehead where a headache caused by lack of sleep and compounded by confusion throbbed painfully.

"Not in the same way. He has another life, you know. He's one of the best art curators in the Southwest. I think his role as a conquistador is a hobby—like china painting. Makes him feel important. Monique, on the other hand, doesn't have another life. From the time she was a young girl, all she talked about were her moldy French ancestors and building a castle. I've always believed she married Bill Whitney because he was the only man she knew who had enough money to afford that architectural monstrosity. Why he married her I'll never know."

She caught her breath and crossed her hands over her bosom. "Gracious, I'm dithering again. What I'm saying, John Lloyd, is that while I can imagine Monique Whitney murdering someone if he discovered she wasn't French, I can't imagine Roberto murdering for the same reason."

"I can't either, John Lloyd," said Lydia. "In the first place, Ortiz couldn't find a blunt object because his field of vision is impaired. Try sticking your nose as far in the air as he does, and you'd see."

"That is a ludicrous reason, Miss Fairchild."

"I'm not finished yet. In the second place, you're jumping to conclusions. The scenario is all wrong. Hemphill and Ortiz? The wimp and the phony? It doesn't play."

John Lloyd impatiently tapped his cane on the floor. "Miss Fairchild, when all other possibilities have been excluded, what remains must be the truth, however unlikely. Roberto Ortiz had a motive, and he signed out at five-forty, which would have allowed him enough time to murder Brad Hemphill. He arranges to meet Hemphill after hours, they argue, Ortiz picks up an instrument from the livery stable, strikes at Hemphill, who falls into the pump, knocks himself unconscious, and subsequently drowns. Ortiz flees through the gallery and thus circles around to Pioneer Hall and the front desk. Abe Yates discovers the body, hides it until he can concoct an alibi that includes the false memos, then moves Hemphill's body away from Pioneer Town. Thus we can explain the references to an impulsive murder that occurs within the greater context of a carefully planned theft."

Lydia thought a moment, then pulled the visitors' map from her purse. "But, John Lloyd, if Ortiz ran through the gallery, he would have had to go through the guns and saddles display, and Abe Yates would have seen him and known who the murderer was. He wouldn't have needed to write those memos."

John Lloyd lost his self-righteous expression for a moment, then smiled. "Ortiz could have taken the stairs by Pioneer Town to the second floor, gone across the museum to the annex, and back to the first floor, Miss Fairchild. In those circumstances Abe Yates would not have seen him."

Lydia's headache was getting worse. "But why would Brad Hemphill meet Ortiz at all if he knew Ortiz was angry? Everyone said Brad Hemphill wouldn't argue with anyone. And why was he scared to death, and Margaret said that when she left him, he was terrified."

"That's right, John Lloyd," said Margaret. "Poor Brad was just shaking. He'd never have been scared of Roberto. They'd known each other for four years. Brad knew Roberto was mostly hot air."

"Brad Hemphill was afraid of the dark, and this late in the year, darkness falls early. Pioneer Town is none too brightly lit even during the day. At dusk, with the lights in the displays dimmed, it must have been terrifying."

"But that's not what Rachel told us," said Lydia slowly.

"Miss Fairchild, no one keeps a year's supply of candles because he fears that Southwestern Public Service will suddenly go bankrupt and stop generating electricity. Rachel may have believed he feared the electricity's failing, but it was a pathological fear of the dark."

Margaret grasped his arm. "Because of Lindsey?"

John Lloyd patted her hand. "Brad was six when Lindsey was murdered, and he interpreted events from a child's perspective. Lindsey was murdered in the dark. Therefore, the dark was to be feared. I am certain he was terrified of electrical storms for the same reason. Brad Hemphill was terrified not of Roberto Ortiz but of remaining in the dark and empty museum after five o'clock. I am afraid, Miss Fairchild, Margaret, that Roberto is guilty. We need to convey our conclusions to Sergeant Schroder and rescue Abe Yates from whatever hiding place he has found."

He pulled out Lydia's chair. "Come along, Miss Fairchild. The whys are answered, and the puzzle solved. We have only to point Sergeant Schroder in the right direction, and like a lumbering bear, he will embrace the culprit."

"Wait!" said Lydia, refusing to move.

"What is it now, Miss Fairchild?"

"Didn't you say Brad Hemphill always checked his facts, Margaret?"

Margaret looked puzzled, then nodded her head. "Definitely. He was a fanatic about it. Checked everything six ways to Sunday."

Lydia poked John Lloyd in the belly. "Then tell me how Brad Hemphill checked the translation against the journal if Rachel gave the journal back to Ortiz?"

John Lloyd sat down again and laid his cane on the table. "Miss Fairchild, he had begun translating the journal before Ortiz reappropriated it. Surely he could determine the accuracy of Roberto's grandmother's translation by comparing it against his own incomplete one."

"There is no incomplete translation in this folder, John Lloyd."

"A damning mark against Roberto Ortiz, Miss Fairchild. Obviously he destroyed it after he murdered Brad Hemphill. Who else would have a motive for doing so? And just as obviously he left this one intact because he was unaware of it."

Lydia felt she was swimming upstream against the current. John Lloyd had an answer for every question. "But how did Ortiz know where to find it?"

"If Brad Hemphill spent the afternoon in the archives and did not return to his office, obviously his notes could only have been left here."

Lydia wished John Lloyd would stop saying everything was so *obvious*. "I'm just saying that this is all too easy."

"Miss Fairchild, you constantly accuse me of having a convoluted mind, and Sergeant Schroder accuses me of wanting to complicate matters. When I finally do propose a simple solution to a complex problem, you accuse me of oversimplifying. You simply cannot have it both ways."

"But the references are wrong, John Lloyd. Roberto Ortiz is an irritating, pretentious prick, but is he violent? Would he pick up a weapon and slam it against Brad Hemphill's ribs? And would he do it over whether or not Brad Hemphill would gossip about him? And why didn't he do it as soon as he received the journal back from Rachel? Why did he wait?"

"I do not know, Miss Fairchild. It may be something so simple as his dread of confronting Hemphill. Or it might very well be that he was waiting for the costume ball to provide him with an alibi of sorts."

"Then that would mean it was a premeditated murder, not an impulsive one," Lydia pointed out triumphantly. "And that screws your precious context all to hell."

"We can do without the vernacular, Miss Fairchild. In any case, I shall ask Mr. Ortiz about his delay."

"I wonder why Brad didn't say anything to me about the journal being gone?" asked Margaret curiously. "It must have happened a month ago because that's the last time I remember seeing Brad with that journal. And I wonder why he didn't mention finding the translation?"

"See, John Lloyd! What did I tell you? Ortiz should've had his secret meeting with Hemphill a month ago, not last night. Why did he wait?"

"And why, Miss Fairchild, are you so certain that Roberto Ortiz is innocent?"

"Because . . ." She stopped and pressed her fingers against her temples. Why was she so sure? Maybe Ortiz didn't live his whole life in ancestor worship like Monique Whitney, but his make-believe family history was important to him. And anyone can kill, she reminded herself.

"I don't know," she replied, feeling defeated. "Maybe because he bowed to me when I first met him."

"Another singularly ludicrous and illogical reason for exempting him from suspicion, Miss Fairchild. I have known several courtly murderers. I have even defended a few." John Lloyd rose. "If you ladies are ready, it is time to find Sergeant Schroder and confront Ortiz."

"I hate this, John Lloyd," said Lydia. "I hate destroying anyone."

John Lloyd took her hand. "It is much less painful to be objective, is it not, Miss Fairchild? But being objective does not free the innocent and capture the wicked. Commitment does, and commitment often hurts. And knowing the secrets of our fellow men can move us to either pity or disgust. You are moved to pity because you are a proud woman and would despise being humiliated. Thus you identify with Roberto Ortiz. But remember, it was wicked to kill a man over such a trivial secret. It is even more wicked to allow an innocent man to be blamed."

"Abe Yates isn't exactly innocent, John Lloyd," protested Lydia.

He stroked her cheek, then took her arm. "My dear Miss Fairchild, our clients are seldom innocent, but they are frequently not guilty—as charged, that is."

* * *

Lydia decided immediately when she and John Lloyd entered the director's office that the people already there were not happy campers. Jenner sat on the couch with a wet rag around his throat in the guise of a whipped puppy who wasn't sure what he'd done wrong but was very, very sure he wouldn't do it again—as soon as he figured out what the offense was. He also looked pissed off. It was an interesting combination of expressions.

Schroder, on the other hand, seemed like a man who wanted to shake somebody until his teeth rattled, but couldn't decide whose teeth he wanted to hear rattle. He also appeared worried and impatient.

The third person in the office was Darrell Farmer. He sat in one of the armchairs looking confused and angry. His face was the color of pavement—dirty pavement—and he kept emitting sharp little sounds like a bat in search of a cave.

"Didn't you see a goddamn thing, Jenner?" demanded Schroder, leaning over the arm of the couch and staring into the younger man's face.

"If I'd seen where Yates went, don't you think I'd tell you? Hell, if I'd seen where he went, I'd have gone after him."

"I can't believe you just let him get away again," squeaked Farmer.

"Shut up, Farmer," said Schroder. "If you hadn't stuck your oar in the water, maybe Jenner could've gotten a handle on the situation."

"How?" asked Farmer, shifting in the chair, turning grayer, and emitting another little squeak. "Jenner's the one that let himself get taken hostage."

"By Yates?" asked Lydia, glancing at the three men.

Everyone ignored her. "Yeah, and you could've gotten me killed, you incompetent asshole, running up on Yates like that. Didn't you see that .45 earplug I had sticking out of the right side of my head? What the hell did you think it was? A hearing aid?"

"Gentlemen! What has happened?" asked John Lloyd, banging his cane on the coffee table to get their attention.

"I'll tell him," said Jenner.

"You shut up, son," said Schroder. "You ain't capable of giving an objective report right now."

"You try being objective with a .45 scratching your eardrum."

Schroder recounted Jenner's adventures on top of the derrick. "So now, thanks to Mr. Farmer's interference, we got an armed and dangerous man loose again."

Farmer flushed, then turned gray again. "All I know is that you had Yates and he escaped. I don't think I've acted any more like an incompetent asshole than the professionals."

Thinking it over, Lydia decided she couldn't argue with Farmer's evaluation.

"Gentlemen, attempting to assign blame is futile. I think Mr. Farmer's time would be better used attempting to repair the security system than indulging in petty squabbles."

Schroder's nose twitched slightly, as if he smelled something in Branson's speech. Evidently the odor of sanctity. "Take a hike, Farmer," said Schroder.

When the door closed behind the security chief's limping form, Schroder turned back to Branson. "Well?"

"You have no idea where Mr. Yates is?"

"No, and my men have looked the place over—again. The son of a bitch has done a vanishing act."

"I doubt that Abe Yates has dematerialized, but he is at liberty again, at least temporarily. If you had considered my theory that he was innocent of the murder, then Sergeant Jenner's recent unpleasant experience need not have happened." John Lloyd sat on one end of the couch, stroking the silver head of his cane and sounding, in Lydia's opinion, like a pompous ass. He was so certain he was right. In spite of Yates's attack on Jenner, John Lloyd was still so damn certain.

"Stuff it, John Lloyd. I don't care what we found out in the archives. Yates is a murdering son of a bitch, and you're a stubborn one."

"Miss Fairchild, your language is both unprofessional and unattractive."

Lydia didn't think her language was all that improper. A

little frank maybe, but not unattractive. Besides, she was right.

"Okay, Branson, suppose you tell me how your theory could've saved Jenner from being caught with his pants down by Yates." Schroder was nearly nose to nose with the lawyer, and Lydia hoped the sergeant had remembered to brush his teeth recently. On the other hand, it probably didn't matter. Schroder had terminal tobacco breath.

"The only reason that Abe Yates is acting in such a remarkably uncivilized fashion is because he knows that a murder charge is pending against him."

"Damn right," interjected Jenner. "Signed, sealed, and I'm going to deliver it right in his ear when I catch the son of a bitch again."

John Lloyd ignored the interruption. "If it were not for the murder charge, I believe that he would have long since surrendered himself and taken his chances in court. With adequate legal representation, it is possible that he would have served only minimal time in the Texas Department of Corrections for his thefts. A professional, such as Mr. Yates has demonstrated himself to be by his very carefully organized and nonviolent looting of the museum, would consider time served as merely a cost of doing business."

"Nonviolent! How would you like a six-gun stuck in your ear?" demanded Jenner.

"An action I consider to be out of character for Mr. Yates, Sergeant Jenner. Not that he is incapable of killing—Miss Fairchild has pointed out that we are all capable—but I do not believe he would kill to prevent knowledge of his thefts. He did not, for example, kill Miss Fairchild, although from a certain perspective, it would have been in his best interests. But more revealing of his common sense is the fact that he did not kill Farmer, who was a direct threat to him. Nor did he kill Sergeant Jenner. The average violent criminal would have shot both men instead of leaving them unharmed. He had no guarantee that Sergeant Jenner would not have pursued and captured him. Consider also that his refusal to leave the building with a hostage may have had as much to do with his reluctance to fire that revolver he brandished so persuasively as it had to do with his fear of being shot himself. Finally, a man who puts a cushion under the head of an unconscious woman is not a man who waits for another to drown. All of these acts are not those of a vicious criminal."

"You're saying Yates is just a misunderstood boy, and if the nasty police hadn't hassled him, he wouldn't have been bad." Schroder belligerently stuck his chin out.

"You are oversimplifying."

"Bullshit! That's exactly what you're saying, Branson."

Lydia noticed that John Lloyd's chin was also jutting out at what she considered a belligerent angle. Instead of nose to nose, the detective and the lawyer were chin to chin. "Sergeant Schroder, if I might be permitted to elaborate."

"By all means, Mr. Branson."

"Yates is not a murderer, but circumstances are limiting his choices to remain free of that crime. Eventually, when he feels his options are entirely gone, he will either surrender or shoot his way out in the best approved wild West fashion. I do not want to give odds on which course of action he will take. A desperate man takes desperate measures, and Abe Yates is desperate. However, if you consider the possibility that there is another explanation for the facts of the case, then Mr. Yates may choose to surrender without further incidents. It is like my illustration of so many hours ago, Sergeant Schroder. Sometimes a fingerprint on a murder weapon is perfectly innocent when considered within a certain specified context. The facts indicate an impulsive murder that cannot be considered within the same context of Mr. Yates's carefully planned thefts. Therefore, the other explanation is that Mr. Yates did not kill Brad Hemphill; someone else did. Two people are involved."

"You're back to that, Branson. Don't you think it's stretching credibility to believe there are two criminals running around loose in the museum: Yates and someone else?"

"It is unfortunate that Mr. Yates was a victim of coincidence, yes. Brad Hemphill's murder was inevitable, and it had nothing to do with Mr. Yates. It would have occurred even if Mr. Yates had never been employed by this museum, had never decided to ply his trade as a thief."

Schroder expelled a breath and opened a new pack of cigarettes. "All right, Branson. Who are you accusing as your alternate murderer?"

"If you would ask Mr. Ortiz to join us, Sergeant Schroder, I believe you will see the case from another point of view."

"Ortiz?" asked Schroder, his eyebrows pulling together into one long, sandy-red, fuzzy line.

"If you please."

Lydia straightened up and walked around the couch when Roberto Ortiz marched into the director's office. And marched was the only way to describe the stiff-legged manner in which the art curator walked. She could almost hear the drums beating cadence. It would have been quite a military performance if Ortiz hadn't stumbled against the coffee table, an inevitable misstep, considering he had his head tilted too far backward to see anything occurring below chin level.

"Mr. Ortiz," said John Lloyd. "You requested that Rachel Applebaum return your ancestor's journal, is that correct?"

Ortiz made a right angle turn and sat stiffly in an armchair. His blue eyes darted like hummingbirds between John Lloyd and Schroder without lighting on either one. "Yes, that's right. I didn't steal that journal."

"Did you at least agree to allow the journal to be copied?"

"No, it's too valuable to risk handling."

"Such a shame that so much historical data is lost to the scholarly world," remarked John Lloyd. "Not to mention the proof of your lineal descent from a member of Coronado's expedition. Without allowing anyone access to the journal, you have no legitimate right to claim such a birthright."

"Are you calling me a liar?" demanded Ortiz, his chin jutting upward another fraction of an inch.

"Yes, Mr. Ortiz, I am. Your grandmother bequeathed more than the journal to the museum; she also bequeathed a translation. You are not descended from a member of Coronado's expedition."

"Son of a bitch," breathed Jenner.

"Lies, lies," said Ortiz, huddling against the back of the

chair, as if John Lloyd had punctured his skin, leaving the bombastic curator shrunken.

"You got the journal back, but that was not enough. Brad Hemphill had been translating it. Did you worry that his incomplete translation included the entry revealing you as claiming a blood heritage to which you are not entitled? Did that worry finally spur you into meeting Hemphill after hours? Or did Hemphill ask you about the entry? Checking his facts as I am assured he was wont to do?"

Ortiz's face turned the color of a sun-bleached bone, and Lydia felt betrayed. John Lloyd was right after all, and she was wrong. Ortiz had felt the need to kill.

"Ah," said John Lloyd. "He did ask you, and you met him in Pioneer Town last night, possibly demanding his translation on the basis that it violated your privacy."

"No!" exclaimed Ortiz. "I didn't! I never met him last night. I hadn't even talked to him in nearly a month. I was"—he hesitated—"too ashamed. He translated part of the journal and asked me about that entry. Like you said, Brad always checked his facts. That was the first time I knew Grandmother had left the journal to the archives. I thought she had destroyed it, when I couldn't find it after her death. She always said false pride would lead me into sin."

"Your grandmother was a perceptive woman. It is unfortunate you did not heed her. Murder is surely the greatest of sins. Particularly this murder. To assault Brad Hemphill is one thing, but to leave him to drown is the cruel and vicious act of an indifferent man."

"Why should I need to meet him after hours? I had no reason to kill him, Mr. Branson. He's the one who told me about the journal. He's the one who voluntarily destroyed his own translation."

"Why should he do that?" asked Schroder, finally breaking the silence that John Lloyd seemed not to notice.

Ortiz looked at him from dull eyes. "He couldn't check his facts." The art curator laughed hysterically. "He said that in those days, dying without issue most probably meant dying without legitimate issue. No one counted the various bastards running around the streets of Mexico City, offspring of the Spaniards by the native women. Remember, this was barely twenty years after Cortez's conquest. There weren't a lot of Spanish women in the country. Brad said that I might be a descendant of one of these bastards, except he didn't say bastards, and that I was technically right to claim my ancestor, but that there was no way to prove it. He advised me to ask Rachel to return the journal because he said it might mislead historians into embarrassing my family. He never implied that my family was guilty of doing the misleading. Brad always assumed that everyone had the most innocent motives. I'm sure he never even realized I was ashamed that he knew I was a fraud."

"So you're telling me that Brad Hemphill told you to take back the journal and tore up his own translation because he didn't want you to be embarrassed?" asked Schroder incredulously.

"Yes."

"Did anybody witness these conversations?"

"No."

"So that means Brad Hemphill was a pretty good guy?"

"Yes."

"But I thought you said he lied to you."

Ortiz wiped a shaking hand across his forehead. "He didn't tell me about my grandmother's translation, but maybe I didn't give him an opportunity. I stayed in my office or upstairs in the galleries and left late so I wouldn't have to see him. I'm sorry I thought of him as a liar for even a moment. Brad Hemphill was an honest man."

Ortiz braced his elbows on his knees and covered his face with his hand. To Lydia, he looked like a shirt with no starch.

Schroder cleared his throat and looked at John Lloyd. "What do you think now, counselor? You got any proof except this translation and a good story?"

John Lloyd watched Ortiz, a brooding expression in his eyes. "No more than you do against Mr. Yates, Sergeant. As I have said from the beginning, this is a murder of whys, not of facts, of references to events, not witnesses to the events themselves. Mr. Ortiz has a motive and only his unsupported word that it is meaningless. Mr. Yates has a motive, but he has not yet given us the benefit of his word. I think perhaps it is time we heard from the elusive gentleman."

Lydia felt a chill of foreboding creeping up her spine at the peculiar tone of John Lloyd's voice.

Schroder must have felt the same foreboding because he gave John Lloyd a look that would have pinned anyone else's body to the seat of the couch. John Lloyd simply raised one eyebrow in polite inquiry. "Branson, you son of a bitch, do you know where Yates is hiding?"

"I believe so, Sergeant."

CHAPTER TWENTY-FOUR

JENNER WAS CERTAIN SCHRODER WAS LITERALLY GOING TO explode and spread tobacco-infused tissue all over Rachel Applebaum's office. The sergeant's face was crimson, and his cheeks were puffed out like a squirrel's full of nuts.

"Branson!" Schroder's voice sounded like the call of a wounded moose. "Branson, I always credited you as a cut above most defense lawyers, but I guess I was wrong. All that crap about cooperating. I should've remembered that you can't teach an old dog new tricks or a criminal attorney to play on the cops' team. Our deal is over." He made a slashing movement with his hand. "No more marriage of convenience. No more cooperation. You want any more information on this investigation, you go file your motions like everybody else."

John Lloyd finally switched his attention from Roberto Ortiz to Schroder. "Sergeant, I have not been dishonest with you, but we have been walking divergent paths."

"If that's a fancy way of saying you've been hiding Abe Yates while I've been running around this fucking museum like a dog with its tongue hanging out looking for the son of a bitch, then you're right. But our paths ain't going to diverge anymore. You cough up Yates's hidey hole, or I'm hauling your ass in for obstruction of justice, interfering with an officer, giving false evidence, aiding and abetting a criminal, and whatever else the D.A.'s office can find in the way of chárges."

"Sergeant Schroder," said Branson, his face taut, "you misunderstand me. I could not permit a miscarriage of justice by allowing Abe Yates to be arrested, so I did nothing to aid in your capturing him. That does not mean I am hiding him. I am not. I merely know of a room in the museum which your men undoubtedly have not searched for the simple reason that we had been occupying it during the greater part of the evening. We did not vacate it until after Yates's first disappearance, when he took up residence on top of the derrick. Still, I doubt that it has occurred to either you or your men to give the auxiliary room, or volunteers' lounge, more than a cursory look. Why should it? If Sergeant Schroder and Sergeant Jenner saw no hiding places in the several hours they spent there, then obviously there were no hiding places to be found. What better place for a hunted man to hide? It is a case of the purloined letter, although I doubt that Abe Yates is so obviously in plain sight as was the stolen letter in Poe's story."

Schroder's upper lip curled slightly away from his teeth, just enough to suggest he was surprised, but not enough that he dropped his cigarette. "You're telling me Abe Yates is hiding under the sofa, or maybe he put a shade over his head and is playing like a floor lamp?"

Roberto Ortiz stirred out of his slump. "The dark room, Mr. Branson?"

Branson nodded, although Jenner thought the lawyer was reluctant to finally reveal the hiding place. "It has occurred to me that it would be the ideal place to hide. There's also the added advantage of having the sinks still in place and the water lines still connected. I am certain that a hunted man gets thirsty."

"What dark room?" said Schroder. "I never saw a dark room in the lounge."

John Lloyd got up and retrieved his cane from the coffee

table. ''Remember that the museum has undergone numerous changes over the years. It is a maze of odd corners and adapted spaces. During one of the changes or additions, a room was literally lost. As time passed and staff changed, its existence was forgotten. Had Margaret Clark not had occasion to refile the original blueprints to the oldest part of the museum, I have no doubt it would still be lost. As it is, I doubt that any know of it except Margaret, Mr. Ortiz, who, as I recall, requested the blueprints for use in setting up an exhibit, and myself as a member of the museum committee. I examined the room and regretfully ruled out remodeling it as an office for the volunteers, due to renovation costs. Its door was closed, and to my knowledge, the subject has not been mentioned in at least seven years.''

''Then how did Yates find out about it?'' asked Jenner. God, what a case! Ghosts, dinosaurs, and now a lost room.

Ortiz lifted his hand, a guilty look on his face. ''I may have mentioned it in passing. Yates—''he licked his lips ''—Yates was very curious about the museum. It was flattering to be asked so many questions.''

''You want to watch that ego of yours, Ortiz,'' said Schroder. ''It nearly got you ass-deep in trouble, and if Mr. Branson had pushed it, I just might have hauled you in on the basis of your grandma's translation. In a lot of ways his theory made sense and answered some of those damn whys.''

Lydia touched John Lloyd's arm. ''Why didn't you push it, John Lloyd? Upstairs in the archives, you were acting like Moses with the Ten Commandments—God had faxed you the right answer, and you weren't listening to anybody. What changed your mind?''

John Lloyd looked past her at Roberto Ortiz. ''Mr. Ortiz finally asked the right question, Miss Fairchild, the single *why* of this case that rearranged all the references into a new and very different context. I only need for Mr. Yates to elucidate a few remaining references to finally obtain a clear picture of what happened to Brad Hemphill.''

Schroder grabbed Branson's arm. ''What the hell is that supposed to mean? Have you got another substitute you want to run in for the last few seconds of the game? Well, you can go to hell, Branson. I've heard enough of your bullshit.''

''Sergeant Schroder, do you wish to see the wrong man arrested? Do you wish to even chance that happening?''

''I've got a good case,'' began Schroder.

''You have nothing!'' Branson snapped his words off with no suggestion of a drawl. ''Nothing but circumstantial evidence. Do you expect Yates to confess to murder when he is guilty of nothing but being a thief? He will not! And you will not see him convicted because I will defend him.''

''At least you're showing your true colors,'' said Schroder. ''You're back to defending thieves and murderers.''

''Suspected murderers, Sergeant, and only one of those. I am defending Abe Yates because he is innocent.''

''John Lloyd!'' Lydia couldn't contain her curiosity any longer. ''What question did Roberto Ortiz ask?''

''Later, Miss Fairchild. First let us persuade Mr. Yates to come out of hiding.'' He strode toward the door, his limp more pronounced than when he had entered the room a few minutes before, and Jenner wondered if John Lloyd Branson's crippled knee was physical as much as it was mental. The lawyer had that stiff-necked look that suggested he was about to face an ordeal he'd rather avoid.

Branson stopped at the door. ''Sergeant Schroder, you and Miss Fairchild seem to share a penchant for dawdling. Come along. Our most important witness awaits in the dark room.''

''And if he isn't, Branson?'' asked Schroder, lumbering after the attorney.

The attorney looked pained. ''I see that you do not play poker, Sergeant Schroder, because you have no faith in the rules of chance. After an evening and a morning of misinterpretations and theories based upon incomplete answers, do you not think that, statistically speaking, we are due a lucky guess?''

Jenner saw Roberto Ortiz blanch at several expressions Schroder muttered more or less under his breath—mostly less—that dealt with John Lloyd Branson's legitimacy, his sexual practices, and what the lawyer might do with the dark room should it prove empty of one assistant curator. Jenner thought that all the dark room suggestions called for physically impossible feats.

Surrounded by what looked like a battalion of Canyon cops, the four of them plus Roberto Ortiz stood in front of the closet in the volunteers' lounge. Schroder noticed Ortiz and frowned. "Out of here, Ortiz."

Ortiz got as far as the door to the lounge when Branson stopped him. "Please, Sergeant Schroder. After being unjustly stripped of his dignity by my questions and accused of a foul murder, I believe Mr. Ortiz has earned the right to participate in the first scene of the final act in this drama."

Schroder looked indecisive, then nodded. "Yeah, as long as he stays out of the range of fire." He nudged Branson. "You ain't even apologized to the man."

John Lloyd failed to look embarrassed. "I can hardly apologize for what I only halfheartedly regret, Sergeant. Had I not questioned Mr. Ortiz, this murder, like that of Lindsey Clark, might have remained forever unsolved, with the staff of this museum living out the rest of their lives in less than pleasant circumstances. To be the unceasing object of suspicion by your neighbors and your co-workers is not conducive to anyone's peace of mind."

He turned to look at the art curator. "Mr. Ortiz, I trust you will feel more charitable toward me when you understand your role in the solution of this case. At present, I do not expect you to wish me well."

He turned to face the closet, lifted his cane, and nodded at Schroder. "Sergeant, if you would please open the closet door, then stand back. I do not wish to provoke any violent reaction from Mr. Yates. One door being blown apart with a firearm is sufficient."

Schroder gestured. "Jenner, the door."

"Why the hell me? I've already had my ass in a crack when I climbed that derrick. Why do I have to open the door? Let one of these boys do it." He waved his arm in the general direction of the encircling Canyon officers. None of them looked too anxious.

"Yates likes you, remember? He didn't shoot your ass off when he had the chance. Maybe he won't do it now. Besides, we're the homicide detectives. It's our job to catch murderers."

"*Suspected* murderers," said John Lloyd.

Schroder gave him a sour look.

Jenner stood to one side and opened the closet door, then jumped back out of any possible range. Branson stepped into the closet and put his face next to an almost invisible seam in its back wall. "Mr. Yates, while I cannot promise you that all is forgiven, I can guarantee you the services of an excellent attorney: myself. I know that you did not kill Brad Hemphill, but I would very much appreciate your help in revealing the identity of the man who did. Whether you surrender voluntarily, or you engage the police in a gun battle is entirely up to you. As your attorney, I recommend the former option. Gun battles are almost always physically dangerous, and one can hardly guarantee either a clean kill or a clear miss. You might contemplate what the results of a bullet to the spine would be, or possibly the consequences of a head wound that would leave you alive but in an irreversible coma."

Jenner shuddered and resolved to always wear a bulletproof vest to a gunfight. Better yet, he resolved to check into the educational requirements of a reference librarian.

The back of the closet creaked and a section of it pushed outward from the wall. "Branson, you guarantee you'll be my lawyer? That's not just bullshit?"

"I so guarantee, Mr. Yates."

"And you know the son of a bitch who murdered Hemphill?"

"I do, Mr. Yates."

"Okay, I'm coming out."

The waiting battalion, or maybe it was a full division, of cops pulled their guns. Major wars had been started with less firepower than Jenner saw in the confines of the lounge.

"Mr. Yates, perhaps you should throw your weapon out first," said Branson quickly. "Then walk out backward with your hands locked behind your head. And please be aware that the police are well armed."

"Yates!" called Schroder. "Most of the cops out here are

the same cops you told to stand in the corner. I've seen them in better moods, so don't try any fancy moves."

"I get the picture, Sergeant Schroder." An antique .45 Colt revolver came sliding through the door, followed by Yates's long, lanky body.

Within five minutes the assistant curator had been searched and handcuffed, most of the officers crowding the lounge had been dispatched back to their regular duties, and Jenner found himself sitting at the conference table next to Schroder. Across the table sat Branson and Lydia—still alert despite the mauve smudges of sleeplessness under her blue eyes. Yates, on the other hand, looked exhausted. Jenner guessed that having a gang of cops chasing your ass for hours didn't allow much time for resting.

Branson cleared his throat. "Sergeant Schroder, before you read Mr. Yates his rights, I have a proposition to make."

"Nothing doing, Branson. One of your propositions per investigation is enough."

The attorney held up his hand as if he were stopping traffic. "If you will hear me out, Sergeant, before making any precipitous decision. As I told you before, Mr. Yates will not confess to murder, nor will he confess to felony theft. He is a professional, and I suspect he knows the ramifications of our legal system as well as you or I. Thus you must prove the theft charges without any help from him. However, I should very much like to hear an account of what went on in the museum last night, and much of it may be prejudicial to Mr. Yates's interests. But it is necessary that I hear it. I cannot again risk arriving at a wrong conclusion. Therefore, I propose in the interests of proving the greater charge—murder—that you do not Mirandize Mr. Yates until after he answers certain questions. You cannot use anything Mr. Yates says against him, but he would not speak a word after receiving the Miranda warning in any case. You will lose nothing, and we may discover the final missing reference."

Schroder locked glances with Branson. "You're crazy! I never heard of any lawyer proposing anything like this. It's probably illegal. I know damn sure it must be unethical. I might lose my badge. You could lose your license."

Branson's sigh was loud and held a tone of disgust. "Sergeant, I could make a practice of committing a foul and disgusting felony every weeknight and twice on Sunday, and as long as I did not steal from my clients, I doubt that I would be disbarred. As for your badge, I fail to see any difficulties. After the questioning concerning the murder, you read Mr. Yates his rights, then you may question him about his practice of liberating certain valuable artifacts, and the game of cops and robbers goes on according to the rules laid down by our several state and federal courts. But before you begin that game, I propose we act for the sake of justice. However irregular or even illegal it might be, it is right that we should do this."

Schroder rubbed his hand over his thinning sandy hair, stuck a cigarette in the corner of his mouth, and gave a sigh of his own. "All right, Branson. I'll go along with you, but it's at my discretion. Anytime I get a whiff of Mr. Yates lying or hedging or trying in any way to cover his ass on a murder charge, I Mirandize him, and we start playing for the record. Understood?"

Branson nodded and Yates looked up at Schroder. "I'll play it straight, Sergeant, because I want to see the bastard who killed Hemphill do some hard time. Otherwise I would've cut my losses and been out of here last night."

Branson rested his arms on the table and laced his fingers together. "So you did deliberately stay."

Yates nodded, looking amazed, as though he couldn't believe it himself. "Yeah, I did. He was so damn scared of everything and everybody that I felt sorry for him. He was even afraid of the dark. The idea of anybody scaring him any worse than he already was just gets to me, Branson. I can imagine how terrified he was when somebody came out with that pair of tongs. Jesus!" Yates covered his face and shuddered.

"Tongs?" asked Schroder.

Yates lifted his head. "Yeah, from the blacksmith's display. I found them on the floor next to Brad's body. I had to put them back, of course, so nobody would know where he was killed for a while, but I was real careful. You might find some evidence on them. No fingerprints—metal's too rough—but maybe a hair or fiber."

"You knew Brad had drowned?" asked Branson.

"I found him facedown in the water, pulled him out, and tried to revive him, but hell, he was full of water. It just kept pouring out of his mouth for a while, then stopped unless I pushed on his back."

"If you'd called a doctor," said Lydia, "maybe he could've been saved. If you hadn't been so interested in saving your own skin."

Yates shook his head. "Lady, his eyes were dead! You ever seen dead eyes? There's nothing like them—blank and glazed over like a frosted window—and you don't do anybody any favor when you start up his heart after his eyes have died. He's a fucking vegetable! Do you think Brad Hemphill would've thanked me? Hell, he was scared of dark places anyway. How do you think he would've felt being locked up in a black mind for as long as doctors could keep his body alive?"

Lydia turned chalk-white, and she hid her face against Branson's shoulder. Jenner felt a little queasy himself.

"So then what did you do, Yates, after your first aid failed?" asked Schroder.

Yates slammed both handcuffed fists on the table. "Don't get sarcastic with me, Schroder! I did my best." He rubbed his hands together and continued. "I knew I was up shit creek. I had been substituting cheap replicas for genuine artifacts for months, and I knew any decent investigation would eventually uncover my scam and I'd find my ass in the slammer for murder. The most ironic thing about it is that I was planning on cutting out last night after one last haul because I was feeling guilty about taking advantage of the timid little bastard. It was like taking candy from a baby. Funny, isn't it, me developing a conscience?"

"Perhaps there is hope for you, Mr. Yates. However, at the risk of stunting your fledgling moral development, I must tell you that Hemphill had begun an inventory of Pioneer Town artifacts. Eventually he would have confronted you."

"Brad wouldn't have confronted me. He wouldn't have

confronted anybody. He was too damn scared. Anyway, he would've asked me about it first, checking his facts and sort of begging to be wrong. That's the way he did things. Like that cleaning woman breaking that dish in the home display and blaming it on a ghost. He believed her because it was less frightening than telling her to stay out of his exhibits. That's probably when he started checking the artifacts. Damn woman and her ghost!"

"You mean you didn't break it?" asked Lydia.

"Hell, no. That dish was worth a ton on the antique market. Why the hell would I break it?"

"If you didn't break it, and Maude Young didn't break it, who did? Do you believe in Sarah Jane?"

"Miss Fairchild, if you could refrain from tracking down your ghost stories. Please continue, Mr. Yates."

"I knew the best thing to do was get the hell out, disappear for a while, pick up another identity, but I was mad, you know. I was pissed that somebody killed Hemphill; then I was pissed that he was laying it off on me. Besides, there's no statute of limitations on a murder charge. I'd have been running forever. I didn't want to do that, and I didn't want the son of a bitch who killed him to walk. So I hid the body, signed myself and Hemphill out just before Walter came in, went to the party and ducked out that woman's back door. Had a hell of a time getting out of there without swimming that moat, and I didn't want to have to do that. Jesus, there was more dead bugs and duck shit in that water than I've ever seen."

"But you signed out at a quarter to six," said Jenner.

Yates grinned. "That asshole Farmer never looks at that sheet, but I figured I could count on him to swear himself black-and-blue that it was accurate. Old military type. Never admit you might be wrong in front of your superiors. Anyway, I got back to the museum about eight and came in the side door. I knew the cleaning crew would have finished the offices and that end of the annex. I'd had time to think while I was driving to and from that party, but I couldn't figure out who killed Brad, except I knew it wasn't Walter Goodwin. I saw him drive up in his old Ford when I was walking around the building. That's why I didn't write a memo on him. I like Walter, but I didn't like Maude Young lying about that damn dish, so I included her, even though I didn't think she was guilty. I used every bit of museum gossip I'd heard about everybody else. I thought if you started looking, maybe you'd find the murderer."

He paused to take a breath. Jenner noticed he was looking less exhausted, as though telling the story was reviving him. "Then I started covering my tracks. I cleaned out some artifacts I had hidden in the Horror of Horrors, but I missed that damn china doll that Miss Fairchild saw. I don't know why. I'm generally careful about that sort of thing. Professional, you know."

"Maybe Sarah Jane hid it from you," suggested Lydia, and glared when everyone looked at her.

"Please, Miss Fairchild," murmured Branson, while Schroder just shook his head.

Yates just nodded. "The ghost, you mean. Maybe so. Who knows? Where was I? Oh, yeah, after I put the artifacts back in storage, I waited around until the cleaning crew left, then I moved Brad." He shuddered and took a deep breath. "Jesus, that was the hardest thing I ever did—besides changing his shirt."

"Why did you do that, Mr. Yates?" asked John Lloyd.

"Brad was always so clean. Always wore those damn white shirts, like he was an accountant or something. When I hid him under the bed, his shirt got filthy. I knew Brad wouldn't be comfortable in a dirty shirt, so I got a clean one out of his office. It was the only thing I could do for him besides sticking around to maybe see to it that his killer got caught."

"Why did you put him on that goddamn skull?" asked Schroder.

"I wanted him found under circumstances that would keep you away from Pioneer Town, at least until after the autopsy. I wanted you to look at somebody else besides me. I didn't do it, but I am a thief. I figured once you knew that, you'd slap the murder charge on me, too. So I gave you a chance to find the real killer first. Then I saw Miss Fairchild looking at the bridles and other tack in Pioneer Town. When Branson said she was taking a break to enjoy the museum, I had a feeling she was onto something. I followed her, saw her pick up that doll, and knew my time was up. But I still couldn't leave—not as long as there was a chance that you would drop on somebody else. I thought maybe I had that chance because of what Branson had said to all of us in Pioneer Town. He thought the killing was impulsive and didn't fit with the sabotage of the security system. I thought maybe he might be smart enough to figure out what happened, so I hid on top the derrick to await unfolding events, so to speak. I never expected Schroder to send Jenner up the derrick. Sorry I scared you, Jenner, but I couldn't let you take me. I was afraid even Branson would stop looking then, so I pulled the macho gangster bit and ran again. God, I'm tired of running. I'm glad it's over."

"Tell me about the sabotage, Mr. Yates. When did you do it?"

"After six o'clock. I'd planned on doing it anyway because I had one more load of artifacts to take, but after the murder, I knew I had to get back inside the museum. I signed out at the south entrance, came back in the north entrance about three minutes later. I knew I had about thirty minutes to do the job before Walter would settle down in the monitoring room. I've done the same kind of thing before. It doesn't take long when you know what you're doing. I rewired the sound and motion detectors, then went in the security office to switch tapes. That's when I discovered somebody had been there before me."

"How did you know that?" asked Branson urgently.

"There weren't any tapes in the recorder. Somebody had swiped them. Good idea, really. If you think you've been recorded on a video surveillance camera, just take the damn tape. I couldn't do it that way because I didn't want anybody seeing me on the monitors. Even if there's no tape in the camera, anybody watching the monitors will see you. They just won't have a record of it. That's why I played back a tape for Walter. But if the monitors are playing to an empty room, like they do from five to half past six every day, and you steal the tape, then it's like you were never there. Because nobody saw you on the monitor, and the camera can't tell what it saw if somebody stole its videotape."

"And as I recall from Sergeant Schroder's account of Darrell Farmer's testimony, the only three cameras on after five o'clock are the ones filming the outside entrances?" asked John Lloyd.

"Damn right. So why the hell did somebody steal the videotapes, when the inside cameras that would've filmed the murder were turned off anyway?"

CHAPTER TWENTY-FIVE

LYDIA LEANED AGAINST THE CORNER OF THE HOME DISPLAY in Pioneer Town. Her stomach hurt, and she couldn't decide if it was hunger or nervousness. Probably both. She hadn't eaten since dinner the night before, and it was nearly noon. She covered her mouth to prevent hysterical laughter from bubbling out. It was high noon, and John Lloyd was standing in a mock street in a mock Western village preparing to face a dangerous killer.

Of course he had more support than Gary Cooper did in the movie. Schroder and Jenner were standing beside and just slightly behind him. There were cops at the north entrance, cops cutting off the gallery exit, cops in front of the elevator just outside the door to Pioneer Town, and there were cops in front of the stairs. Gary Cooper should've had so much help.

She took four deep breaths to settle her nerves and studied the suspects who bunched together near the water trough, which looked odd with its pump now dismantled and carried off by Special Crimes. Bill Whitney held Rachel Applebaum's arm as if he were afraid she would collapse without his support. And she might, too, thought Lydia. Rachel looked every year of her age plus some.

Monique Bancroft Whitney, on the other hand, looked fresh and smooth-skinned, surgically impervious to anything so tasteless as middle age. More than that, Monique looked untouched by the tragedy of Brad Hemphill's death—unless one noticed her impatiently tapping her foot. Poor baby was probably missing her aerobics class or her appointment to have her nails redone, but was graciously making the sacrifice in order to remain a thorn in her husband's side. She certainly wasn't staying to lend moral support to Rachel Applebaum, who she was eyeing with all the warmth of a bad-tempered poodle.

Abe Yates, still in handcuffs, stood on the edge of the group with Officer Evans hovering at his shoulder. The assistant curator and professional thief was countering the accusing looks from the other staff members with an accusing look of his own. He had nothing to be ashamed of; thievery was his profession, and murder had not been his game. Lydia's head ached with thinking about the convoluted mental processes such a complex moral code must require. Much easier to be either a villain or a saint; in-between felons must expend a lot of energy making complicated moral decisions.

Schroder had argued against this gathering of the suspects around the scene of the crime as overly dramatic, unnecessary, and "not worth a fart in a high wind," while John Lloyd had countered that it was an exercise in group dynamics and peer pressure.

"It is a classic example of *res gestae*—an excited utterance, Sergeant Schroder," John Lloyd had explained earlier. "Surely you have read the mystery novels by Ms. Christie in which her odd little detective with the egg-shaped head gathers all the suspects together and explains the crime, thus spurring the guilty party to confess."

"Jesus H. Christ, Branson!" exclaimed Schroder. "This isn't a mystery story; it's a damn murder investigation."

"Which has netted you nothing but the wrong man. Standard police procedure, your collecting of bits and pieces of evidence, will not convict Brad Hemphill's murderer because you have no contact evidence directly linking anyone to the murder. There is, however, enough testimony to provide outside support to an oral confession should I prove successful.''

Jenner looked confused. ''What's that got to do with this Christie woman and *res gestae*?''

John Lloyd looked pained at Jenner's slighting reference to Dame Agatha. ''Ms. Christie wrote extensively about the British middle and upper-middle classes, their servants, and their exercises in domestic malice. In other words she dealt with a social class composed of people much like those involved in our present case. Ms. Christie used the legal principle of *res gestae* as a literary device with devastating effectiveness. Her use of it was firmly grounded in law and supported by her knowledge of human psychology. When confronted in the presence of one's peers by an account of his or her wrongdoing, the respectable, law-abiding person is quite likely to make the excited utterance. If that utterance is *not* made in response to police questioning, then it is legally admissible in court. I suggest we borrow from art, Sergeant Schroder. What do we have to lose?''

What indeed, thought Lydia as she watched John Lloyd straighten his shoulders and study each person's face in turn. She imitated him, examining each suspect—and coming up with a blank. She had no idea who was guilty, and John Lloyd had remained closemouthed on the subject.

She stepped closer to him as he tapped his cane on the tile floor. ''Ladies and gentlemen, I know who killed Brad Hemphill.''

If John Lloyd was waiting for *his* excited utterance, then he must be disappointed, thought Lydia, because the silence in Pioneer Town was absolute. One could hear the proverbial pin drop. No one broke the silence with questions. No one looked guilty. And certainly no one confessed. They all stood about glancing surreptitiously at one another.

Except one.

A single individual stared with fixed intensity—but not at John Lloyd—at someone else, someone who couldn't and wouldn't possibly have killed Brad Hemphill.

Unless.

Lydia rapidly reexamined her references.

Unless the object of the stare felt more than an impulse to kill, felt instead a desperation. That made more sense. Brad Hemphill's murder wasn't the act of an impulsive individual; it was the act of a desperate individual, an individual compelled by hopelessness and despair to make one last, ill-conceived, violent attempt to protect a secret.

But how, and most important of all, why?

John Lloyd's lips tightened as the silence continued. "Let me recount the events of last night. Brad Hemphill met his murderer by this watering trough after five-fifteen last night. After a very short conversation, Brad was struck and left to die, and the murderer hurried to the security office and stole the videotapes, the only record of who left the museum by any door except the south entrance, where Mr. Farmer stood guard with his sign-out sheet. Once I learned that fact, then the central question of the case became why a man like Brad Hemphill, a man so terrified of the dark that he kept candles in his desk, would stay after hours in a darkened museum in order to meet someone. The answer to that question also explains why the videotapes were stolen. Brad Hemphill met his murderer after hours because he could not arrange a meeting during what might be considered business hours. The tapes were stolen not because they filmed anyone's leaving the museum, but because they filmed someone entering the museum, someone whose presence could not be easily explained, someone not on staff. Only one person possessed keys to the museum, yet did not work here. Only one person was tied up all day in business activities until after five. Only one person had an important enough motive to kill Brad Hemphill—and that is Bill Whitney."

Whitney cast a despairing look at Rachel, who stood frozen, tears running down her shocked and ravished face. He turned away from her, his face that of an old and disillusioned man. "I killed him," he said in a toneless voice. "I took a set of tongs from the blacksmith's shop, and I waited for him. I meant to kill him, to batter him to death. But when the time came, I couldn't do it. I took a halfhearted swing and hit him in the ribs. He fell against the pump and I heard his skull crack. I swear to God, John Lloyd, I thought that he died that instant. I didn't know he was still alive when he rolled over into the trough. I wouldn't have let him die. Not if I'd known. But I didn't, and I panicked. I stole the videotapes and got the hell out of here through the north entrance. I drove back to Amarillo in a sweat, knowing that Walter Goodwin would discover the body when he made his rounds. When there was no phone call, I was ready to fly to pieces. Then when Monique told me Rachel had taken the money back to Canyon with her, all I could think of was that Rachel might be in the museum when Hemphill's dead body was found. I knew, you see, that our affair would eventually be exposed, and I was afraid Rachel would be automatically suspected because of it. I was right."

He rubbed his hand over his face, and glanced at Rachel who was sobbing quietly. The police were staying well away from him, as they had been instructed to do. Once he was under arrest, then he must be advised of his rights, and that would undoubtedly be the end of any confession.

"When it turned out that Yates sabotaged the security system, I figured I was home free. He sort of muddied the waters. But I guess that didn't fool you any, did it, John Lloyd? When Yates told you he found the recorder empty, you knew it had to be me."

John Lloyd shook his head. "The tapes were only confirmation. I knew before that, when Roberto Ortiz asked me why he should have to meet Brad Hemphill after hours. A sensible question under the circumstances. Hemphill could have met a staff member at any time. That left you. The question was why, and the answer had to do with a picture in a family history, a picture of three people in clown suits, and a small boy who grew up with a pathological fear of the dark and the color red. These references only had significance in one context: Lindsey Clark."

"You bastard!" screamed Margaret as she launched herself at Bill Whitney, her hands curved into talons.

"Get her!" yelled Schroder.

Walter Goodwin grabbed the archivist around her waist

and swung her away from Whitney. Jenner ran over, and the two men subdued a screaming Margaret. "Why did you do it? Why did you murder my Lindsey?"

It was a good question, thought Lydia, as she studied Bill Whitney's face.

John Lloyd didn't take his eyes off Whitney, either. "Brad Hemphill was six years old at the time of Lindsey's murder, old enough to be observant, but young enough to have a child's frame of reference. Perhaps he was looking out his bedroom window at the time of the murder. It was Halloween night, after all, and there were interesting things to be seen by a six-year-old boy who might have resented being sent to bed. Lightning flashes lit up the landscape at intervals, and that's when little Brad Hemphill saw the bogeyman run out of Lindsey Clark's house. He didn't realize it was a man in a Halloween costume until twenty years later when he saw a photograph in a family history—a photograph of that same man in that same costume. Clown suits are frequently red and white, which I believe accounts for Brad's fear of red. Since Brad always checked his facts, he called Bill Whitney to ask about the photograph. One might say the need to be sure killed Brad Hemphill."

"You're brilliant, John Lloyd. I don't suppose anybody else could've figured out the motive but you. I killed Lindsey Clark twenty years ago, and I killed Brad Hemphill last night. It's over now, and I'm glad. I'm not really much of a killer, I guess. I just feel sorry about the whole thing."

Schroder stepped up and pulled a card out of his pocket. "William Bancroft Whitney, you're under arrest for the murders of Brad Hemphill and Lindsey Clark. You have the right to—"

"Wait!" Lydia stepped up to John Lloyd's side and clasped his hand. "The story isn't over yet, John Lloyd. The references are wrong."

Bill Whitney jerked around to stare at her, his face white and strained and despairing.

"What are you talking about, Miss Fairchild?" Schroder turned to John Lloyd. "What's she talking about, Branson?"

John Lloyd's black eyes locked with Lydia's blue ones,

and Lydia again felt the sensation of having her thoughts read. "I am certain Miss Fairchild will tell us, and I am equally certain we should listen."

Lydia smiled at him and took a deep breath. She was on her own now, and she sensed John Lloyd wouldn't provide her with a safety net. It was her maiden voyage as a deductive solver of crime—and she hoped she didn't strike an iceberg. "You are a very inept murderer, Bill Whitney. If Brad Hemphill hadn't hit his head so you thought you'd killed him, he would still be alive. A real murderer plans ahead. You didn't. You didn't even steal the videotapes before you met Hemphill. It seems to me that would have been the sensible thing to do. And the weapon. A big strong man like you didn't really need a weapon. You could've very easily strangled Brad." She saw Whitney briefly close his eyes and shudder. "But you couldn't do something so cold-blooded as that. You couldn't even hit Brad Hemphill anywhere that it counted. So what makes you think anyone will believe you deliberately smothered Lindsey Clark?"

"John Lloyd, your clerk is making a fool out of herself. You ought to shut her up until you can train her better. I killed Hemphill and Lindsey Clark. I confessed; I feel better, and now I want to go to jail. I don't want to have to listen to this crap from Miss Fairchild." Whitney's chest was heaving, and his face was beaded with greasy sweat.

John Lloyd put his arm around Lydia's waist. "I rather think I have trained her well indeed. Please continue with your argument, Miss Fairchild. I find it fascinating, and I am sure Dame Agatha would approve."

Lydia returned from Whitney to the museum director. "Dr. Applebaum, why didn't you marry Bill Whitney? You were engaged to him after Lindsey's murder. What happened?"

Rachel lifted her face to look at Lydia from sunken eyes. "I don't know. He never asked me."

"Goddamn it, Sergeant. Does she have the right to harass Rachel?" demanded Whitney.

Lydia turned to look at him. "I'm righting an old wrong, Whitney, one you should've righted years ago. It's too late to save Hemphill, but in the name of all that's right, it's not too late to avenge Lindsey. It's not much, but it's the only good thing that'll come out of this mess. You killed Brad Hemphill, and you married Monique for the same reason: to protect Rachel Applebaum."

There was a collective gasp, and everyone turned to look at the museum director who stood frozen in place, her face almost bloodless.

"Rachel," whispered Margaret Clark, her face slack with disbelief.

"Look at Margaret Clark, Whitney. Look at her!" Lydia insisted when he continued staring blankly ahead. Reluctantly he turned his head. "Look at Margaret's face, Whitney. Even she doesn't believe it. Why did you?"

"What?" asked Schroder.

Whitney turned his head back toward Lydia, his face taut with dawning awareness. "My, God, no."

Lydia nodded. "You didn't check your references twenty years ago, Whitney, and you failed again to check them last night. There were three figures in that picture, and they all wore clown suits. Brad Hemphill was checking to make sure that the woman in the clown suit whom he saw running from Lindsey Clark's house was correctly identified in the photograph, but you misunderstood his reference. Brad Hemphill wasn't talking about Rachel Applebaum; he had no reason to question her identity. She wasn't wearing clown makeup, and she hasn't changed much since the photograph was made. He wanted to check the identity of the other woman in the photo, the one who wore white clown makeup and a wig—your wife, Monique Whitney."

There was a scream, and Monique Whitney broke from the cluster of suspects and raced up the stairs. Lydia pounded after her. "You're not getting away from this, you bloody, artificially enhanced bitch!"

"Miss Fairchild, stop! Let the police handle this!" John Lloyd exclaimed.

"Hold her, Lydia!" screamed Margaret Clark, kicking Walter Goodwin in the shins and escaping.

Lydia hesitated at the landing. Second floor or third? Second floor, she decided, since the archives were on the third, and they were locked tighter than Margaret Clark's corset.

"Lydia, damn it, wait!" bellowed John Lloyd, catching her arm as she ran through the costume hall and turned down the corridor toward the petroleum wing.

"I'll catch her," panted Lydia, but her lungs already felt squeezed. No sleep and her own experience with a ghost must have sapped her more than she realized.

Jenner and Schroder passed her, along with a wedge of Canyon cops. Margaret Clark was close behind, dragging a limping, panting Walter Goodwin with her. Lydia didn't see Whitney and Yates, but suspected each had about six cops holding them down to prevent their joining the chase. She shook loose of John Lloyd's grasp and ran after Jenner and Schroder.

She heard John Lloyd's uneven gait beside her before she realized he'd caught up with her again. "Don't you ever listen, Miss Fairchild?" he asked.

"Nope," she answered as she burst out on the balcony just behind Jenner.

Monique Whitney was at its other end, ready to cut around the theatre and lose herself in the bowels of the oil patch exhibit. The woman stumbled, as if something had tripped her. She staggered sideways, her hands slapping at something only she could see; then she seemed to leap into the air with an awkward kicking motion, hit the balcony railing, and topple over, as if someone had tipped her feet over her head.

Lydia heard Monique Whitney's body hit the tile floor two stories below.

EPILOGUE

"SO HOW DID YOU KNOW, MISS FAIRCHILD?" ASKED Schroder, stepping out of the way of the ambulance crew as they carried past the stretcher with Monique Bancroft Whitney's crushed, paralyzed, but still living body strapped on it.

Lydia swallowed, but didn't avert her eyes. She'd been responsible for the broken woman on the stretcher. Or had she? Who had tripped Monique Whitney? Who had tipped her over the balcony railing? She looked back over Schroder's shoulder toward the annex and thought she saw a shimmer in a dark corner by one of the windmills. She sniffed the air.

"Miss Fairchild, Sergeant Schroder asked you a question," said John Lloyd gently.

Had she smelled sage and sunshine and wildflowers? Or not?

"Miss Fairchild!" John Lloyd's voice was louder and more emphatic. He reached out and touched her arm.

She shook her head. "I'm sorry; I was thinking about something else."

Schroder turned around and stared curiously at the dark windmill display. "Evans? Is that you? I told you to haul your butt back to the Canyon cop shop."

Lydia peered more closely, but the shimmer was no longer there.

Schroder shook his head. "Must be getting old, Branson. Thought I saw something back there."

John Lloyd looked back. Lydia watched him smile and tip his hat. "What are you doing, John Lloyd?"

He cocked an eyebrow. "Saying farewell to the past, Miss Fairchild. A whimsy of mine whenever I visit this museum."

Lydia tilted her head and looked at him suspiciously. "I thought you were saying goodbye to someone."

His face went blank for a second. "I have already bade farewell to Bill Whitney, Miss Fairchild."

She took his hand. "I'm sorry, John Lloyd. I know he was your friend."

He shook his head. "Only part of him, Miss Fairchild. The other part I did not know. Each person's ghosts are his own, and I was not introduced."

"What do you think he'll get, Branson?" asked Schroder as they walked through Pioneer Hall toward the south entrance. It was still locked and guarded until all the paperwork could be completed and the police could formally turn the museum back to the staff.

John Lloyd motioned for the guard to unlock the huge metal doors. "With a good attorney, and considering all possible extenuating circumstances, perhaps twenty years. If one adds the past twenty years of regrets to that, then he will have paid dearly."

Schroder nodded, then looked at Lydia. "So answer my question, Miss Fairchild, how did you know Monique Whitney murdered Lindsey Clark?"

Lydia stepped into the sunshine. "She immediately stared at Bill Whitney when John Lloyd said he knew who killed Brad Hemphill. She knew he killed Brad, and she knew it must have something to do with Lindsey Clark's murder and Rachel Applebaum. Now, how could she know that unless she knew more about Lindsey Clark's murder than she had ever told? There were two possible reasons for her knowing but not telling: either she knew Bill did it, or she did it herself. Which reference made more sense in context? Monique's guilt, of course. Bill Whitney just didn't strike me as a murderer."

They walked halfway down the sidewalk and stopped. "Then I wondered why he would murder Brad Hemphill," continued Lydia. "He certainly wouldn't do it for money; he didn't appear to enjoy his wealth that much. He would, however, do it for love, and whom did he love? Rachel Applebaum. But why kill to protect Rachel unless he believed she murdered Lindsey Clark? And why would the oaf think something that stupid unless a witness told him so, a witness who offered to keep silent in exchange for marriage. To be a witness, one must be on the scene, and why should Monique Whitney have been on the scene except to murder Lindsey Clark?

Schroder scratched his head and then stuck a cigarette in the corner of his mouth. "Wait a minute, Miss Fairchild. I'm not saying you're wrong, because it's obvious to a blind man that Monique Whitney wouldn't have taken off like a jackrabbit if she hadn't killed Lindsey Clark, but why in the hell did she kill her? Canadian is a small town, and it wasn't much bigger twenty years ago. Why take the chance of murdering somebody you know?"

John Lloyd chuckled. "You want to know the whys rather than the facts, Sergeant Schroder? We may make an attorney of you yet."

"Just let the young lady answer without all your sarcastic remarks, Branson."

Lydia pinched John Lloyd's arm. "I'm certain she believed that once Lindsey was dead, she would have a clear path into Whitney's bank vaults as his wife. Self-confidence has never been her problem. It must have been a shock when Whitney and Rachel patched up their relationship. It was decision time for Monique. If she murdered another woman in Canadian who was engaged to Bill Whitney, the police might start to ask embarrassing questions. She did the next best thing. She told Bill Whitney that she saw Rachel Applebaum murder Lindsey Clark, or saw her running from Lindsey's house, I don't know which. She offered to stay silent if Whitney married her and said nothing to Rachel Applebaum."

"Why didn't he just ask Rachel?" asked Jenner, scratching at his day old beard.

Lydia shrugged. "Who knows?"

"He was caught on the horns of a dilemma, Sergeant Jenner," replied John Lloyd. "What if Rachel had been guilty? She might have murdered Monique, too. What if she were innocent, but could not prove it? He decided to marry Monique and remain silent. He had an abundance of love, but a scarcity of faith."

Jenner scratched his chin again. "Doesn't make much sense to me. I'd have asked. It would've saved living with Monique Whitney for twenty years. Hell, he should've confessed to the murder himself. Prison would've been better than marriage to that woman."

Lydia tugged at John Lloyd's hand. "Feed me, you Victorian sweatshop employer." She waved at the two cops. "Sergeant Schroder, Jenner, I'll see you next trip." She pulled John Lloyd down the sidewalk toward the brand new Lincoln town car parked at the curb in front of Schroder's old Ford.

John Lloyd stopped beside the car. "There is another possible scenario, Miss Fairchild."

Lydia looked up at him. "You mean, in answer to Jenner's question of why Bill Whitney didn't just ask Rachel?"

"I see that you are aware of the noticeable weakness in your account."

"I don't know that it's so weak. Your remark about the horns of the dilemma might be true, John Lloyd."

He cocked his head. "But you doubt it?"

She nodded and looked back at the museum. A gaunt and wasted Rachel Applebaum stood in the doorway by a handcuffed Bill Whitney. "It would be a reference out of context, John Lloyd. Bill Whitney is a clumsy sort of man in many ways. He would blurt out to Rachel exactly what Monique had said."

"Meaning what, Miss Fairchild?"

"Meaning, I suspect, that Rachel Applebaum had no alibi, and might even have been at Lindsey's house the night of the murder. Maybe they argued over Bill Whitney. Perhaps Monique saw her leave, which gave Monique the idea of accusing her. Maybe Rachel fought with Lindsey—you know, a shoving contest. Lindsey falls, hits her head, and instant unconsciousness. Rachel flees and Monique enters, sees an opportunity, and smothers Lindsey Clark. When Monique makes her accusation to Bill Whitney, Rachel cannot disprove it entirely. That would present a true dilemma to Bill Whitney, one that he would solve by marrying Monique. If they both had been more honest, or less afraid, Brad Hemphill would still be alive."

"No one is ever totally innocent," remarked John Lloyd.

"But we do know that Monique murdered Lindsey Clark, John Lloyd."

"We have a clean solution, Miss Fairchild, one that satisfies the police and Margaret Clark. If our speculations are true, I suggest that we leave Rachel Applebaum and Bill Whitney to the mercy of their ghosts, although in Bill's case, the state will exact its own punishment."

"Speaking of ghosts, John Lloyd. I want to hire someone to do an exorcism."

"Miss Fairchild, I have never known you to be cruel."

"What are you talking about?"

"Banishment."

Lydia felt a headache throb behind her eyelids and blamed John Lloyd. Medically speaking, his obscure responses to her suggestions usually caused her more headaches than did a high pollen count. "Would you care to explain the significance of your comments in the context of this conversation? In other words, I'm trying to check your references, and I got lost somewhere between cruel and banishment."

John Lloyd arched one eyebrow. "Miss Fairchild, exorcism amounts to banishment to some nether region, and I should hate to be responsible for banishing such a playful spirit from an environment where she is obviously so happy."

"She? Sarah Jane? Playful spirit?"

"Her interference with the accession records demonstrates a rich comic imagination and is quite harmless. I also quite enjoyed the account of her tricks in Pioneer Town."

''John Lloyd, she tipped Monique Bancroft Whitney off the balcony.''

''A fate she richly deserved. Our spirit has a highly developed sense of justice.''

''Our spirit? I thought you didn't believe in ghosts.''

He grasped her around the waist. ''Indulge my whimsy, Miss Fairchild. If such a spirit does exist, she reminds me very much of you, and I should hate to see you banished.''

As he pulled her closer and lowered his head to kiss her, she decided not to point out that a whimsy is a fanciful idea. Whimsies, like spirits, tend to disappear when defined too closely.

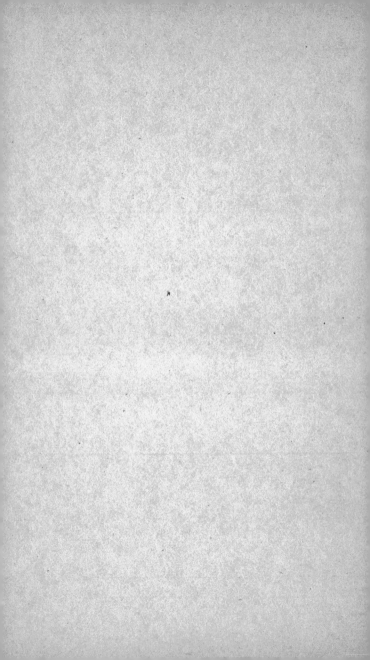